Sensitive New Age Spy

ALBY MURDOCH 2

GEOFFREY McGEACHIN

First published by Clan Destine Press in 2025

PO Box 121,
Bittern Victoria 3918
Australia

National Library of Australia Cataloguing-In-Publication data:

Sensitive New Age Spy

ISBNs: 978-1-922904-94-2 (paperback)
978-1-922904-95-9 (eBook)

Cover design by Willsin Rowe

Design & Typesetting by Clan Destine Press

www.clandestinepress.net

For Wilma

as ever and always

Chapter One

One sunny Sunday morning a few years back, I popped out early to get some milk and fell arse-over-tit over my neighbour's ugly mutt Dougal, who was snoozing happily on my doorstep. While there was minimal damage to all concerned it was a bit of a shock, so I knew exactly how the live-in caretaker on Fort Denison must have felt when he ambled outside to check the tide gauge early one holiday Monday in October and almost tripped over the 80,000-tonne, ocean-going, bulk-transport tanker someone had left tied up to his Hills Hoist during the night.

Now, Fort Denison, a tiny island bang in the middle of Sydney Harbour, doesn't actually have a Hills Hoist, and the giant tanker wasn't so much tied up as parked – or anchored, if you want to get all nautical – but it was definitely a very big ship and the damned thing was right there on this bloke's doorstep, where it really shouldn't have been.

At 2.45 am an inexplicable blackout had shut down the surveillance screens in the Harbour Control Tower high above Millers Point. When they flickered back to life at 5.10 am the duty officer spotted the unexpected visitor anchored right across the Manly ferry route and became both alert and alarmed. Even more so when he couldn't pick up a signal from the ship's Automatic Identification System, or raise anyone on board by radio. He called the local cops, who called the federal cops, who called the government security-service liaison people in Canberra, who called Detective Inspector Peter Sturdee in Sydney, who called me. Julie took the call, which was fair enough since she was closest to the phone.

It was just on 6.40 according to the stainless-steel Omega Seamaster wristwatch on the bedside table, and the taste in my mouth and the mild throbbing in my head suggested that tugging the cork out of that third bottle of Graveyard Shiraz hadn't been such a great idea. Julie, stretched out on the couch in the bay window and looking one hell of a lot better than she had any right to, was listening and nodding. I was trying to remember if I'd topped up the Panadol supply in the bathroom cabinet after her last visit. The opening of a third bottle, followed by a platonic sleepover, was becoming a recurring theme on Julie's visits, and it was giving both my liver and my ego a hammering. Julie and I came under the heading of Work Colleagues and Just Good Friends. The last bit was more her idea than mine.

Julie sat up straight and that was definitely a sight worth looking at. She was wearing one of my old Icebergs windcheaters, her tousled blond hair, those long tanned runner's legs, lacy black knickers and not a whole lot else. I'm pretty sure if Plato had copped an eyeful of that outfit he would have done a quick rethink of his concept of the bonk-free relationship.

Julie nodded one more time in response to whoever was on the line then added a terse, 'It's happening, Peter.'

She tossed the cordless phone across the room in my direction. I came very close to catching it.

'There's a Highway Patrol car double-parked downstairs with the engine running,' she said as I fumbled through the folds of the doona for the phone. 'Better get your hat on, cowboy. Peter Sturdee needs a senior intelligence officer down at the Opera House jetty, and he needs him there pronto. There's a problem on the harbour.'

Why the hell anyone would think that problems on the harbour were a job for me or for our agency, D-E-D, was hard to figure. D-E-D stands for Directorate for Extra-territorial Defence and the E-word should be a bit of a clue. Our job is spying on the world's trouble spots, or what the layman might call covert offshore visual intelligence gathering, and we do a pretty nice job of it.

Domestic incidents are usually left to the local agencies, but it was the last day of a long weekend, perfect sailing and barbecue weather, so I guessed that ASIO, ASIS, and all the other federal security acronyms were as good as shut down for the duration. Since Peter Sturdee's call had come through to me, I must have been the most senior intelligence officer available, which was a bit of a scary thought.

I'd been Acting Director-General of D-E-D for almost six months now – six months in and I was already eight months behind in my paperwork. It was pretty obvious I wasn't cut out to be behind a desk, and recently I'd started a campaign to get myself demoted. So far I hadn't had much success, but hey, I'm an optimist. Right now, though, just when I was hoping to enjoy a lazy holiday Monday like every other bugger in Sydney, Julie had to go and answer that bloody phone.

Lights and sirens and some aggressive driving by the Highway Patrol officer got us down to the Opera House in no time flat. We skidded and slewed through cross traffic at major intersections with headlights flashing and tyres smoking, scaring the living daylights out of a bunch of still half-asleep holiday drivers.

I had my eyes closed and my feet jammed hard against the firewall for most of the trip, and when we reached the CBD, amazingly still in one piece, everything was cordoned off. Police cars blocked every intersection and officers in yellow safety-vests were busily directing traffic away from the city.

We screamed through the cordon and on down to the ferry terminal at Circular Quay without seeing a single civilian. The usually buzzing quay area looked dead as a doornail, the elevated train station was deserted, and a flotilla of abandoned and forlorn-looking ferries was tied up at the wharves. All rail and water traffic had been shut down, and apart from the cops, seagulls, and a CNN news crew setting up a satellite dish, it seemed I had all of Sydney Harbour to myself. Lucky me.

It was just on seven when we skidded to an eyeball-jarring stop at the Man O' War Steps beside the Opera House. I glanced over at the driver. 'Thank Christ we made it. I was starting to wonder if this heap actually had a brake pedal.'

The cop grinned and adjusted his wraparound mirrored sunglasses.

He switched off the siren and lights and pointed to a police launch waiting at the pontoon, engines idling. As a rule I'm wary of all boats smaller than the *QE2*, but I was bloody glad to have a reason to get out of that car. After checking that the World War II Sauer 9mm pistol was still snug in its holster under my jacket, I grabbed my camera bag and headed for the wharf.

My shoulder had finally healed from a bullet I took during an incident earlier in the year and I was champing at the bit to be back on assignment, either photographic or covert ops. That was the reason I was carrying the camera bag. All D-E-D operatives, myself included, operate under the guise of photographers for WORLDPIX International. I'd been a photographer before I got into the spy business and I used that as a cover for one of my first assignments in Afghanistan in the early 1980s. It worked like a charm so I came up with the concept of establishing WorldPix, a real photographic agency that could be used to disguise the activities of D-E-D operatives.

WorldPix provides worldwide hard news coverage, as well as celebrity fluff for the pulp magazines and Sunday trashloids. The agency's snappers roam the globe supplying images to newspapers, magazines and the advertising industry, and the press passes and camera bags are perfect cover for the ten percent of photographers who are also spies.

All D-E-D espionage recruits have to learn to be top-rate photographers, to justify their place on the WorldPix books alongside the genuine snappers. Sometimes it's hard to say if our people are spies who are photographers or photographers who are spies. To maintain cover, D-E-D operatives have to keep up with the drinking and partying that typifies your average photographer on assignment, and we all take this part of our jobs very seriously. No doubt this behaviour that had inspired Julie to christen us Dedheads.

Navigating the swaying gangway to the police launch was awkward, and I'd barely managed to scramble aboard when the engines went to full throttle and the vessel surged forward, throwing me backwards and almost over the stern into the drink. I was about to give the skipper a piece of my mind when I glanced past the wheelhouse towards our destination and the thought went right out of my head.

The huge tanker towered above the Fort, casting its massive shadow over the tiny island. The letters LNG were painted on the side in enormous white capitals, and rising high above the deck and glistening in the early sunlight were four gigantic silver domes, designed to hold liquefied natural gas. They were an awe-inspiring sight, and I'll admit made me more than a little uneasy. My uneasiness increased as we got closer and I could make out the warnings painted at regular intervals on the hull, DANGER! FLAMMABLE CARGO! KEEP CLEAR!

Just last week at the airport some doofus had left his suitcase by the snack bar while he went to the toilet. When he got back the bomb squad had blown up his dirty underwear in the middle of the car park. And here I was heading in the direction of something which was a lot bigger than your average Paklite Million Miler, and possibly holding something a bit more volatile than a load of grubby socks and jocks.

Chapter Two

A travel writer once declared the world's most beautiful harbour to be Sydney by day and Hong Kong by night, and you won't get an argument from me. With a foreshore featuring well-kept parks, small secluded beaches and very expensive homes, the Harbour's main focus is a rough triangle made up of the elegant grey steel arch of the bridge, the Opera House, with its amazing sail shapes mimicking yachts under sail, and Kirribilli House – the Prime Minister's palatial waterfront residence when he's in town.

The PM's joint, a gabled, federation mansion fronting onto the water, has beautifully manicured grounds and panoramic harbour views from the front porch, taking in the Royal Australian Navy's base at Garden Island and Fort Denison. Originally known as Pinch gut, Fort Denison was re-named in the 1850s when it was fortified with a stone Martello tower armed with muzzle-loading cannon. The fortifications were designed to protect Sydney from a Russian invasion that fortunately never eventuated.

The police launch dropped me on the Fort Denison jetty just a few minutes after seven. It felt like we'd broken the world water-speed record to do it, and now I had a touch of seasickness to contend with, as well as a hangover. A bunch of cops were already on the island, among them Detective Inspector Peter Sturdee, acting State/Federal Special Liaison Officer. Sturdee was pacing the paved forecourt, and looked like he was anxious to start specially liaising. He waved off the young uniformed walloper on the dock who wanted to see some ID and have a quick sniff through my camera bag.

'So what have we got here then, Pete?' I said.

Sturdee shook his head. 'Buggered if I know, Alby, and that's the problem. Come and have a look.'

He walked quickly across the forecourt, leading me past old barracks rooms and up a well-worn stone stairway to a courtyard surrounded by parapets with firing steps and more million-dollar views. A flagpole and a battery of small, muzzle-loading cannon stood at one end of the courtyard, and the massive bulk of the Martello tower dominated the other. Everyone else with an interest in the proceedings was gathered in a gaggle on top of the tower, gazing up at the bow of one hell of a big ship. She had looked pretty imposing from a distance, but up close she was gigantic.

I slipped my sunglasses into my pocket, walked across the courtyard and climbed up on one of the firing steps to get a better look. With the uniformed cop back on the jetty well out of earshot and the rest of the plainclothes cops up on the tower, Peter and I could talk freely. Plainclothes was right – very bloody plain. Sturdee was the only detective I knew who didn't look like he'd just fallen out of a tumble drier.

'Around seventy, maybe eighty thousand tons,' he said, staring up at the ship. 'Or so the Water Police boys reckon.'

'And you've got no idea what the hell's going on?' I asked.

He shook his head.

I glanced back past the Opera House and the bridge pylons to Millers Point and the harbour master's control room, a circular, glass-sided observation deck on top of a ninety-metre, reinforced-concrete support column. It gave the duty officer a 360 degree, bird's-eye view of Sydney's maritime traffic.

'Someone asleep at the switch up there?' I said.

'They had their hands full with a blackout. Radar and video surveillance systems went down, along with the backups, about the same time our visitor there would have been coming in through the Heads.'

'That was convenient. And no one got a visual fix?'

Sturdee shrugged. 'Like I said, they had their hands full. Plus the tanker had no lights showing and it's a new moon, which meant a lot of the harbour was dark.'

'So we have to assume it's not an accident. The captain wasn't just as drunk as a skunk and decided to pull her over to the kerb and sleep it off till morning.'

'Doesn't look like it. The Sydney Ports blokes reckon it would have needed an ace pilot who really knew the harbour to get her to this point in the dark, so someone understood exactly what they were doing. They – whoever *they* are – wanted her anchored right here.'

Dammit. Why had Julie gone and answered that bloody phone?

'Your blokes spotted anyone on board yet?' I asked.

'Nope. I'm trying to organise a chopper to do a low-level sweep over the top.'

'So no demands, threats, anonymous phone calls claiming responsibility?'

Another shake of the head from Sturdee. 'Not a peep, so far.'

That would probably change soon. No one would pull a stunt like this just as a prank.

'Jesus, what a mess,' Sturdee groaned. 'A public holiday, weather's perfect, and there's a ferry race scheduled for the afternoon, so naturally the harbour was going to be the destination of choice for everything that floats. Great bloody timing.'

He was right about that. The timing of all this was just too perfect.

'I've declared a full emergency,' he continued, 'and we've started diverting all city-bound bridge and tunnel traffic out towards the western suburbs. I've also set up a total exclusion zone, air and sea, and I've closed the bridge and shut down the bridge climb.'

I was impressed. 'You can do all that?'

'Damned if I know, but I did it anyway. I still haven't been able to raise anyone senior at HQ and nobody at the security services is answering. If Julie hadn't picked up your phone I'd be out here all on my lonesome.'

'I guess you drew the short straw on weekend duty?' I said.

'Worse than that, I volunteered -- wanted the overtime. What can I tell you.'

Peter's wife had recently produced a second set of twin boys and the Sturdee household needed every penny it could get.

'But I figured I'd just be spending the weekend at a desk with my feet up.'

'Bit of a bad call,' I said.

'Tell me about it.' He glanced across the harbour in the direction of Kirribilli House. 'Prime Minister's apparently evacuating right now.'

'Can't say I blame him,' I said. 'When he's finished and washed his hands maybe we should ask him to leave.'

Sturdee looked at me and shook his head, but I did get a smile out of him.

The sky was completely clear and you could feel the heat starting to build. It was shaping up to be one of those late-spring Sydney scorchers. I thought about grabbing the tube of 50+ sun block from my camera bag, but changed my mind – a bloke wouldn't want to look like a wuss in front of all those butch coppers. Besides, I figured that right at the moment the tanker and its contents was potentially a lot more hazardous to my health.

'And if I didn't have enough on my bloody plate,' Sturdee said, 'there's that.' He looked back over his shoulder in the direction of the Woolloomooloo wharves.

'That' referred to the bristling array of antennae rising above the Garden Island naval dockyard, indicating the presence of a United States Navy Ticonderoga-class Aegis battle cruiser, the USS *Altoona*. According to the not-for-publication briefing all the security agencies had received, the *Altoona* had been extensively refitted, with an extended stern wedge to improve fuel efficiency at cruising speed, new reduced-cavitation propellers, and an upgrade to the Baseline 7.5b Aegis Weapons System. Right now she was on a shakedown cruise and the Sydney stopover was a long-scheduled goodwill visit.

In the old days, a navy cruiser was a tad smaller than a battleship but faster, with lighter armour and bloody big guns. Modern cruisers are small by comparison, still very fast, and they mount just one dinky little five-inch gun, if they're lucky. Ships like the *Altoona* made up for this with Harpoon anti-ship missiles, Stinger infrared surface-to-air missiles, Penguin and Hellfire air-to-surface missiles for the onboard helicopters, and Phalanx rapid-firing guns or Sea Sparrow missiles for close-in defence. Chuck in some nuclear-capable Tomahawk cruise missiles, and one modern cruiser packed as much punch as a whole World War II aircraft-carrier battle group. It was about as close as you could get to a floating Death Star.

On the raised helipad at the stern of the warship, I could just make out the shape of an SH 60R Seahawk helicopter, rotor blades slowly turning, and sailors going about their business.

Sturdee turned back towards the tanker. 'The Navy are sending a work boat over from HMAS Waterhen with some clearance divers so we can take a closer look at our visitor.'

'Sounds sensible.'

'And naturally the Yanks on the cruiser are a bit edgy about all this. The captain sent over his executive officer and a couple of specialists to have a look-see. They're up on the tower, ready to give us any assistance we might need.'

Having a ship anchor unexpectedly within spitting distance of your poop deck would make any navy man worth his salt nervous. I looked up at the tower. Amid our very plainclothes cops, the three Americans in neatly pressed khaki stood out like nuns in a brothel. Not as much as the crew-cut CIA man in rust-red chinos and the Hawaiian shirt, though – talk about standing out like dog's balls!

'Lonergan's up early,' I said.

'Yeah. Navy blokes must have given him a shout.'

Carter Lonergan was the new CIA Chief of Station in Australia. His predecessor had copped a full magazine from an M4 carbine in the chest, in a nasty incident at the top-secret US satellite facility at Bitter Springs last February. The same incident saw me catching that bullet in the shoulder, blowing up the base, shooting my boss dead, and getting arrested and then promoted, all in the same week. Probably not a career-advancement pathway they teach at the Harvard School of Business, but I could be wrong about that.

'I don't suppose Mr Lonergan has informed you whether yonder symbol of American might is carrying nuclear warheads for its cruise missiles?' I asked.

'You know how it goes, Alby. "We are unable to confirm or deny the presence of …" et cetera, et cetera, et cetera.'

Same old same old. Not all American warships carried nuclear weapons all the time, and the Yanks had a policy of keeping you guessing.

'Anyway,' Sturdee said, 'I thought you'd know, if anyone did.'

That was a joke. 'I'm just the boss of an intelligence service,' I said, 'so nobody tells me nothin'. Got any binoculars?'

'Fraid not. The caretaker had a pair but Lonergan borrowed 'em.'

I put my camera bag down, popped the clasps and pulled out a Nikon DSLR with the 200-500mm zoom. A quick scan of the tanker's superstructure through the telephoto lens didn't reveal anything out of the ordinary. I aimed the camera down and focused on the hull of the tanker.

'Better have that Navy work boat keep well clear when it shows up, Peter.'

At regular intervals around the hull, thin black rectangular boxes were suspended by wires, just a metre or so above the waterline.

'Yeah, what are those things?' Sturdee asked. 'They look like kids' lunchboxes.'

'They're anti-personnel mines,' I said. 'Perimeter defence weapon. Russian MON 50s, I think, very similar to the American Claymore. Remotely triggered. Anyone gets too close and *bang* – they cop around five hundred high-velocity, steel ball-bearings smack in the kisser. That work boat would end up looking like a piece of grey Swiss cheese. Same goes for the sailors in it.'

Sturdee turned white, grabbed for his radio and started talking very fast.

Chapter Three

There was a rumble of boat engines from the direction of the jetty and a minute or so later a familiar voice asked, 'Coffee?'

The cardboard tray held six takeaway cups with lids. Julie was wearing running shoes, shorts, a singlet top and a light bomber jacket. Only ten minutes behind me, yet she looked clean-scrubbed, fresh-faced, and there wasn't a single blond hair out of place. And she'd even managed to stop to get coffee. I shouldn't have been too surprised. My second-in-command was what some might call an assertive driver.

'I left your truck down by the Opera House,' she said.

I took a coffee from the tray.

'There's supposed to be a total exclusion zone around here, you know.'

'That might be so, Alby, but a winning smile and a dozen donuts can get a girl almost anywhere with the boys in blue.'

I sipped my coffee. It wasn't very good coffee but it *was* coffee. Shame the cops on shore had snaffled all the donuts. I hadn't had breakfast yet.

Peter Sturdee, who had turned round at the mention of donuts, finished his radio call and took a cup.

'Thanks, Jules,' he said. 'Bit of a surprise you answering Alby's phone. I thought maybe I'd dialled the office by mistake.' There was a mischievous twinkle in his eye.

Julie smiled. 'He made me dinner and plied me with wine in the hope of having his wicked way.'

'Hey,' I protested, 'I only wanted to give my new stove a burl.'

Me and Julie and wicked ways was a concept I'd long since given up on.

'Alby's just had one of those swish, stainless-steel SMUG super-kitchens installed,' Julie said, putting down the tray of coffees.

'I thought it was SMEG,' Sturdee said.

'You obviously haven't talked to any of the bastards who own them.'

Sturdee started to smile, then his radio crackled and he turned away.

Julie was staring up at the tanker, then across at the bridge and the Opera House, taking in the situation. 'This looks like it has the potential to get a bit ugly.'

I nodded. 'That's what I was thinking.'

She twisted the top off a Goodie orange juice. Those bloody juices were suddenly everywhere. Some marketing genius was really earning their Christmas bonus.

Sturdee's radio conversation was brief. 'Navy got the message, Alby,' he said, turning back to us. 'They're keeping well clear. And they've spotted some activity at the back end of the boat.'

'That would be the stern,' Julie said. 'Of the ship.'

Sturdee looked at her.

'North Narrabeen Sea Scouts,' I said. 'Merit badge for knots.'

Sturdee took a sip of his coffee. 'Anyway, two bods in black ski masks just unfurled a banner. It says "Halifax" and the numbers "one nine one seven".'

'Jesus H. Christ!'

Sturdee and I both stared at Julie. She's usually not one for religious profanity, though she can do an excellent line in straight-out obscenity if you push her enough.

'My bet is it's supposed to read 1917,' she said.

'I'll bite,' I said, and a few moments later wished I hadn't.

'Halifax, as in the city in Nova Scotia, in Canada,' Julie explained. 'In December 1917 a freighter called the *Mont Blanc* caught fire following a collision and drifted into the main harbour after the crew abandoned ship. Even though she was crammed full of high explosives intended for the allied armies in France, she had no Dangerous Cargo flag flying. At about 9.20 in the morning, with the whole town standing around watching, the burning ship drifted up against the dock and blew herself to pieces, taking most of downtown Halifax with her. Close to two thousand people were killed, and thousands more were badly injured.'

'Bugger me dead!'

I glanced across at Sturdee. 'Couldn't have put it better myself.'

So the guys on the ship were serious, but what the hell did they want? Was this a threat, a warning, part of a demand? But for what?

'Then there's the really bad news,' Julie continued.

'It gets worse?' I asked.

'She's sitting low in the water, which means those LNG tanks are probably full. You need to talk to Emergency Services about the possibility of a blevy.'

I heard a quick intake of breath from Sturdee.

'A blevy? What the fuck's a blevy?'

'B-l-e-v-e – stands for boiling liquid expanding vapour explosion,' Sturdee said quietly. 'It's what happens when a storage container holding flammable liquefied gas under pressure fails as a result of a leak or fire.'

That couldn't be good, I decided.

'As the liquefied gas heats up,' Sturdee went on, 'it produces explosive vapour at a faster and faster rate. When it reaches the point where the tank can't contain the pressure it ruptures, and all the remaining gas vaporises and ignites simultaneously — *ka-boom!* And we're talking about one hell of a big *ka-boom*.'

Now I was really not happy about Julie answering my phone.

'Massive fireball,' Sturdee continued, 'flying chunks of red-hot metal, and a huge pressure wave that flattens everything in its path. You can get a blevy from something as small as a barbecue gas bottle or as big as that.' He indicated the tanker with a tilt of his head. 'It was one of the scenarios in last year's terrorist-attack exercise. Hijacked LPG road tanker set on fire in the CBD. The computer modelling of the blast on a blevy incident simulator wasn't real pretty. And given that each of those four domes there looks like it'd hold about five hundred of those road tankers ...'

No one spoke for a very long minute.

Why hadn't I taken my mate Armando up on his offer of spending the weekend on his farm? Rolling hills, acres of olive trees, a well-stocked larder, and a cellar full of wines that would make you bloody weep.

'So what's the difference between LNG and LPG?' I asked Sturdee.

'I'm a bit fuzzy on that one. We need to ask an expert.'

I looked up at the group on the Martello tower. 'No one from fire services here?'

Sturdee shook his head. 'Three suspicious packages turned up at the oil refineries out at Moorebank around midnight, so the Major Incident bods are all out there.'

'Can we call someone at Moorebank?'

'Nope. The packages look like they're wireless-linked, so they're under total radio silence at the site. They've promised to get back to us as soon as they can.'

'But any fireman should be able to tell us what we're dealing with here, right?'

I looked at Julie, who flipped open her mobile and hit a number.

Julie's younger sister had a penchant for members of the fire brigade. If anyone could put their hands on a fire-fighter at short notice it was Michelle. Julie walked away and started talking as soon as the phone was answered.

Carter Lonergan ambled over and joined us. A lot of men seem to amble over and join me when I'm in Julie's vicinity. I put my sunnies back on. A residual hangover, a wild ride in a cop car, bad coffee and Lonergan's Hawaiian shirt were an unsettling combo.

'Nice shirt, Carter, gives the TV news crews something to focus on. They sell them in the gift shop at Langley?'

'They do as a matter of fact, Alby, right beside the secret-agent radio cufflinks and the suicide pills.'

Crikey, a CIA agent with a sense of humour. What would they think of next?

'So gentlemen,' Lonergan said, glancing at his watch, 'exactly what do we have on our hands here, any ideas?'

The accent was Manhattan, Upper East Side, and the scar on the cheek Afghanistan, post-2001. Carter Lonergan was in his mid-thirties, around six feet, good-looking, I guess, with sandy-coloured Ginger

Meggs-ish hair. He was nowhere near as big a pain in the arse as his predecessor had been, but I was willing to give him time.

'No threats or demands as yet,' I said. 'And as far as I know, no one is claiming responsibility. You have any leads?'

'No, but it's bad timing, what with our new cruiser there in port.'

Maybe I was wrong about the pain-in-the-arse thing.

'Perhaps we can get them to hold off blowing up the city until after she leaves?' Sturdee suggested. 'If it's going to be inconvenient for you.'

Lonergan held up his hands. 'No offence meant.'

'Heaps taken,' Sturdee said with a cold smile.

I was impressed. Peter Sturdee was really shaping up as a special liaison officer.

'So you haven't considered the possibility that whatever the hell is going on here might be due to the presence of that ship, Carter?' I asked.

'No radio chatter, no insider dope, no buzz about anything like this at all. And believe me, we've been watching and listening.'

Ever since an explosives-packed motorboat had rammed the guided missile destroyer USS *Cole* in Yemen's Aden harbour in 2000, the Americans had been ultra-sensitive to the vulnerability of their warships in port. They kept both ears open for even the smallest hint that one of their vessels might be on a target list.

Julie snapped her phone shut and walked back to us. Lonergan, who had developed a severe and unreciprocated case of the hots for Julie as soon as he'd met her, was now smiling at her like a lovesick puppy. It was pathetic. I just hoped he wouldn't make any sudden moves, since Julie held black belts in tae kwon do and karate, and her equivalent of a smack on the nose with a rolled-up newspaper could be pretty awesome.

'Good morning, Mr Lonergan,' she said, smiling sweetly.

I was familiar with that smile. It meant 'Not in a million years.'

'Find out anything?' I asked her.

'We got lucky. Mish was entertaining an off-duty, Hazmat-qualified, Instant Response Team officer.'

'Instant response, eh? Mish would enjoy that.'

Julie narrowed her eyes at me. 'The Hazmat bloke said natural gas is mostly methane, which is liquefied by chilling to minus 260 degrees centigrade, then stored at around normal atmospheric pressure. Those domes are insulated, dual-layer high-nickel steel, designed to keep the gas cool.'

'So what are the odds of a blevy with our mystery ship if things just happen to go pear-shaped?' I asked.

'Moot point,' Julie said. 'The good news is that ocean-going LNG tankers have an almost perfect safety record.'

Like a fool I asked if there was any bad news.

'A worst case scenario would be like Armageddon, only hotter and nastier. The energy potential of your standard LNG tanker is equivalent to 700 000 tons of TNT.'

Sturdee stared at her. 'Seven hundred *thousand* tons of TNT?'

'Or putting it another way,' she continued, 'that ship holds the explosive power of around of fifty Hiroshima-size atomic bombs.'

Chapter Four

Peter Sturdee was looking decidedly pale.

'How long before we can get an OAT in place?' I asked.

OATs, or Offshore Assault Teams, are four-man SAS or Commando units specifically trained for operations against maritime targets. If anyone could sort out what was going on aboard the tanker, it would be the OAT bods. And if anyone on the tanker made the mistake of getting in their way then they'd live to regret it, but not for very long.

'Well, it's just dumb luck,' Sturdee said, 'but there were a couple of OAT units exercising on the Bass Strait offshore oil and gas platforms this weekend. They took off from Sale for Bankstown Airport an hour ago.' He checked his watch. 'They're due to touch down in ten minutes. A pair of army Blackhawks, scrambled from Holsworthy Special Ops Base are standing by to ferry them straight here.'

'Who authorised that?'

'Like I said, I was the only one out here, so …'

It was a ballsy move on Sturdee's part, but at least now we had something in our favour – or we would have when the OATs arrived. I started down towards the Fort Denison flagpole, motioning to Julie to join me.

'Technical question,' I said when we were alone, 'since you've been working in upper management a whole lot longer than I have. Who the hell is actually running this show?'

Julie shrugged. 'Bit of a grey area, I'm afraid. It's probably still a state police matter right at the moment. Officially, if Peter wants the OAT boys to board the tanker he'll have to ask you.'

'But do I have the authority to order an attack on that ship?'

'You know how it works, Alby. If you order an assault and it all pans out okay, then the answer is yes, you do. And every other security department head who took a three-day weekend will be seriously pissed off at their career blunder and will white-ant you for the rest of your life. But if it all goes pear-shaped then the answer is no, you exceeded your authority, and those same departmental heads will be thanking their lucky stars they were smart enough to take the weekend off. And there'll be an in-camera senate inquiry in Canberra where they'll all merrily set about crucifying you.'

'Well, that certainly helped clarify things, Jules, thanks a heap.'

'My pleasure,' she smiled, 'that's what I'm here for. But look on the bright side, Alby, if this whole thing does blow up in our faces we really won't give a rat's anyway. Not if we're standing right here.'

She had a point. I looked at my watch. I had maybe twenty-five minutes before I had to make up my mind about ordering an assault on the ship.

Sturdee joined us. 'I've got a police chopper on its way to do a reconnaissance sweep over the tanker. And the boys on shore are doing a breakfast run.

'That sounds like an excellent plan, Pete, I'll have a bacon and egg roll. And a hash brown. And the part about the chopper is good too.'

'It's nice to see you haven't lost your sense of proportion, Alby. The city is gridlocked, the hospitals are gearing up for a level-one disaster, all emergency services are on full alert, we're on standby to evacuate every building with water views on both sides of the harbour and you're worried about breakfast.'

What I was really worried about was being the one who might have to order eight men in Kevlar helmets and bulletproof vests to do a freefall rappel down ropes from helicopters onto a floating bomb.

Ten minutes later, we heard the *whop whop whop* of rotor blades from over towards Lavender Bay. The police chopper dropped down to a couple of hundred feet above Luna Park and then raced straight towards us, right under the harbour bridge. Sturdee gave instructions on his two-way radio and the chopper began a slow circuit of the tanker, hovering about fifty metres out and around deck height.

It was moving in our direction, towards the front of the ship, when Sturdee's radio crackled with a message from the pilot.

'Movement on the ship,' Sturdee yelled. 'Two men carrying some sort of tube.'

I lifted my camera and focused on two figures moving along the deck, partly silhouetted against the sky. They stopped and one of them knelt down, and when he stood up again I could see a long thin cylindrical shape on his shoulder.

I snatched the radio from Sturdee's hand and before he could react I was speaking as calmly and clearly as I could into the mouthpiece.

'Abort! Abort! Abort! Subjects onboard are armed with anti-aircraft missile. Clear the area immediately. I repeat, clear the area immediately.'

The chopper's nose went up at the words 'anti-aircraft missile' and then it dropped straight down to water level and scooted towards the stern of the ship. The pilot was good – putting the bulk of the tanker between himself and the missile was exactly the right thing to do as surface-to-air missiles need a rough visual fix so that the infrared tracking can lock on. The chopper made a straight run up the Harbour towards Point Piper, still using the hull of the tanker as shelter. It zoomed up over the trees and then ducked down out of sight on the other side of the headland.

When I looked back at the deck of the tanker the two men had disappeared. I put my camera in my bag and handed Sturdee his radio.

'You sure that was what you thought it was?' he asked.

I nodded. 'Grail. Russian surface-to-air missile. Popular black-market item for people who like that sort of thing.'

Sturdee took a slow deep breath. 'Fuck this for a game of soldiers.'

His mobile rang and he answered it quickly. It was a long conversation which mostly involved Sturdee nodding his head in agreement with whoever was on the other end.

'Incident room at HQ,' he said when the call ended. 'They monitored your radio message about the missile and reckon this puts the whole thing squarely in federal hands. Alby, over to you, mate. What do you think we should do next?'

'Close Kingsford Smith and Bankstown airports immediately, shut down all air traffic. The only things I want flying are the Blackhawks with the OATs.'

'Gotcha. They've just left Bankstown. ETA fifteen minutes.' Sturdee punched the buttons on his phone.

I looked over at Lonergan, who was on his mobile. He finished the call, glanced at his watch and walked across.

'CNN picked up the story of a mystery tanker moored off the Sydney Opera House,' he said. 'They've been running it live in the UK and some Scottish insomniac just rang CNN's London office to say he recognised the ship. Says she was Clyde-built and then laid up in a deepwater bay opposite his house for the last six or seven years.'

'Did he know why she was laid up?'

'Apparently she failed certification to carry LNG. The stuff kept leaking out of a couple of badly built tanks. She was too expensive to repair so they mothballed her. Then she disappeared one night a couple of months back.'

'If she won't hold gas because of shonky construction,' I said, 'what the hell is she doing tied up here with anti-personnel mines hanging off the side and anti-aircraft missiles on deck, scaring the brown out of everyone?'

'It could be a decoy,' Julie suggested. 'Or maybe a distraction.'

'Distraction from what?' Lonergan asked. 'This would have taken a lot of money and time to organise. What kind of operation would justify a distraction on this scale?'

Even as he said it I saw a strange look on his face – part comprehension and part fear. He spun around and stared across the water towards the American cruiser moored at the dock. And that was when the shooting started.

Chapter Five

It was hard to place where the gunfire was coming from. When I looked around the guys on the tower had taken cover behind the parapet, Lonergan and Julie were down flat on the ground with me, Peter Sturdee was in a half-crouch with one hand on his still-holstered police-issue Glock, and the uniformed cop by the jetty was looking about in confusion. I had my Sauer 38H out and cocked, Lonergan was gripping a Khar K9, and Julie had a black, Teflon-coated ASP. No question about it, Julie had the coolest gun.

The cop by the jetty was staring in our direction now, probably trying to figure out why the bloke from the press, the girl with the coffee, and the Yank in the loud shirt were so well tooled up. I was trying to figure out where Julie had managed to put her hands on that nifty little ASP, and where the hell she'd had it hidden in the outfit she was wearing.

The firing picked up – M16s, I reckoned – but nothing in the form of hot lead seemed to be coming our way, so I stood up. I could see muzzle flashes on the stern of the American cruiser. There was the sound of a helicopter lifting off at full revs, and the firing suddenly stopped. Seconds later, I was surrounded by people yelling into two-way radios.

Everyone was looking towards the cruiser, except for the young walloper who was pointing at the top of the LNG tanker and shouting.

Two men, dressed in black and wearing ski masks, were clambering up a metal stairway on the front dome. It looked like one hell of a tricky climb to the top of that thing, with a bastard of a drop down to the steel deck if you missed your footing.

Suddenly the wash from a US Navy Seahawk was lifting dust from the ground at our feet, and there was heat and a strong smell of burnt jet fuel. The helicopter went into a hover over the front LNG dome, its massive rotor blades thrashing the air. A masked, black-clad figure in the chopper's open doorway was pointing an M16 down in our direction. We had absolutely no cover, but luckily no one on our side was stupid enough to point a firearm back.

The noise from the engines was deafening. Lonergan was shouting into his mobile and Sturdee was yelling in my ear.

'We've got police snipers stationed on top of the bridge pylons and on the Opera House,' he screamed. 'What do you reckon we should do? It's your show now, Alby, and you're bloody welcome to it. I'm sure as hell not about to tell anyone to open fire.'

Good idea. It would be an almost impossible shot from either position, but bringing down a US Navy Seahawk in a friendly port in front of a CNN live-satellite feed couldn't possibly be good for US/Australian relations and would definitely put a serious crimp in the Free Trade Agreement. And a six-tonne aircraft chock-full of fuel dropping onto the Fort would put a serious crimp in us.

'Everyone holds their fire until we figure out what's happening,' I yelled.

Sturdee nodded and put his radio to his ear.

Above us, the Seahawk pilot manoeuvred in close to the top of the dome and the first of the waiting men leapt the narrow gap between the dome and the chopper and scrambled into the cabin. I dropped my pistol into my camera bag, grabbed my Nikon, and rattled off a burst of twenty or so frames of the hovering aircraft. The pilot swung away from the ship momentarily and then eased back in, but the gap was wider this time and the second man jumped too soon. He hit the metal cargo deck of the chopper with a thud you could almost feel, the lower half of his body hanging out the doorway, legs kicking. A black-clad arm grabbed him by the belt and hauled him inside.

Lonergan stopped shouting into his phone, covered his other ear with his hand to block out the chopper noise and listened intently. Then, swear to God, he turned as white as a sheet. You think it's just an expression until you see the blood drain right out of a man's face like that. Suddenly he was yelling, 'Don't shoot! Don't shoot! Don't shoot!' with an urgency that got everyone's attention.

The chopper lifted away from the tanker, and with both engines screaming started a run up the harbour. In sixty seconds the Seahawk was out of sight and it was suddenly very, very quiet. There was only the sound of waves lapping against the fort and the wail of sirens in the distance

'Peter,' I yelled, breaking the stunned silence around me, 'get the OAT guys on board *now*! We need prisoners, information, anything.'

We could see frantic activity on the *Altoona*'s empty chopper deck and ambulances were screaming onto the wharf.

'You were right on the money, Jules,' I said. 'That tanker was an 80 000 tonne distraction. We were set up, and I bloody fell for it.'

Two army Blackhawks roared overhead as we jumped aboard the Yank Navy inflatable with Lonergan and the American officers. The coxswain had the engines screaming and the nose up as soon as we left the dock and we bounced off every damn wave between the island and the cruiser, with the bitter salt spray soaking everyone on board. No one spoke a word on the three minute journey. Looking back at Fort Denison, I could see the Assault Teams rappelling down onto the tanker from the hovering choppers.

Sturdee, Lonergan and I clambered awkwardly onto the dock near the stern of the *Altoona*. Julie and the officers were a lot more graceful about it. As we ran towards the cruiser a bunch of nervous-looking American sailors in helmets and flak vests, members of the ship's Security Alert Team, pointed combat shotguns and M16s in our direction. They lowered their weapons when they saw the US officers. There was a neat row of plastic body bags, what the Americans call *human remains pouches*, on the dock near the gangway. So we had three dead already.

Dockside, Navy medics and local ambulance officers were working frantically on the injured. A motorcycle paramedic with his helmet still on was doing vigorous chest compressions on a sailor who had a hole in his thigh you could drive a bus through. He was desperately chanting, 'Breathe, you bastard, breathe, you bastard,' as he pushed down. More ambulances were speeding onto the dock with lights and sirens going full tilt and I could see a TV news crew setting up out in the street just past Harry's Café de Wheels. A bunch of press photographers were milling about the dock gate, held back by a couple of cops and some Naval Police. Diego Vega, a new member of the WorldPix team was elbowing his way to the front of the pack.

I was keeping well back, trying to stay out of everybody's way. Lonergan joined me after a brief conversation with a group of American officers. He was confused and angry, which he had every right to be since, as local CIA chief, the fallout from all this would land at his feet.

'Maybe we should go talk to the captain,' I suggested.

Lonergan thought about it for a moment, then nodded. 'He's on the helicopter deck with some medics. Got a bullet through the shoulder.'

Lonergan led Julie and me up the gangway to the helicopter deck. Deep gouges from close-range bullet hits scored the sides of the empty hangar. The usual post-gunfight stink of cordite hung in the air, and the deck was spattered with blood and littered with empty cartridge cases.

A medical officer was bandaging the captain's left shoulder. The captain waved the medic away when he saw Lonergan and they had a brief conversation, most of which involved the captain shaking his head. Finally he relented, and Lonergan called Julie and me over and did the introductions. The captain glanced warily at Julie, then at Lonergan.

'Ms Danko knows more about my job than I do,' I said, 'and she's cleared to hear everything I am.'

'You know I can't tell you much,' the captain said.

'Maybe I should just guess, then. Had a bit of trouble and lost a helicopter?'

He looked at Lonergan again who nodded.

'We have three men dead,' the captain said after a long pause, 'God knows how many wounded, eight men AWOL and a missing Seahawk.'

'Lose anything else, Captain?'

There aren't too many things that can make a career CIA operative like Carter Lonergan turn white, so I took a punt. 'Like a nuclear warhead, for instance?'

The captain's jaw was clenched so tight I expected to hear the sound of exploding molars.

'You understand that I can neither confirm nor deny the presence of nuclear weapons on my vessel.'

The way he said 'my vessel' told me he understood it wasn't going to be his ship for very much longer. If there's a constant in navies worldwide – besides the predilection for grey paint, buggery and bell-bottom trousers – it's that no one gets away with a major screw-up. This poor bastard's next command would probably be a desk, if he was bloody lucky.

'So I guess, Captain,' I said, 'that means you can neither confirm nor deny the absence of a nuclear warhead?'

Again he glanced at Lonergan who shrugged, nodded and looked down at his shoes.

'Hell, Mr Murdoch,' the captain said quietly, 'I couldn't even confirm or deny the absence of *two* nuclear warheads.'

At that he turned and vomited over the side of the ship, into the sun-kissed, pale-blue waters of Sydney Harbour. I knew exactly how he felt.

Chapter Six

THE *ALTOONA*'S CAPTAIN INSISTED ON WALKING OFF HIS SHIP RATHER than being carried. He saluted the quarterdeck, paused momentarily on the dock beside the body bags, shook his head slowly, then turned and walked to the waiting ambulance.

Carter Lonergan was in conference with a group of navy officers. He broke away from them and walked across the deck to where Julie and I were standing.

'Ship's executive officer wants to put out a press release saying there was a small electrical explosion in one of the galley storage bays.'

I looked at the body bags and the TV crews and the ambulance carrying the captain roaring out of the main gate, siren wailing.

'Exploding baked beans? That should work,' I said, 'especially if you redirect the wounded to the emergency department at Saint Stupid's Hospital and have them examined by a bunch of legally blind medical students.'

Lonergan's right eye twitched and the scar on his cheek tightened.

'This isn't the kind of situation you can spin away with a press release and your fingers crossed, Lonergan. This is two missing nuclear warheads, for God's sake!'

'So what the fuck do you suggest?' he snapped.

'Well, for starters, how about not bringing nuclear weapons into our front parlour. And if you do bring the bloody things in, at least have a responsible adult keep an eye on them.'

I figured Lonergan's fist was just about to start on an anger-fuelled, upward trajectory towards my jaw when a khaki-clad US Navy lieutenant joined us. The lieutenant had been sitting on the helicopter deck when we boarded, leaning back on a bulkhead looking totally exhausted. A less evolved person than myself might have noted that this particular sailor had rather perky breasts under her neatly pressed shirt. She was tall, with tawny-blond hair and dark brown eyes and was wearing a blue baseball cap with NAVY in big yellow letters on the front. The whole package was accented by a webbing belt and a pistol in a holster on her right hip. I'm a sucker for a girl in uniform, especially when she's packing a gun.

'I'm Lieutenant Kingston,' she said, 'and I would like to point out, without confirming or denying the existence of fissile armaments, that our security systems for transport, storage, sterile containment and safe disbursement of said armaments are second to none.'

'Bully for you but right now your security systems are looking a bit shabby, so let's cut to the chase. What's missing exactly, who took them, and why? We can leave the *how* to the secret commission of inquiry down the track.'

There was a Beretta semiautomatic pistol in that holster on her hip, and I could see she was very tempted to take it out and use it. If looks could kill I'd already be pushing up gerberas. The Beretta is a bit of a hefty gun, but the lieutenant looked like she could handle it. Right about then I noticed some red spatters on the left shoulder of her shirt.

'That looks like blood,' I said. 'You get injured in the gunfight?'

She shook her head. 'It's not mine. I was next to the captain when they fired back at us from the helicopter.'

'Sorry, must have been a bit grim. But your skipper looks like he's going to be okay.'

Lieutenant Kingston seemed to soften a little.

'And I'm sorry if I was short with you, Lieutenant, but I haven't had a decent cup of coffee this morning and someone played me for a sucker with that tanker out there, and things like that tend to put me in a bad mood.'

I held out my hand. 'My name's Alby Murdoch, and to all intents and purposes I'm a member of the local press. But I'm covert ops with D-E-D, I'm the senior Australian operative on the ground this morning, and I have clearance at the highest level, which Mr Lonergan here can confirm. So let's see what we can do about getting your missing, non-confirmable, non-deniable items back.'

The Lieutenant glanced at Lonergan, who nodded, then she shook my hand.

'Apology accepted,' she said. 'The name's Clare.'

'Nice to meet you Clare. Now, while everything's still fresh in everyone's mind, why don't we have a debrief.'

The lieutenant looked at Julie.

'This is my associate, Julie Danko,' I said. 'She has clearance to hear whatever I hear, which Mr Lonergan can also confirm.'

'I'm limited in what I can tell you,' the lieutenant said. 'However, it appears that eight members of our ship's crew conspired to illegally obtain two items of United States government property and remove them from the USS *Altoona* by helicopter.'

'Can you describe these items?' I asked. 'Without confirming or denying what they are, of course.'

'The items in question are cylindrical, around thirty inches long, twelve inches in diameter, and weigh in at approximately two hundred and fifty pounds each.'

What a wonderful age of miniaturisation we live in, I thought. Video cameras that fit in your hand, iPods the size of business cards, and nuclear warheads no bigger than a beer keg. A bit bulky, but at a smidge over a hundred kilos, easy enough for two or three strong men to handle.

'Your eight missing sailors weren't gym junkies, by any chance?'

'They were all bodybuilders. Spent most of their free time in the weight room.'

That made sense. 'Apart from the crew-cuts and the rippling muscles, did these blokes have anything else in common? Regular meeting place? Similar hobbies or interests?'

The Lieutenant nodded. 'They had their duty rosters arranged so they could get together at least four or five times a week to rehearse, and always on Sundays, of course.'

'Rehearse what, and why always on Sundays?'

She looked slightly embarrassed.

'Because, Mr Murdoch, the eight men involved make up our ship's choir.'

Chapter Seven

The Sydney office of WorldPix International Photo Agency is located on the eastern side of an old wooden pier, a relic from the days when the harbour was a busy international shipping hub. The office looks like any other successful photo agency: open-plan, minimalist, floor-to-ceiling windows, award-winning pictures on the walls, computer workstations interspersed with lounge areas, a well set-up studio, and the ubiquitous pool table in the corner near the kitchen.

We've also got a small darkroom, just for developing and printing black and white. I'm the only one who ever uses it, and all the young guys who shoot exclusively on digital like to point and laugh. I'm pretty sure they'd call me a Luddite if they knew what it meant. While I shoot digital on assignment, for my personal work I find the traditional wet darkroom very relaxing. I enjoy splashing around in the developer and fixer fumes under the amber glow of the safelights, making prints that I know are going to last a lot longer than I will.

If you unlock the chemical-storage cupboard at the rear of the darkroom and then lean hard on the back wall, you hear a click and next thing you're standing in a stationery cupboard, which opens out into the D-E-D office – a nifty shortcut for us Dedheads who work on both sides of the business.

The Sydney HQ of D-E-D fronts the western side of the pier and the sign on the door reads WorldPix archival storage – management only. This justifies Julie's presence there from time to time. Publicly, Julie is the Sydney manager of WorldPix, enabling her to coordinate the assignments of the real WorldPix photographers and the D-E-D operatives working undercover.

The windowless space used to be a secure document-storage facility and we left it pretty much as we found it, just putting in the connecting darkroom door, a bathroom, a galley kitchen with a heavy-duty espresso machine, and a gun safe –everything the modern office needs.

By the time Peter Sturdee and I arrived, Julie had the computers booted up, the espresso machine humming and the conference table set up. I had a quick shower and shave and was grinding a batch of coffee beans when Lonergan and Lieutenant Kingston arrived in his big black Chevy Suburban. I couldn't tell from our surveillance monitors whether the vehicle had cia agent vanity plates, but with the tinted windows, multiple radio antennae, and the throb of a turbo-charged V8, it might as well have.

Lieutenant Kingston was in civvies now: khaki chinos, Converse one-star runners and a white polo shirt. She was carrying a large black zippered folder and a leather shoulder bag. The polo shirt confirmed my earlier assessment of perky and the shoulder bag made a solid, Beretta-ish thump when she put it on the floor.

She smiled, and I thought I detected a definite shift in her attitude towards me. I'd been checked out by sailors before, but never by one that good-looking.

I returned her smile. 'Coffee, Clare?'

'Yes please. You have decaf?'

'Nope. Just coffee.'

'Soy milk?'

''fraid not.'

This wasn't a good sign. But I had to make allowances – the poor woman had probably been raised on Nescafe and caramel frappuccinos.

She settled for a flat white, and once everyone was right for coffee we sat down at the conference table.

Lonergan spoke first. 'Washington, via Langley, obviously wants this resolved as quickly and as quietly as possible. I've had a flash authorising me to form an interim taskforce from the people in this room to track down the missing items. Crisis teams from the Navy, NSA, FBI and other interested agencies will be flying in under the cover of a standard investigation into the accidental death of on-duty US military personnel.'

The Americans liked to make a big deal about how the Russians weren't able to keep their nukes safely under lock and key after the break-up of the Soviet Union, so having a couple of their own go missing would be embarrassing. But nowhere near as embarrassing as it would be if the nukes went off.

'Until the crisis teams are on the ground and organised,' Lonergan continued, 'we run with the investigation, with a total security lockdown. The story released to the press is that an accidental fire in a small arms storage locker set off rifle and pistol ammunition, which was responsible for the casualties.'

He glanced at me. I shrugged. It was a bit more plausible than that fire-in-the-kitchen yarn. Our own people were busily working on a cover story for the LNG tanker that was cluttering up the harbour. Engine failure was the current favourite. How they would explain a chopper assault on the tanker by Australian special forces was their problem, and they were welcome to it.

'Lieutenant Kingston here,' Lonergan said, 'is our liaison officer with the Navy.'

'Okay,' I said, 'you want to go first, Lieutenant?

Clare opened a folder. 'Summing up what we know so far, under cover of a possible terrorist threat from a tanker moored in Sydney Harbour, and a reduced crew presence due to shore leave, eight crewman from the USS *Altoona*, acting in concert, illegally removed two items from the ship, by helicopter, under gunfire. The US Navy can neither confirm nor deny that these items were two W80 Model 26J RS/EVY thermonuclear warheads.'

'I know this is probably highly-classified information,' I said, 'but if I Google the W80 what would I find out?'

Clare sighed. 'Possibly that the Model 26J RS/EVY is a reduced-size, expanded variable-yield modification of the W80 warhead and that the maximum yield per unit is 150 kilotons.'

There was a long silence which was broken by Peter Sturdee. 'Exactly how dangerous are these bloody things? I mean as in just standing around them?'

'Since they also may or may not be designated for deployment on submarine launched cruise missiles,' Clare explained, 'the 26J uses super grade low-neutron emission plutonium to reduce occupational radiation exposure.' She smiled. 'Submarine crews on extended patrols are a little averse to having their testicles irradiated – hypothetically, of course.'

The men in the room shifted uncomfortably in their seats. I wondered if Sturdee had hypothetically considered having his testicles irradiated after that second set of twins. Or perhaps at least disconnected.

'As to why these items were removed,' Clare continued, 'that remains very much a mystery. The only common link we can find at this point in time is membership of an off-duty choral group.'

'Ship's Choir Nicks Nukes,' Julie said. 'Now that's a headline the *Sunday Telegraph* would love to run.'

Lonergan looked glum. 'And it's our job to make sure they never get the chance.'

That was how this was going to play out, of course. Priority two would be getting the nukes back. Priority one would be keeping a lid on the story.

Clare handed some folders to Lonergan, who passed them round. 'I thought these might be useful,' she said. The stamp on the front said TOP SECRET.

The folders contained dossiers on each of the eight missing crewmen, with names, ID photographs, personal details and shipboard duties. These boys were all career crew and only two were from the same state. One was a chopper pilot, three were electronic-warfare specialists, two were helicopter mechanics, one a weapons technician, and the last was a culinary specialist, military speak for a ship's cook.

'Do you have any record of unusual activity by these choirboys during the last week?' I asked.

Clare checked her files. 'Nothing out of the ordinary. Just their regular work roster, rehearsals and gym time. And they were all back on board and accounted for by midnight last night.'

That made me sit up. 'Back on board from where?'

'They sang at Evensong at the First Church of The Lord's Bounty in Martin Place, and afterwards at a private recital, some place called Jindivick. Does that mean anything to anyone?'

If Lieutenant Kingston had been on the bridge of the cruiser as it came up the harbour she might have noticed a neat little point on her left with a number of palatial mansions built right down to the water's edge. There were some pretty glitzy joints on Point Piper, but the jewel in Sydney's waterfront crown was Jindivick, a 1930s Spanish Mission-style extravaganza that was even more opulent than Elizabeth Bay's famed Boomerang.

When people talk prime waterfront in Sydney they talk Point Piper and Jindivick. And when they talk Jindivick they start at about 35 million dollars. As anyone who watched tabloid television or kept up with the Sunday papers' social pages knew, the current occupant was the Reverend Laurence LaSalle Priday, former business tycoon and white-collar felon and now head of the First Church of the Lord's Bounty.

The church itself was located in Martin Place, smack in the middle of the financial district, in what was originally the headquarters of the Rural Colonial Bank. No dicking about in the leafy outer suburbs for this preacher. The fully restored, heritage-listed, eight-storey pile was built back in the days when money was no object, and today, prime central business district acreage doesn't get much more prime.

But what the hell was the Reverend Laurence LaSalle Priday doing entertaining a ship's choir on the night before what was shaping up to be some pretty unholy business?

'Okay,' I said, 'we need to start somewhere. Carter, see if you can track down exactly who brought the LNG tanker into port and how. Clare and Peter, you head back to the cruiser and turn our missing choirboys' bunks and lives upside down and inside out. Look for anything that links them together besides hymns and larceny. Julie will co-ordinate everything from here; it all goes through her. We haven't got time to be doubling up or tripping over ourselves. And Julie, hit your network and see what you can dig up.'

Julie had extensive contacts in local and overseas intelligence services, and in the military, law enforcement, law breaking, and some other areas that were just plain weird. In five minutes she'd be researching on the Net, emailing, phoning, and for all I knew flashing a heliograph or sending smoke signals from up on the roof.

'I'll be on my mobile if you need me, Jules.'

Lonergan looked at me. 'Where're you headed?'

'With two missing nukes in the hands of God knows who, I think now is the perfect time for me to seek some spiritual guidance.'

Chapter Eight

WHEN SHE OPENED THE DOOR I WASN'T SURE IF SHE WAS THE REVEREND'S wife or his daughter. Then I remembered Julie's briefing: the stunningly gorgeous nineteen-year-old brunette is the daughter, the totally gorgeous 24-year-old blonde is the wife. Totally gorgeous was a bit of an understatement – Mrs Louise Priday was a knock-out. The Reverend Laurence LaSalle Priday had so much to be grateful for.

Mrs Priday was barefoot and wearing very short shorts and a pale-pink midriff shirt knotted under her breasts. The knot was straining a little at holding everything in. Her stomach was flat and tanned and toned and so dammed tight I bet bullets would bounce right off. She pulled the huge wooden front door back and invited me in, after first eyeing me like I was the last lamb chop at a barbie. Flirtatious was an understatement for Mrs Priday, and no matter how hard I tried to keep my mind on the job as I followed her down the hall, the back view of those shorts was extremely distracting.

We entered the biggest reception hall I'd ever seen in my life. Whole forests of old-growth trees must have given up their lives for the panelling in this room alone.

'My husband should be back shortly, Inspector Murdoch,' the Reverend Mrs Priday said.

The fake police ID comes in handy in a situation like this, or when someone gets curious about the concealed pistol under my left armpit.

'Can I offer you a little something in the meantime?'

She smiled and gave me that look again. Downright predatory.

I settled for a glass of water, and Mrs Priday ushered me out to the sunny terrace and disappeared back into the house to organise it.

The terrace was bigger than my whole apartment, and 35 million gets you a rather nice view. It included a curvaceous brunette in a bikini sunning herself on a slatted wooden deckchair, sipping a Goodie watermelon juice. This would have to be the teenage daughter. She glanced up from her book and smiled. It was a really lovely smile.

'I'm Cristobel,' she said, sitting up and closing her book.

'My name's Alby, Alby Murdoch,' I said. 'I'm just waiting for your dad. Good book?'

She held it up.' It most certainly is, Mr Murdoch. The very best book, in fact.'

The combination of a King James Bible and a Tiger Lily bikini was pretty arresting and I found myself lost for words.

'It's very hot today, isn't it Mr Murdoch? Is Louise getting you a drink?'

I nodded. 'Nice place you've got here,' I said.

'We *are* blessed. A generous benefactor donated this wonderful home for the use of the church, and Daddy feels we should live here as an inspiration to others.'

The way she said it sounded totally genuine, even a little touching. By sheer force of will I took my eyes off Cristobel's tanned, lithe body and looked out over the harbour. In the distance I could see Fort Denison and the moored tanker, which was now surrounded by police and Navy launches.

'Nice view. Must have been a bit scary this morning, though?'

Cristobel shook her head. 'We saw the tanker and heard about the proposed evacuation order on the radio, but Daddy said there was nothing for us to worry about.'

That was interesting. While half the city's emergency personnel were panicking about the possibility of a great big bang, the Priday clan were happily sipping their fruit juice and coffee without a care in the world.

'You studying any part of the Bible in particular, Ms Priday?'

'I help Daddy with his sermons sometimes. Right now we're looking at the story of Jonah.'

'And the whale?'

'Exactly! Did you know we had a pair of whales right here in the harbour this year, Mr Murdoch? I think whales are the most wonderful of all God's creatures.'

That pair of whales, like thousands of Japanese tourists, had chosen Sydney for their honeymoon. I'd photographed them getting hot and heavy in the waters near the Opera House. WorldPix had made a stack of money syndicating the images internationally.

Cristobel stood up and tied a tropical-print sarong around her waist. 'I'll see what's keeping Louise with your drink, Mr Murdoch.'

With that body and in that bikini I should have been thinking lustful thoughts, but she was just too dammed wholesome. Plus I was wondering why the Reverend had dismissed the evacuation order. Was he just a father reassuring his daughter, a man of the cloth putting his faith in the Lord, or was there some other reason?

Louise and Cristobel wandered back out onto the terrace a few minutes later, side by side and smiling, arms around each other's waist. Louise handed me a glass full of ice and Cristobel filled it with Italian sparkling mineral water from the bottle she was carrying. She beamed at Louise. 'Isn't she beautiful, Mr Murdoch?'

'What wonders God hath wrought.'

Cristobel stared at me. 'Are you saved, Mr Murdoch?'

I shook my head. 'Bit of a lapsed Presbyterian, actually. I was expelled from Sunday School for disruptive behaviour. After that I sort of lost interest in religion.'

'You shouldn't say something like that around Cristobel, Mr Murdoch,' Louise said, 'she might just decide to take you on as a challenge.'

'Is she making any headway with you?' I said, and immediately felt a little embarrassed for saying it.

Louise smiled. 'With Cristobel's guidance I have come to understand the reasons for some of my earlier indiscretions.'

I'd seen some of those indiscretions, as had anyone else who'd bought the June 2003 issue of *Bloke*. They'd also seen a whole lot more besides. *Bloke* wasn't the kind of magazine anybody bought for the articles, so there weren't any, and the pictures left nothing to the imagination.

The Sunday gossip columns had had a field day when the middle-aged convicted fraudster and the spunky young centrefold and party-girl became pen pals, in the truest sense of the word. When Priday was finally paroled Louise was waiting at the gate. The fact that the marriage had now lasted three years surprised everybody.

There was a melodic toot and the crunch of tyres on gravel, and we headed out to the driveway to greet the master of the house.

Back in Sunday School I was taught that when God talked directly to one of the faithful it was to ask them to help the sick or the lame, or to lead His people out of slavery. These days the first thing the Almighty appears to request is that His spiritual representative here on earth set himself up with some really smooth wheels. And wheels don't come any smoother than the sleek silver-grey Mercedes-Benz Maybach 57S that the Reverend Laurence LaSalle Priday was driving. A particularly nice automobile that got you very little change from a million bucks.

Priday climbed elegantly out of the Maybach's leather drivers seat. He was tall, tanned, fifty-ish and fit-looking, his carefully styled hair greying gently at the temples. His suit was beautifully tailored and when he smiled at the Priday women you could see why tens of thousands of people who really should have known better had invested hundreds of millions of dollars in his many and varied and – as it panned out – downright dodgy enterprises. The Reverend Laurence LaSalle Priday was as smooth as a rat with a gold tooth.

Surprisingly, though, he'd had the decency not to flee the country after the biggest financial collapse in Australian corporate history. While doing his seven years in minimum security, with three off for good behaviour, Priday had discovered God.

The lovely Cristobel had shown her old man the Light on her twice-weekly visits to the country-club prison where he was doing penance, planting gum trees as part of a bush-regeneration project. Priday had altered the Light slightly, and discovered his own special flock. Old money really didn't give a damn about how wealthy they were or where it all came from but the nouveau riche could be a bit uncomfortable with success and its earthly rewards. Priday had crafted the First Church of the Lord's Bounty just for them, creating a haven for the aspirational and upwardly mobile middle-class, where making scads of money was God's will and actually a valid form of worship.

Priday's faithful flock became rich *because* they were faithful, and this was the way it was meant to be. Of course they did good works and made modest donations to worthwhile causes, but the major draw was that they were under the care of a God who was glad they were rich and would be even happier if they became richer still. As the Internet-ordained Reverend Priday preached it, God was the chairman of their board and Jesus was his CEO. And generous donations directed to the church would be rewarded ten and twenty and thirty times over sometime down the track. It was a very sweet deal, and one with tremendous tax advantages.

The Reverend kissed his wife and his daughter, shook my hand and led me into the study, where the polished-oak shelving groaned under the weight of leather-bound first editions, the andirons in the walk-in fireplace were Toledo steel, and the whisky on the bar was a 21-year-old single malt at two hundred dollars the bottle. He offered me a drink, and though the sun wasn't quite over the yardarm no-one in their right mind would say no to a lead-crystal tumbler full of Glenfarclas.

'A splash of water?' he asked, holding up a crystal decanter. 'It's melted ice from an Antarctic glacier. One hundred per cent pure and 10 thousand years old.'

'Who could resist?' I said.

The amber coloured liquid was almost as smooth as the Reverend.

'Now, what can I do to help you, Inspector Murdoch?'

'I'm investigating an incident involving members of the choir from the USS *Altoona* and I'm looking into their movements yesterday.'

'I heard about the accident on my car radio,' Priday said, sipping his whisky. 'Don't tell me any of those wonderful young men were injured.'

'No, they're all fine as far as I know,' which was technically correct. 'Can you tell me how they came to be performing at your church?'

'Of course. One of my parishioners told me about the choir, Inspector. She heard them on a visit to San Diego and found them inspirational. When we learned that they were coming to Sydney we invited them to celebrate Evensong with us. We held a little reception here last night as a way of saying thank you. It was a joyous night. Very uplifting.'

Their performance on the *Altoona* this morning had been pretty uplifting too – they'd uplifted a couple of nuclear warheads right out from under the nose of the US Navy.

'Was there anything unusual in their behaviour last night?'

'No, nothing at all. They sang beautifully for us then mingled pleasantly with the guests. Why do you ask?' He tried to make it sound like a casual question but I could see he was edgy.

'Just routine, Reverend.' I ran my eye around Priday's study and stopped at the signed Chagall etching over the fireplace. 'I see you don't buy into that *rich man and the camel through the eye of a needle* business?'

'I'm just a simple man trying to do the Lord's bidding, Inspector.'

'Here's to the simple life,' I said, raising the glass and finishing my whisky. He didn't offer me a refill.

'Churches have to move with the times, Inspector. Hopes for a reward in the hereafter may have sufficed once but life is more complex now and people expect to see a tangible return on the time and effort expended in worship.'

'Isn't that a bit more Milton Friedman than Jesus of Nazareth?'

'Modern religion is all about niches. There is a particular spiritual need out there right now and I fill it.'

'And in return you get all this.'

'It's about inspiration, Inspector, and aspiration. I lead my flock by example.'

'So if Jesus came back tomorrow your flock would be happier if he was less of a carpenter and more of a property developer in an Italian suit with a Rolex and a Beamer.'

Priday smiled. 'These days, I'm afraid, it's about whatever floats your boat.'

'Which in your case would be a hundred foot cruiser with a full crew, a helipad and an indoor swimming pool.'

'The good lord provides, Inspector.'

I had a sudden urge to smack the smug bastard. Maybe the Sunday school incident had scarred me for life when it came to organised religion.

Priday glanced at the Tag Heuer Aquaracer on his wrist. It was a nice watch but it definitely looked better on Brad Pitt.

'Is there anything else I can help you with?' he asked.

'It doesn't seem so, Reverend,' I said. I thanked him for his co-operation and hospitality, shook his hand and took my leave.

At the front door of Jindivick, the two women in the Reverend's life were waiting to say goodbye. Louise Priday was now wearing a bikini. It might not have been yellow polka-dot like in that song from the sixties but it sure as hell was itsy-bitsy, teeny-weeny. I smiled at the Reverend's spunky missus and equally spunky daughter and imagined them together in the pool downstairs, Cristobel frolicking like a dolphin while the tanned and toned Mrs Priday swam laps, cutting silently and purposefully through the water like a grey nurse shark.

On the long trek back up the gravel driveway to normal land, I made a special effort not to yield to residual working-class angst and key the immaculate paint job on the Maybach. While I might not have found out anything useful about the choir, my visit to Jindivick hadn't been a complete waste of time. When Cristobel had gone to check on my drink and left me alone on the terrace, I'd come across a beautifully restored antique brass telescope mounted on a set of polished wooden legs. Being the inquisitive type, I naturally took a quick squiz. Bugger me if I wasn't looking right at a nicely in-focus image of two blokes having an argument on top of the front gas storage dome on the LNG tanker.

One of the blokes in the shouting match I recognised as Chapman F. Pergo, special assistant to the Minister for Defence and a well-known political hard man, fixer and head kicker. The other was the CIA's Carter Lonergan. I probably didn't need the telescope, you couldn't miss that bloody shirt at a mile.

Chapter Nine

Back at the D-E-D office, Julie had been working the phones hard. She updated me on the team's progress. Lonergan had been out on the LNG tanker, but I already knew that. Peter Sturdee and Lt. Kingston had visited the *Altoona*, picked through the choirboys' rubbish bins and lockers, questioned every single crew member on board and come up with nothing. Now, they were on their way back from the hospital after interviewing the captain and the wounded sailors. The *Altoona*'s crew hadn't given in without a fight, but who in their right mind would have expected the God Squad to pop up from below decks in flak jackets, guns blazing, and a couple of nuclear warheads in tow?

Julie buzzed Lonergan in through the front door.

'That Scottish insomniac was right,' he said, pulling a wad of papers from an impossibly thin stainless-steel attaché case. 'Preliminary reports from Glasgow confirm the tanker was mothballed around seven years ago. Her engines were totally overhauled recently, so she made it out here under her own power, and those gas-storage tanks were partially filled with seawater for ballast, so that she sat low in the water like she was carrying a full cargo. The anti-personnel mines are dummies, and the crew's quarters have been recently used but swept clean. No food, no clothes, no books, not even toilet paper. Looks like they may have dumped all the incriminating evidence over the side before they came through the heads.'

'There's harbour-surveillance footage from the Sydney Ports cameras showing the tanker cruising up the western channel around 3 am and anchoring off Fort Denison at 3.45,' Julie said.

'So the surveillance cameras were working?' Lonergan asked.

'They were recording, but nothing was received in the tower because of the blackout. Apparently the tapes also show three people leaving the tanker in a zodiac soon after she moored. Cops found the zodiac sunk at the Rose Bay wharf. Forensics have been all over it but it's the same story as the tanker, clean as a whistle.'

'Could have been the pilot going ashore,' I said. 'Pete said the harbour master reckons you don't run something that size up the harbour in the middle of the night without bumping into things unless you really know what you're doing.'

Julie, as usual, was one step ahead. 'I've been onto Sydney Ports and they say all of their pilots can be accounted for, including those on holiday or sick leave.'

'What about RAN pilots?' I asked. The Oz Navy has warships popping in and out of the fleet base at Woolloomooloo all the time and have their own harbour pilots. One of them would have been on the bridge of the *Altoona* when she docked, making sure she was neatly parked between the white lines before slipping a couple of dollars into the meter.

'I checked with a contact in the Defence Department in Canberra and your Navy guys are all accounted for too,' Lonergan said.

How nice that the CIA had a direct line into Defence. I wondered if his contact was Pergo, but the barney I saw them having on the tanker didn't look like Lonergan had been asking for a list of pilots.

'I've already put in a request to Sydney Ports for the surveillance tapes,' Julie said. 'And for the names of every harbour pilot who qualified in the last thirty years. Since it's a public holiday, it might take a while.'

'If the bad guys just kept banker's hours like the rest of us,' I said, 'things would be a whole lot simpler.'

It was after two when Peter and Clare got back from the hospital and they had very little to report. The ship's choir had been formed in San

Diego earlier in the year and they pretty much kept to themselves. Expressions of interest from other members of the crew had been politely but firmly rebuffed, which seemed a bit unchristian to me, and the ship's company had become used to having a choir whose members were as thick as thieves, which is quite literally what they turned out to be.

I was just considering a plan for a late lunch when I saw Julie staring up at one of the security-surveillance monitors. She glanced at me. 'Ducks on the pond,' she said quietly.

That meant trouble.

I walked across to her desk and watched on the monitors as three white Commodores rolled onto the pier, the trailing vehicle neatly blocking the main entrance to our office. Two men in dark suits climbed out of the first car and another seven, also in dark suits, emerged from the two other vehicles. Even on our surveillance monitors you could see that the Hugo Boss threads on the bloke in the lead car would have cost twice as much as the other eight suits combined.

'Well, well, well,' Julie said. 'Chapman Fucking Pergo.'

Jules sometimes has a problem with authority but since she is an unerringly accurate judge of character and consistently shoots the tightest groups on the pistol range she gets away with it.

Pergo was standing in front of the surveillance camera, waiting.

'Shall I buzz him in?' Julie said.

I shrugged. 'Guess so.'

Julie's fingers moved rapidly over her keyboard, then she reached across and pressed the button that opened the security door. As Pergo walked into the office, she looked at me and said, just loudly enough for him to hear, 'So I guess this means our no-arseholes policy is out the window then, Mr Murdoch?'

One of Pergo's heavies accompanied him into the office while a second stationed himself outside the front door. On the surveillance monitors, I could see the others take up positions along the pier. They were all about two axe-handles wide across the shoulders, had their suit jackets fitted loose to hide a pistol in a shoulder holster, and appeared to be wearing earpieces with tiny microphones in their jacket cuffs. The body language suggested ex-Special Ops, and their bulk said almost certainly steroids.

A dangerous combination, definitely not the kind of dudes you wanted to mess with.

The thug who accompanied Pergo into the office had bleached white hair and wraparound sunglasses with mirrored lenses. He kept the glasses on, which was a good thing since I was damn sure he'd have seriously creepy eyes.

Chapman Pergo was just a little taller than me, forty-ish, lithe, and he carried himself like the amateur boxer he claimed to have been. He flashed an icy smile at Julie.

'Good afternoon, Miss Danko, always a pleasure. Enjoying the weekend?'

'Up until quite recently, Mr Pergo.'

'And Alby, dear fellow, how are things with you?'

Pergo was using his best Sloane Square drawl. He liked to play the superior Pom slumming it out in the colonies, and he was rather good at it.

'That's *Mister* Murdoch,' I said.

He smiled again, with the practised insincerity that only working in Canberra can give you. 'Of course, of course, you do outrank me – slightly. You're *acting* department head now, aren't you?' He put a lot of emphasis on the 'acting' part.

'And maybe you should starting acting like it,' I said. I hadn't pulled rank on anyone since being been promoted, and it was surprising how much fun it was.

'My apologies, *Mister* Murdoch.'

'Apologies accepted,' I said, 'but let's not be so formal. You can call me sir.' ,

I could see him making a mental note to break me in half at some later date.

'So tell me, *Chapman*,' I went on, 'what brings you out of your burrow on such a fine afternoon?'

Pergo was a fixer for the Defence Minister, and his methods, while they suited the tenor of the current government, had made him few friends. Pergo's style could best be described as a steel fist in an iron glove, clutching a set of brass knuckle-dusters and an electric cattle-prod just for good measure.

The rumour was he'd been serving with the British paras in Iraq – a gung-ho defender of Queen, flag and country – until he was chucked out after being sprung by a BBC news crew while conducting an over-enthusiastic, boots-and-all interrogation of a local in a back alley in Basra.

Things being what they were in Iraq, Pergo was immediately recruited at ten times his army salary to head the Black Falcon Group, one of the many dubious private security companies running mercenaries in Baghdad, and it wasn't long before things really got nasty. So nasty in fact that after six months, with a dozen different government factions and terrorist groups offering big money for his head on a stick, Pergo was forced to flee the country.

He shipped out one evening covered head to foot in a burkah, reportedly leaving close to a million bucks in US dollars in his private safe. If he hadn't turned up down under and got himself married to the Defence Minister's daughter, he'd probably have been unemployable.

'Perhaps you might like to introduce the rest of your associates, *Mister* Murdoch,' He looked at Clare, Carter and Peter. 'I'm Chapman Pergo, Special Assistant to the Minister for Defence.'

I made the introductions and Pergo shook hands and did the 'very pleased to meet you' bit with each of them, including Carter Lonergan. This seemed a little strange, given the barney I'd seen the two of them having not three hours earlier.

'You still haven't mentioned what brings you and the heavy cavalry down to this neck of the woods, Chapman,' I said when all the insincere gladhanding was over.

'I am the bearer of good news,' he smiled. 'By mutual agreement, the investigations into this morning's awkwardness on the harbour will now be handled by the Department of Defence. You are relieved of any and all involvement in this operation and are free to enjoy the rest of the holiday.'

'On whose authority?' I asked. From the corner of my eye I saw the bleached blond heavy unbuttoning his jacket. It looked like Pergo wasn't going to take no for an answer.

He took a single sheet of A4 paper from his pocket, unfolded it and held it up.

'You may read this, but you may not retain the original or a scan or photocopy. In essence it says you are to turn over all files, notes, recordings, and any other pertinent data on this investigation collected thus far. You are to retain no copies of said files, notes, recordings or data. The letter is signed by the Defence Minister, both in that role and in the role of Acting Minister for Homeland Security. It is countersigned by the Ambassador of the United States of America on behalf of the US Director of Homeland Security and the US Secretary for Defence.'

He smiled once more. 'The letter further advises that the people in this room are forbidden to reveal any details of this morning's events to anyone, under penalty of any or all secrecy acts and security regulations that pertain to their particular jurisdictions. And by anyone we mean anyone. I am also authorised to use deadly force in ensuring compliance with this directive. Are there any questions?'

No one spoke. When you're screwed you're screwed, and we were well and truly screwed. But Pergo wasn't finished yet.

'Lieutenant Kingston is to report to her ship within thirty minutes or she will be listed as AWOL, and Mr Sturdee I believe has an urgent meeting with the Commissioner of Police. Something about exceeding his authority I'm told.'

Pergo's goon pulled a file box from a shelf and casually emptied the contents onto the floor. He placed it in the centre of the conference table. 'All notes, diaries, recording devices, mobile phones and photo memory cards in the box please.'

He murmured into the microphone on his cuff and on the monitor I saw one of the other heavies on the dock approach the office door. 'Buzz him in, would you, babe,' he said to Julie.

For a second I thought Julie was reaching for the Fairbairn-Sykes commando dagger she kept on her desk as a letter opener but she calmly buzzed the guy in. Such restraint – must be all the martial arts training.

The two heavies began disconnecting computers from their monitors and keyboards and handing them out the door to another goon, who was placing them in the boot of the lead Commodore.

'These will be returned once we've removed all the data pertaining to this investigation,' Pergo said.

When the heavies were satisfied they'd collected everything of value, they backed out of the office. Pergo did one final sweep and his eyes landed on the camera bag on my desk. 'You had that with you this morning, I believe.'

No sense denying it. Lonergan had seen me shooting pix on the island. Pergo opened the bag and removed the half-dozen memory cards from the holder in the lid. He put them in his pocket and reached for the Nikon. That really pissed me off. Nobody touches my cameras without asking.

I grabbed him by the wrist. 'Let me do that.'

He twisted his arm to break free and I tightened my hold. The more he twisted, the tighter I made my grip. His jaw was clenched and the tendons in his neck were standing out with the strain.

'Er, Alby,' Julie said, and I looked over Pergo's shoulder to the doorway. The blond heavy had a Glock pointed in the general direction of yours truly.

I released Pergo's right wrist, flipped open the memory-card panel on the Nikon and popped out the card. Pergo took it with his left hand and slipped it into his pocket. He started massaging his right wrist.

'That was fun,' I said, 'we should do it again sometime. You ever go anywhere without Snow White and the Seven Psychos?'

Pergo smiled at the challenge. 'Any time you like, boyo. Just name the place.'

Boyo? Sloan Square to Belfast in one easy step.

'Queensbury Rules, old chap?' I asked.

'If you prefer. But you should remember the first rule of boxing, Murdoch – never punch above your weight.'

'I'll take my chances, Chapman, I heard your nickname in the ring was the Glazier. One win, one draw, seven losses – five by knockout. Smart money says you had a glass jaw and no bottle.'

Pergo stared at me. 'Like I said, boyo, any time.'

He turned quickly on his heel and walked out the door.

Julie started a slow hand-clap. 'Well played, Mr Murdoch. Nothing like a couple of blokes having a dick-measuring competition to liven up the afternoon.'

Clare was staring at the doorway. 'Can someone tell me what is going on?'

'We've been shut down,' Lonergan said. 'We are off the case.' He glanced at his watch. 'I think maybe I'd better give you a ride back to the ship, Lieutenant.'

Something in Lonergan's matter-of-fact summing up of the situation made me think he had known exactly what was coming, even before Pergo's cowboy convoy rolled onto the dock.

Clare was looking at me.

'Probably wise to make a move,' I said to her. 'You don't want to have an AWOL charge on your service record.'

She kept looking at me. And it was a look that made the hairs on the back of my neck stand up, but in a nice kind of way.

'Maybe we can have lunch sometime,' she said. 'Given the circumstances, I think the *Altoona* will be in port a little longer than we expected.'

She was right about that. I couldn't imagine the cruiser upping anchor any time soon. As for having lunch together, I'm never one to knock back the advances of a beautiful woman, and, well, a man has to eat.

I handed her my WorldPix business card. 'Sounds great. Why don't you email me your contact details?'

'That might not be a good idea, Lieutenant,' Lonergan warned. 'This is an extremely sensitive situation.'

'Don't worry, Carter, I'm an extremely sensitive guy.'

'Why Carter,' Julie said, 'haven't you heard? Alby here's done all the gender sensitivity training going. He's a genuine, all-round sensitive new age spy.'

I ignored that. 'Lieutenant Kingston, is there anything you don't eat?'

She smiled. 'I'm omnivorous, and I have rather a voracious appetite.'

My kind of girl. That made up for the decaf and the soy milk.

Carter and Clare drove away in the Chevy Suburban and Peter left straight afterwards for what looked to be a very unpleasant meeting with the top brass.

Julie surveyed the wreckage of the office. 'Too bad Pergo got your images from the island.'

I pulled a memory card out of the coin pocket of my jeans.

'You must have heard me say it to the Dedheads a hundred times: always take the memory card out of your camera as soon as you finish shooting something important. You can replace your hardware, but when the images are gone they're gone forever. Luckily, I followed my own rules for once.'

'You went to a lot of trouble to stop Pergo getting a blank card.'

'Couldn't let him think I was giving it up without a fight. Pergo's no fool – if I'd made it too easy he would have been suspicious.'

'He's going to be very pissed off, Alby,' Julie said. 'And more so when he tries to access those hard drives. I've got them configured to reformat themselves after three failed attempts to bypass the security system.'

'Can they get around that and retrieve the data?'

'Of course, but it's going to take them a lot of time and effort.'

She kicked a side panel on her desk, a concealed drawer slid open and she took out two mobile phones, tossing me one.

'A bit basic but they're prepaid, so we should be secure for a while. I don't fancy using a mobile after Pergo's had his greasy mitts on it.'

'Good thinking, Miss Danko,' I said, dropping the phone in my pocket. 'And now, what do you reckon, should we call it a day?'

'Fine by me. But don't forget to check your email when you get home.'

'You think Clare's that keen?' I asked.

'Settle down, Alby, she just left. But God yes, she's gagging for it. Especially after that little display of testosterone with Pergo.' She shook her head slowly. '*Is there anything you don't eat?* Jesus, I thought I was going to have to throw a bucket of cold water over the two of you.'

'That obvious, eh?'

'And then some. However, Mr Murdoch, I think you should remember what happened last time you got romantically involved with the American military.'

She did have a point. Besides having my heart broken by a gorgeous US Army major named Grace Goodluck, it had been suggested at the secret commission of inquiry into my destruction of the US spy base at Bitter Springs that I owed the United States government almost half a billion dollars. Julie had worked out that even with overtime and bonuses I wouldn't be able to retire until I was close to nine hundred years old. Luckily they decided it was in everybody's best interest to forget the whole thing.

'What's so important about my inbox at home,' I asked, 'if it's not a pash note from the lovely Lieutenant Kingston?'

'When I saw those cars driving onto the pier I smelled trouble, so I emailed our files to your private mail box. While Pergo was busy shooting his mouth off, all the pertinent data collected so far was winging its way through cyberspace for safekeeping.'

'You mean, if I want to I can just log on in Bondi and this investigation is back in business?'

'I know you like to keep your options open, Alby.'

'Thanks, but no thanks, Jules. You saw Pergo's letter. Someone else can find their missing nukes. I'm going to salvage what I can of this long weekend by doing what I do best. Care to join me?'

Chapter Ten

We fronted up for a very late lunch or an extremely early dinner at the Blue Eye Dragon in Pyrmont. Muriel, the owner, does Taiwanese dining and she does it very well. I ordered the pan-fried dumplings as we walked in the door. Her mum, Jade, makes them by hand and they are bloody amazing with a dash of chilli sauce.

While we waited for the pork belly slow cooked in soy, aniseed, garlic and chilli, and prawns in Jade's 'Bloody' plum sauce, Julie called Sydney Ports and redirected the list of harbour pilots to the fax at my place. Just in case, she said when I reminded her once again that I was off the investigation, and staying off.

Neither of us spoke while we ate, but I knew Julie was trying to figure out if I was really serious about dropping the investigation. I was trying to figure out if I could snaffle an extra dumpling without her noticing, but she had eyes like a hawk.

Public transport was back up and running and the city was open again, so after lunch I dropped Julie at Circular Quay to catch a ferry to Manly and headed back to Bondi. It was a warm evening on a public holiday in a beachside suburb, so parking was never going to be easy, especially since my building was right on Campbell Parade, the main drag.

The name Luxor Mansions might conjure up visions of an Egyptian palace overlooking the Nile, but my apartment block was more a 1930s copy of an English seaside hotel. My place was on the top floor, with views stretching from the seawater pool at the Icebergs swimming club right round to the rocks at Ben Buckler Point, but unfortunately no parking.

It took twenty minutes of cruising the streets before a space big enough for my four-wheel drive opened up. I carefully avoided bumping the kerb since the Bondi salt air had reduced the old Pathfinder's body to several small areas of metal held together by paint and rust. Even a decent slamming of the driver's door had the potential to cause the vehicle's total disintegration.

I stopped in at Nirvana Beach Liquor to grab a couple of bottles of red, and on my way out I caught the tempting aroma of drunk noodles coming from Nina's Ploy Thai round on Wairoa Avenue but it was a bit too early for dinner, considering I'd just finished lunch.

Back home, I started rummaging through the kitchen drawer for a corkscrew. Then I remembered the events of the previous night and found it next to my bed. I noticed my bed had been made, the room straightened up, and my plants had been watered.

The only reason I still had any living houseplants was my next-door neighbour, Mrs Templeton, who watered them when I was away on assignment, or busy, or just plain forgot. She also collected my mail and popped the odd shepherd's pie and tub of homemade soup into my freezer for those times when I needed a bit of comfort food. Mrs T was a pretty dammed good cook when it came to comfort food. Every bloke should have a Mrs T next door.

She had moved into Luxor Mansions when she arrived from Scotland with her husband in the early 1950s. Mr Templeton was a marine engineer who'd survived three ships being torpedoed out from under him on the Atlantic convoy runs in World War II. He walked away from the chronic unemployment of post-war Glasgow and into a job at the Garden Island naval dockyard within a week of arriving in Sydney. Mrs T was widowed and still living in the Mansions when I bought the building in the eighties with the profits from the sale of pictures I'd done for WorldPix, well before the smart set discovered Bondi and sent the prices through the roof.

I kept my ownership quiet and ignored the managing agent when he told me I could turf her out, give the place a splash of paint, whack down some seagrass matting and quadruple the rent. I didn't need the extra money, and besides, it was nice to drink tea and chat in Mrs T's sunroom while Dougal, her wheezing and flatulent pug, grunted and snuffled under my feet like a small black asthmatic vacuum cleaner, sucking up the crumbs of her delicious homemade biscuits.

I poured a glass of wine and wandered into Mrs T's flat through the front door I could never persuade her to keep closed. 'Dougal can protect me,' she'd say, and given the lethal quality of the little bugger's farts, she may well have been right. When I walked in the ugly mutt was snoozing on a shawl on her lap and he didn't even bother to look up. So much for a watchdog.

The Cooking Channel was on the box and some Scottish chef was doing something mouth-watering with a whole salmon. I think Mrs T fancied the bloke, but maybe it was just his accent.

'You left early this morning, Alby,' she said, looking up, 'and Julie not long after.' She paused. 'She's a lovely wee girl, Alby. Just lovely.'

Mrs T had plans for Julie and me, but I couldn't seem to explain to her that Julie wasn't interested. I'm not too sure she bought my stories of the platonic sleepovers either.

'I had to go and take pictures of the tanker that broke down in the harbour,' I said.

'Aye,' she nodded, 'and all the press photographers were being picked up in police cars this morning, I suppose?'

Mrs T might have been well into her eighties but she was nobody's fool. Along with kilted soldiers and ship's engineers, the Scots had produced more than their fair share of denizens of the secret world. Maybe it was something in the porridge. I figured Mrs T had probably worked out some time back that things in my life weren't exactly how they seemed, but she appeared to be content to play along.

The Scottish chef had plated up his salmon and Mrs T switched over to the ABC News as I finished off my glass of red.

The ashen face of Rupert Hall-Smith, the Defence Minister, got my attention. He looked like death warmed over. According to the caption on the bottom of the screen, the Minister was speaking at a press conference recorded earlier in the afternoon at Sydney Airport. The top brass of the NSW Police were lined up behind him, and none of them looked all that happy either.

The press briefing commenced with the minister putting on a pair of rimless glasses and reading from a prepared statement.

'As you are no doubt aware, there was some excitement on the harbour this morning. Around three a ship experiencing mechanical difficulties entered the Heads and dropped anchor off Fort Denison to await repairs. Overreaction by an inexperienced police liaison officer resulted in local police and Defence Department anti-terrorism teams being mobilised, causing major disruption in the city. For this the New South Wales Police Service apologises unreservedly.'

Some of the top brass shuffled uncomfortably and stared down at their feet.

'There will be a full inquiry at ministerial level,' Hall-Smith went on, 'and I am advised that the police officer in question will be stood down without pay until this investigation is complete.'

Shit. So Peter Sturdee's head was on the chopping block and Hall-Smith was handing the Police Commissioner the axe.

'Hmmphh. All sounds a bit fishy to me,' Mrs T said. 'Wouldn't trust those politicians as far as I could throw them.'

'I'm with you there, Mrs T.'

'Also this morning,' the Minister continued, 'two crewmen from the disabled tanker were injured while trying to effect repairs. They were evacuated for medical treatment by a helicopter from the visiting US warship *Altoona*. We would like to thank the US Navy for its prompt assistance in this operation.'

Well, that explained away the TV footage of the Yank chopper hovering over the tanker. Jesus, these bastards could spin anything.

Hall-Smith finished with a brief mention of an unrelated accident onboard the US cruiser, and sent the government's condolences to the families of the dead and injured. When Chapman Pergo walked up and stood next to the Minister it was pretty obvious the press conference was over and there'd be no questions, unless any members of the press corps were sniffing around for cancelled media accreditation and multiple fractures.

The item ended, I said goodnight to Mrs T and reminded her to lock her door. Back in my place I dialled Peter's number. The phone was answered after exactly half a ring.

'Sounds like you might be in a spot of bother, mate?'

'Well, I'm suspended without pay pending an inquiry which could be months away. Pergo's quoting the new anti-terrorism laws, which no bugger understands and which seem to mean I can't say anything in my own defence, so yes, I guess you could say I'm in a lot of trouble. I think the scenario involves that well-known creek and a barbed-wire canoe. And no paddle.'

'You don't think they'll make all this go away when things calm down?'

That was usual government practice when embarrassing things like this came up.

'Alby, every cop in this state senior to me was either out on their luxury cabin cruiser, living it up at their beachside holiday home, or shacked up with a call girl in the penthouse suite of some five-star hotel in Fiji. All of them need a scalp to cover their arse, and right now my head's up highest.'

'You okay for money?'

He laughed softly. 'I'm a straight cop with a wife, four kids under two, a mortgage, six maxed-out credit cards and a rust bucket of a Tarago. I'm bloody rolling in it, mate.'

I heard a baby start crying in the background and Peter said, 'Shit, the twins are awake, gotta go,' and hung up.

Peter Sturdee was a little fish in whatever was going on here and he was being hung out to dry as part of the cover-up. That really pissed me off.

I called Julie's mobile number. 'Looks like they're planning to scapegoat Peter.'

'I know, I saw the news.'

'Someone's got to watch his back.'

I heard a car door slam and Julie said, 'I'm in the taxi now.'

'You understand you could be putting your career on the line here, Jules. Officially we're both off the case.'

'Why don't you fire up the espresso machine. I'll be at your place in twenty.'

My landline rang about five seconds after Julie hung up. I didn't recognise the number on the caller ID, so I picked it up and said, 'Alby Murdoch.'

'Oh,' said a male voice on the other end, and then there was silence.

'This is Constable Whitfield from the Kings Cross Police,' the voice continued after a pause. 'I guess you're not dead, then.'

'Mate,' I said, 'it's not for the want of a lot of people trying.'

Since I'd had a couple of glasses of wine, I grabbed a cab. Julie's taxi was halfway over the bridge when I called so she had the driver take the Woolloomooloo exit and beat me to the Cowper Wharf Road car park by five minutes. I'd had more than enough of the 'Loo for one day but here I was back again, and trying not to stand in more blood.

The Navy's staff car park is a grim-looking, five-storey concrete building directly opposite the navy wharf. Despite trying to hide the functional ugliness behind some scrawny trees a prolonged drought had given most of the greenery a severe case of death.

A couple of police paddy wagons were parked on the footpath by the northern entrance, lights flashing, and I was directed up to level three. The dingy grey structure had the usual car park smell of oil, urine and vomit. Julie was waiting with Constable Whitfield and some crime-scene examiners. She did the introductions.

'Sorry about the weird phone call,' the constable said, 'but your name and phone number were inside his camera bag so I figured …'

He pointed to an area roped off with police tape. It looked like there was a severe case of death inside the car park too.

From time to time, I get invited by the Australian Centre for Photography in Paddington to talk to photo-journalism students about my career in photography, and occasionally I'll let a promising young talent do some work experience with me. Most recently that was Max Gallagher.

Max was nineteen, enthusiastic, and had a great beginner's portfolio. Frankly, all his boyish enthusiasm had been becoming a bit of a pain in the arse, but he was committed and he did have a good eye. We'd had our last meeting a month ago and I'd encouraged him to find a project he could put all his energy into. I'd also given him one of my old camera bags. And now young Max was lying face-down behind a pillar in a dingy car park with a bullet in the back of his head.

'Security guard found the body about an hour ago,' Constable Whitfield said. 'He took one look and spewed his dinner all over the hood of some poor bastard's Toyota.'

That explained part of the car park's aroma.

'Guard reckons he didn't see him on his rounds, but the doc said the kid's been dead since early this morning. As it's a public holiday, I figure Mr Rent-a-Cop wasn't doing his job with a lot of diligence.'

'Anything stolen?'

'There's no wallet, which is why I was going on the name in the camera bag. But all this camera gear is still lying about and it looks like pretty expensive stuff, so I'd say it's not a robbery.'

There was a Canon camera with a telephoto lens attached next to the body. The camera's memory-card compartment was open and the card was missing. Pockets in the lid of the camera bag designed to hold spare cards were also empty.

Standing up I looked over the rail and tried to figure what might be interesting to a photographer with a telephoto lens from this particular vantage point. Maybe it was a window in the hotel on the pier opposite, or maybe it was Heath or Nicole some other superstar shacking up in one of the multimillion-dollar apartments. Or perhaps it was the USS *Altoona*, docked just across the other side of the street.

Glancing down over the wall I said, 'Looks like a wallet on the ground. Down on the next level. Maybe it belongs to the kid.'

When the crime scene bods took off to investigate I caught Julie's eye, indicating the constable with a tilt of my head. Within a couple of seconds he had his back to me and an apparently enraptured Julie was getting his life story. I fumbled around under Max's body and quickly found what I was looking for in the coin pocket of his jeans. After slipping the memory card into my pocket I stood up.

'Do you need us for anything else tonight Constable Whitfield?'

He shook his head. 'I've got your details, and since you've identified the body I think we can leave it at that. The detectives will probably be in touch later this week. Right now they've got their hands full with that business on the boat.'

'Ship,' Julie said, smiling.

'Right, ship. Do you want me to get one of the boys to run you somewhere?'

'That would be nice,' I said. 'You got anyone who drives within the speed limit?'

As we walked down the ramp to the waiting police car, Julie said, 'Sorry about Max.'

'Yeah, me too. He was a good kid.' This was all starting to get a bit personal

Mrs T's apartment was in darkness when we got back to Bondi, so she was spared having to see me starting and ending my day in a police car.

While Julie made tea I downloaded my images of the helicopter hovering over the tanker to my computer and moved them to a folder on the desktop. Max's memory card held about sixty images, and I opened them in preview to have a quick look. Whatever had been on the card taken from his camera was now gone for ever, but maybe we'd get some clues from these shots.

They were happy snaps from a party, and it didn't take me long to realise that the event was last night's little shindig at Jindivick.

Julie put a mug of tea on the desk beside me and looked over my shoulder as I scrolled through the images. 'So Max was at the reception for the choir at Jindivick last night, and today he turns up dead, with an empty camera at a perfect vantage point overlooking the scene of the heist.'

I nodded. 'And what are the odds of that being a coincidence?'

I scrolled through more images. The Reverend Priday, Mrs Priday and the choirboys featured in several shots, and Cristobel was chatting to a tall, white-haired woman. None of the other guests rang any bells.

'The Reverend Priday caters well,' Julie commented, indicating several shots.

Besides photographing the guests, young Max had snapped elegantly dressed waitresses balancing silver trays laden with tempting snacks. There were several close-ups of the food, which included Vietnamese rice paper rolls, samosas, Peking duck crepes, and skewered char grilled Tiger prawns with a chilli-flecked mayonnaise. There was also some thinly sliced beef on squares of toasted ciabatta which looked bloody fantastic. I couldn't fault Max there – photographing delicious-looking canapés was one of my weaknesses. Great finger food is rare and deserves to be immortalised.

'I think maybe I need to have another chat with the Reverend tomorrow,' I said.

'Don't forget you've got that thing in Canberra tomorrow night.'

'Bugger,' I said. I had forgotten.

'I booked you on a one o'clock flight. Want me to cancel it?'

I shook my head. 'If I can track down the Revered in the morning I can still make that flight. And a chat with some Canberra insiders might be just what I need right now.'

Suddenly I was very, very tired. It had been one hell of a long day. Jesus, I bloody hate Mondays.

Chapter Eleven

The Video Oz TV production studios were located in an industrial park in inner-city Alexandria. It had taken me close to twenty minutes to track down the Reverend Priday through his church switchboard, which had me chasing through an automated menu with over thirty options, most of which encouraged me to give the First Church of the Lord's Bounty money in varying amounts, by cash or by credit card. Eventually I got through to a real live person who told me the Reverend was in Alexandria, recording his weekly televised sermon for the God Network.

The receptionist at Video Oz was young and female and gorgeous, which is the way it seems to go in TV, or any media industry for that matter. She directed me to Studio Four where the Reverend was recording.

'He's definitely not in Studio Two,' she called helpfully after me as I headed down the corridor. Naturally I had to take a peek in through the Studio Two door, even though the red light was on.

On a fake bathroom set, under bright lights, a couple of voluptuous, young women were responding to the state government's plea to conserve water by taking a bubble bath together. Judging from the dialogue, there appeared to be a problem with a blocked drain. Luckily for them, a very buff plumber in Blundstones, Stubbies and a tool belt was just passing and offered to help. He dropped his tool belt and shorts and produced a rather spectacular piece of equipment which looked like it could do the job.

Things were much more sedate in Studio Four and I caught the Reverend, all Max Factor and whitened teeth, mid-sermon. His topic was the story of the prophet Jonah and the lessons to be learned from it. Cristobel had done her homework well and I found myself drawn into the drama of the tale. We were just at the bit where Jonah jacks up about having to pop over to Nineveh for a bit of a chin-wag with the Assyrians regarding God's wrath and their possible total annihilation, when a deep voice rumbled from somewhere high above, 'Reverend Priday, we've got a slight problem with audio, can we take five and then go again from the top?'

The audio problem didn't seem to stop the microphones picking up the Priday's next muttered line. 'Jesus H. Christ, why can't you people get your heads out of your fucking arses so we can get this damn thing finished.'

So the good Reverend didn't buy into that *meek inheriting the earth* caper, either.

I was standing next to a catering table covered with plates of pastries, pots of tea and coffee, and an esky full of those ubiquitous bottles of Goodie fruit juice. Priday smiled politely when he saw me, and walked over and picked up an almond croissant. A nervous wardrobe girl stuffed a paper napkin into his collar to keep powdered sugar off his Armani suit.

'Nice sermon, Reverend,' I said. 'Cristobel must be a big help to you.'

'My daughter has a way with words, Inspector Murdoch, and I value her input when it comes to interpreting God's message.'

Priday studied the selection of juices and chose an apple, beetroot and carrot. Its bright red colour sent the wardrobe girl into a panic and she draped a smock across his shoulders. 'And now what can I help you with today? I only have a moment, you understand.'

'Max Gallagher was taking photos last night at Jindivick,' I said. 'Was that for the church newsletter?'

The Reverend smiled. 'Mr Gallagher approached me several weeks ago about doing a photo-essay on a modern evangelical church – some sort of school project. I couldn't see any harm. He's a charming young fellow, and doesn't seem to get in the way.'

'He's a dead young fellow now, so he must have been in someone's way.'

All the colour drained from the Reverend's face. 'It wasn't an accident, then?' he said after a long pause.

'Nope. He was found in a car park overlooking that American warship where all the fuss was yesterday. You know, the one your guest choir called home.'

Priday took a sip of his juice. I could see his mind working at a million miles a minute.

'I'm very sorry to hear of the young man's death, Inspector Murdoch. That's most unfortunate. God bless his soul.'

'Any idea what Max was doing in the car park?'

'I'm afraid not.'

The deep voice from on high announced that they were ready for the Reverend again and he smiled at me, relieved at the interruption.

'We're installing our own broadcast facilities in the church, you know, Inspector Murdoch. We'll have 24-hour web-streaming for my parishioners, and I won't have this weekly disruption to my schedule.'

'Yeah, I hate disruptions to my schedule. Bet Max did too. Bit of a major disruption to his schedule.'

'Indeed. May he rest in peace.'

I was sure Priday knew more than he was saying, but it was obvious I wasn't going to get any more out of him. He'd composed himself and was back in full Reverend mode.

'Would you like to stay for the end of my sermon, Inspector? Cristobel has an interesting take on the story of Jonah. She says it can be interpreted as a satirical attack on prophets and the self-righteousness of the pious. Fascinating.'

Apparently irony was lost on the Reverend Priday.

'No thanks,' I said. 'I know how it comes out.'

It was actually the Jonah story that had led to my dramatic expulsion from Sunday School and my early and enduring schism with the Church. That 'whale swallows man whole and chucks him up again in one piece three days later' business just hadn't rung true. My relentless, week-after-week questioning was too much for the earnest young Sunday School teacher with his teenage acne and Fletcher Jones blazer and he finally screamed at me that I was a bloody little heathen and told me to fuck off in front of a class of stunned five-year-olds.

Perhaps he had been wrestling with profound theological questions of his own. I knew for a fact that he'd been wrestling with our minister's giggling fifteen-year-old daughter, because I'd caught them at it behind the church hall once or twice. I suppose it was at that young age I first became aware that teenage girls were trouble.

'Please give my regards to Cristobel,' I said as I turned to leave. 'And by the way, if you're looking for content to keep your parishioners entertained on that 24-hour web-streaming, you might want to have a squiz at what they're shooting in Studio Two on your way out.'

I flew into Canberra because they'd forgotten to build the high-speed train again. When the Australian colonies joined together to form a Commonwealth in 1900 they needed a permanent national capital, and to stop all the bitching from Melbourne and Sydney about which city should get the job, they settled on a couple of thousand square kilometres of bleak sheep-grazing country located inconveniently halfway between the two. A high-speed rail link connecting the three cities had been on the cards since the advent of high-speed trains, and this being Australia and there being two states and a federal territory involved, the project was proceeding at the normal snail's pace.

Canberra is apparently an Aboriginal word meaning a place where one's tax dollars are pissed away. A self-governing territory and the seat of our federal government, it also has the country's most liberal liquor laws, a thriving black market trade in fireworks and is home to the nation's mail-order dirty-video business. All in all, a combination guaranteed to make a bloke's chest swell with patriotic pride.

Since large parts of it were designed and built in the 1920s and '30s, Canberra features excellent examples of late-deco architecture. It also has great public parks and gardens, wide roads, and sections of the city are beautiful in a lethargic, public service kind of way.

Parliament was in recess, so the airport arrivals lounge was blissfully free of journos, pollies, hangers-on, and high-priced call girls. The only jarring note was the security, as heavy this end as in Sydney, and that was pretty heavy. With a couple of nukes on the loose, this was understandable, but the total cover-up of the theft meant none of the airport security people knew what they were supposed to be extra vigilant about.

There was actually a second jarring note, which was the sight of a Com Car driver holding up a card reading 'MISTER Murdoch'. And sure enough, standing next to the driver, smiling, obviously pleased with himself, was my old mate Chapman F. Pergo.

'Twice in two days, *Mister* Murdoch,' Pergo said. 'We'll have to stop meeting like this. People will talk.'

'That would suit me down to the ground, Chapman. I'm not all that particular about the company I keep, but you have to draw the line somewhere. How'd you know I was coming?'

'There's very little that I don't know.'

I didn't like the sound of that, especially as it was probably true.

'The Minister wants to see you,' he said.

'Okay, I'll drop by when I've checked into my hotel.'

Pergo shook his head. 'The Minister wants to see you *now*. Why not let me drive you?'

'I've got a rental car booked.'

'Give the paperwork and your baggage-claim stubs to the driver here,' Pergo suggested. 'He'll drop off your bags and arrange for the rental people to deliver your vehicle to the hotel. The keys will be with the Hyatt's concierge.'

It looked like he did know everything. I handed over the claim stubs and paperwork to the driver, who seemed very relieved to be getting away from Pergo. We walked outside to a shiny black Holden VEE Thunder SS ute parked in one of those *don't even think about parking here* zones. The vehicle had a hard tonneau cover, black-tinted windows and flashy mag wheels. To finish off the look, great streamers of red and yellow airbrushed flames licked along the side panels.

'Very subtle,' I said. 'Maybe you could get the Minister to give our new second-hand Abrams tanks the same paint job. It would sure scare the crap out of the enemy.'

By the time we reached the exit gate the G-forces from the ute's V8 had slammed me back in my bucket seat and I realised that Chapman

Pergo, besides being a thug and a total pain in the arse, was also a seriously crook driver.

Pergo had that *red lights are optional* and *tailgating is a good thing* driving style so beloved by teenage P-platers and taxi drivers from Bombay to Brisbane. I tucked my legs up close to the seat, double-checked the seatbelt, and prayed that the airbags wouldn't rupture my eardrums when they deployed.

The drive to Parliament House took seven minutes and ten years off my life. It was worse than my ride to the Opera House in the patrol car. Doesn't anyone watch those road-safety commercials on TV? I wondered. A couple of times I tried to snatch a quick glance at the instrument panel, just so I'd know what speed the cops would put in their report after they pulled my mangled body from the wreckage, but Pergo's hands on the wheel blocked my view. He had French cuffs on his shirt and was wearing gold, diamond-studded, monogrammed cufflinks. Bloody typical. What a wanker.

We rocketed past the entrance to the Duntroon military college, a blur of poplars – a golf course, I think –then we were zooming over the Kings Avenue Bridge and suddenly on a rise dead ahead was the breathtaking dullness of Parliament House.

The new Parliament House replaced the classic 1927 building in 1988 and was cunningly designed to look like it was half buried under a grassy hillside. I don't think the Australian public would be too fussed if someone brought in a fleet of bulldozers and finished the job, especially if they locked all the pollies inside before firing up the machinery.

In deference to the 40 kph speed signs, Pergo dropped the ute back to eighty, hung a left at the top of the hill and roared up to a driveway marked Members of Parliament Only. We zoomed past all the high-security car park checkpoints like they didn't exist, and less than twenty minutes after hitting the Canberra runway I was inside the Defence Minister's office.

Rupert Hall-Smith was in a very big chair at a very big desk, head down, reading the contents of a folder. He studiously ignored me. Pergo was the only other person present. I timed out the three minutes in my head. *The Boy's Own Book of Office Power Plays* says that three minutes of ignoring a visitor to your office establishes dominance.

Right on the one-eighty count the Minister glanced up, having demonstrated who was top dog. I wondered if I was supposed to roll over on the carpet and put my legs in the air. He closed the folder and stared at me. He looked even worse in the flesh than he had on TV the night before.

'And who exactly the fuck do you think you are, Murdoch?' he said slowly.

Great, so it was going to be one of those meetings.

Rupert Hall-Smith did an excellent line in intimidation. Maybe it's in the job description. I remembered the pathetic spectacle in a recent Senate Estimates hearing when high-ranking, be-medalled defence force personnel were forced to sit uncomfortably close to the Minister, as if they were at a headmaster's interview with their mums. You could see them praying they wouldn't give a wrong answer and find themselves demoted and out in the car park washing the bastard's car.

'Hands off means hands off, Murdoch,' Hall-Smith said. 'Mr Pergo showed you my directive, yet you seem unable to understand simple English. The matter of that tanker and the USS *Altoona* is now out of your hands. It's over and done, do you understand me?'

I understood perfectly. News of my visit to see Priday had obviously reached the Minister's office already.

'And the missing nukes?' I said.

The Minister's face twitched. 'I can assure you, I have it on the authority of the highest levels of the American government that the *Altoona* was not carrying nuclear weapons.'

If it *was* the highest levels of the American government they would have said 'nuke-u-lar weapons'. My personal theory on the non-proliferation of atomic weapons was if you couldn't pronounce the word nuclear correctly you shouldn't be allowed to have any.

'So all the warheads the ship wasn't carrying are fully accounted for?'

'I've spoken on this, Murdoch. I'm not getting into a discussion with you.'

'Fine. Then all you have to do to get me off this case is send a signed minute on your ministerial letterhead addressed to me as Acting Department Head. Just put it all in writing and everything will be dandy.'

The Minister smiled pleasantly, which was a bit disconcerting. 'No,

Mr Murdoch, all I need to do to get you off this case is to terminate your temporary appointment, effective immediately. And that's what I'm doing. You are returned to your previous position and pay scale forthwith.'

Damn. Much as I wanted out of the top job at D-E-D, there was no way I was giving up on the investigation now, and this was going to cramp my style somewhat.

'Furthermore,' the Minister continued, 'the Honourable Gwenda Felton is your new Head of Department.'

Struth. The Honourable Gwenda Felton, AO, Companion of the Order of Australia and former Member of Parliament, was generally regarded as having the compassion of Vlad the Impaler, the dress sense of Bozo the clown, and the subtlety of one of Marshal Zhukov's World War II Red Army artillery barrages. It was also universally agreed that she was dead from the neck up. What the Honourable Gwenda Felton AO did have going for her was loyalty. When the Prime Minister said jump all the party faithful asked how high, except for Gwenda, who rushed out and got herself a trampoline.

Having made a total hash of her last three portfolios, without career consequences, Gwenda had recently been forced to resign her seat in parliament after an unfortunate incident involving refugees, a talkback radio shock-jock, and a comment she made when she thought the microphones were turned off. Even in a government whose code of conduct was so slackly enforced that clocking the Leader of the Opposition with half a house brick during question time would only get you a smack on the wrist, Gwenda had to go.

She got the usual golden handshake, lifetime use of the honorific, and the promise of the next available cushy public service appointment. How Hall-Smith could justify making her Director-General of an intelligence service in these days of a war on terror was hard to fathom. Then again, she pretty much terrorised everyone who worked for her.

'I think D-E-D will benefit from a new broom,' the Minister said.

'A new broom can be useful for sweeping things under the carpet.'

'Very droll, Murdoch.'

'Look, the official line might be that the two warheads don't exist, but everybody in this room knows they do and that they've been stolen, and people are dead because of it. Nothing you do to me can change the facts, so somebody better find those nukes and find them fast, because if they go off there won't be broom big enough to clean up that mess.'

The Minister's face turned a strange shade of purple. He looked like a man whose blood pressure was in the high triple digits and climbing.

'Now, if you'll excuse me,' I said, 'I need to shower and frock up. I've got a birthday party to go to.'

It was just a short walk down the hill to the Hyatt. I still had plenty of time to check in and freshen up, and I was confident my luggage would be in the room and the rental car in the car park. The Com Car driver would know better than to screw with Pergo, that was for sure. I wondered why I didn't have that kind of smarts.

Working for Gwenda Felton was going to be interesting. I couldn't wait to tell Julie but I decided to save it for when I got back to Sydney, since I really wanted to see the look on her face.

But it was the look on Hall-Smith's face that occupied me most as I headed up the drive to the Hyatt. The Minister was running scared and that had me worried. When the people who are masters at putting the frighteners on the rest of us get edgy, maybe it's time we all got nervous.

Chapter Twelve

It took a very long, very hot shower to get the Minister's ire out of my pores but by 7.45 I was all glammed up and ready to party. I splashed on some Geoffrey Beene Grey Flannel aftershave, grabbed the rental car keys from the concierge, and stepped out the front door of the Hyatt into a media scrum.

The journos and photographers were focused on the steady stream of luxury cars dropping off a series of handsome, elegantly dressed, bejewelled couples. From the plates on the limos I deduced there was a diplomatic reception happening, and I hoped the Hyatt bouncers would manage to chuck out the last of the drunks and the strippers before I got back from my night on the tiles. I knew how much the Corp Diplomatique liked to party; some nights they were still hitting the mineral water as late as 10.15.

A limo glided to a stop right in front of me. A muscular bloke in the front passenger seat jumped out to open the door for the Japanese ambassador and his missus. The lady was beautiful, petite and delicate, swathed in silk and pearls, and as she smiled for the press pack a couple of camera flashes lit up the driveway.

'*Murderers!*'

It was a woman's voice, almost right in my ear, and it scared the crap out of me. Immediately afterwards a great stream of red liquid arced upwards and then down towards the ambassadorial couple. A bodyguard stepped in front of the ambassador's wife and copped the liquid full in the chest as a barrage of camera flashes went off.

Was it blood? I wondered. An anti-fur demo? But the ambassador's wife was wearing a silk wrap, with not a bit of mink or ermine to be seen.

'Whale murderers!' the voice shouted again.

So that was the story. It was whales, not fox or sable, that the protest was about. And I could smell it now, not blood, paint – red plastic paint. But there was no mistaking the symbolism.

The Japanese couple were whisked into the hotel while security and the press pack closed in on the paint thrower – a woman in her fifties with long white hair and dressed a bit like a rich hippie. She looked familiar. The journos were shouting over each other, and all the questions started with 'Miss Gaarg, Miss Gaarg …'

So it was the famous Artemisia Gaarg, reclusive multi-billionairess, philanthropist, and champion of the world's whales. There was quite a little press and security scrum developing around me, so after quickly checking for paint splashes on my dinner suit I headed to the car. Right now the last thing I needed was another bunfight.

The rental Toyota was in a front parking bay, and as I unlocked the door I looked back at the melee outside the hotel. Flashes were still going off and I could just make out Artemisia Gaarg as she shouted anti-whaling slogans at the TV cameras.

It was quite a well-staged media event, as these things go. The photographers had been ready and waiting for the paint hurling, and even though Artemisia had missed the ambassador's wife, the incident would be on the front page of every newspaper in the country tomorrow morning, and probably on the international wires as well, thus proving that what they said in the ads was true – you *do* get great coverage from a four litre can of Dulux Wash & Wear semi-gloss.

As I pulled out of the driveway I glanced in the rear vision mirror and in amongst the jostling journos and cameras and microphones I caught a quick glimpse of an attractive brunette standing just behind Artemisia – and blow me down if it wasn't the lovely Cristobel Priday.

The sign outside the winery read RESTAURANT CLOSED FOR PRIVATE PARTY. The car park was chock-a-block so I parked on the gravel on the edge of the road, and as I rolled to a stop there was a slight *pop* from the front of the car. When I climbed out to have a look the driver's front side tyre was hissing softly as it slowly deflated. Bugger. I was all shiny and clean and the last thing I felt like doing was changing a tyre in the dark.

I decided to sort it out later and headed up the pathway to the winery. It was a typically crisp Canberra evening and my exhaled breath condensed to white mist in the cold, wood smoke-scented air. A beautiful vintage Indian motorcycle was parked right outside the restaurant's main door. It was a '47 Chief with the full-skirted mudguards front and rear. Painted all white, the bike was pristine, right down to the leather seat and the thin leather streamers hanging off the handlebars. Damned thing looked brand new, which I knew it wasn't since they'd stopped making Indians in the early 1950s.

It was warm inside the restaurant. The place had low ceilings and dark wood panelling and was looked like a 1930s Bavarian hunting lodge. The smell from the crackling log fires and the aroma of smoked meats added to the effect. All that was missing was a couple of boar's heads on the wall, some yokels in lederhosen, and Herman Goering warming his fat arse at the fireplace.

The joint was packed and there was a lot of laughter and the sound of clinking glasses. Candles in brass holders on the tables threw off a warm glow. A quick scan of the room revealed that all the guests were women.

'Jesus,' I said. 'Lezzos by lamplight.'

A tall woman standing at the bar turned around and looked at me. 'You sucking round for a knuckle sandwich, shit-for-brains?' she said.

I sized her up. She was wearing tight white leather trousers and a white leather motorcycle jacket over a white silk shirt. The leather looked butter-soft and screamed Italian tailoring. She stood around six feet tall but her motorcycle boots, also white, added another inch or two. A blazing mane of curly red hair, a slender but curvy figure, and a face like an angel completed the picture.

'Oh yeah,' I said, 'and who's going to give it to me? You and whose sister?'

The woman suddenly jumped across from the bar and grabbed me. When Gudrun Arkell, five times Walkley Award-winner and doyenne of the Canberra Press Gallery, kisses you, you know you've been kissed. There were a lot of women in the national capital who could attest to that.

'Happy Birthday, Goods,' I said, disentangling myself from her embrace. 'And so I don't put my foot in it tonight, we're still sticking with that just-turned-thirty story, right?'

Gudrun grinned and used her thumb to wipe a smear of red lipstick from the corner of my mouth. 'Did you see the bike?' she said.

'Couldn't miss it, babe. It's bloody beautiful.'

'Did you know he was restoring it for me?'

'Maybe,' I said. 'But I know how to keep a secret.'

Gudrun's dad Morris had spent more than a year working on the bike for her fortieth birthday. Some of the WorldPix guys had brought parts back for him from their overseas assignments. I'd even lugged a gearbox from Holland on one of my trips. Since the Indian Motorcycle Company had been out of business for more than fifty years, original parts were as rare as hen's teeth.

I'd met Morris Arkell about fifteen years ago when he'd just retired from a career in aircraft maintenance and opened the winery. I was sipping an abrasive young pinot at the cellar door when three dickheads on a winery crawl had started getting stroppy. Just as I was about to go over and give the old pensioner a hand he deftly dropped the trio on their arses with some moves I hadn't seen since my days in spy-school self-defence classes. There were multiple bruises, one broken nose and a dislocated wrist. And Morris may have dropped his glasses as I recall. I stuffed the kids back in their car and gave them directions to the closest hospital while Morris opened a rather nice shiraz.

'Where is the old bastard?' I said.

'In the kitchen,' Gudrun said, 'annoying Mum as usual.'

Morris and Marta had equally fiery personalities. They'd met in post-war Berlin where Morris was stationed with a British commando unit and Marta was cooking in the military-base kitchen. Even after sixty-odd years of married bliss, there were still days when Gudrun reckoned it was like the war in Europe was still going full tilt. The smoked meats and German dishes that had made the winery's restaurant famous were from Marta's traditional family recipes, but Morris couldn't resist giving her advice. Marta's opinions on English cookery were well known and not at all complimentary. The restaurant's kitchen was a famous octogenarian battleground, but the food was fantastic.

I looked around for Gudrun's better half. Amy was a Kiwi winemaker who'd taken a job at the winery and fallen head over heels for Gudrun. They made a good couple. I spotted her at a table in a group that included a female senator well known for her outspoken opinions on the sanctity of marriage and family. Amy waved when she saw me, and the family-friendly senator, who had her arm around the shoulder of a brunette in a red bustier, turned white.

Amy came over and gave me a discreet kiss, then slipped her arm around Gudrun's waist. She was still a bit wary of me, since Gudrun kept telling everyone how we'd once shared a bed for three hot sweaty nights while on assignment. We'd actually been huddled together *under* the bed, in a hotel room in Baghdad with no air-conditioning, and shock-and-awe cruise missiles whizzing past the windows. On the positive side, sharing a room with a stunner like Gudrun had been great for my reputation as a stud. I gave up telling people she was gay when I got sick of watching battle-hardened male war correspondents burst into tears.

'Good you could come Alby,' Amy said, but she didn't mean it.

'Couldn't miss the old girl's thirtieth again, could I?' I said, winking at Gudrun. 'And I was thinking of stripping back some furniture, so I wanted to pick up a couple of gallons of your latest shiraz.'

'Get rooted, Alby,' Amy said.

'Not round here tonight, I won't.'

'Hey, you two, be nice,' Gudrun said.

Amy was sensitive about her wine but she knew I already had my name on a dozen cases of her shiraz. That particular drop had gold medals in its future, no doubt about it.

'So, what do you think of my outfit, Alby?' Gudrun said. 'Amy had it made specially, to go with the bike.'

'It's fantastic, babe,' I said. 'You look good enough to eat.'

It was a comment that resulted in a rather awkward silence.

'I'll leave you two to catch up,' Amy said.

As she headed back to the table, I yelled after her, 'Tell the senator I'm off duty. Her secret's safe with me.'

The senator gave me a weak smile and then I added, 'Until I want something.'

'I get the feeling you might want something from me,' Gudrun said. 'Nice and all as it is to see you.'

'Fancy a moonlit walk through the grapevines with your old Uncle Alby?'

'I've had some seriously creepy offers in my life, Alby, but that one really takes the cake.'

'Bloody bike dyke,' I said.

'Career public servant,' Gudrun retorted.

She always was better than me when it came to name-calling.

A full moon was lighting up rows of recently pruned vines that cascaded down the gentle slopes of the vineyard.

'Any idea what's happening in Defence?' I said. 'The Minister seems a bit twitchy.'

'This wouldn't have something to do with that little kerfuffle on the harbour yesterday, would it?'

'Maybe,' I said.

'Can't help you much, Alby. Something has definitely scared the horses, but I can't even get a whisper. All my usual sources in the Department have clammed up. That prick Pergo has everyone terrified, and not just in the Russell Hill complex.'

With the government's policy of falling like a ton of bricks on public servants who openly disagreed with it, or whistleblowers who felt a duty to leak stories that the great unwashed might have a vested interest in knowing about, a lot of journalists had given up on sources lately and were just regurgitating what was in the press handouts. Gudrun was old-school, though, and she understood that in politics the lack of a story was probably a story in itself.

'What I *can* tell you,' she continued, 'is that there've been a heap of crew cut, ramrod-straight Yanks in civvies visiting the Minister's office over the last few weeks. They spend a lot of time forcing themselves not to salute each other when they pass in the corridors. And young Carter Lonergan has dropped by a few times. He was in there this morning in fact, and didn't look like a happy camper, I hear.'

Now that was interesting. There was no way on earth Lonergan would have been able to visit the Minister's office without bumping into Pergo at least once. So they must have had a relationship going back before their little chat on the tanker and all that 'pleased to meet you, Mr Lonergan' bullshit in the D-E-D office.

Heavy US military traffic in and out of the Minister's office wasn't all that unusual, but why in civvies?

'What do you know about Operation Chester?' Gudrun said.

'Never heard of it. What is it?'

'Buggered if I know. I heard a whisper a while back, then nothing. Now, every time I mention it to anyone in Defence, they clam up tight as a drum. But if it doesn't mean anything to you it looks like you've wasted a trip.'

I smiled and pulled the small package from my pocket.

'If you're hinting around for your present …'

Gudrun ripped the paper off the box, opened it and slipped the heavy, polished-silver bracelet onto her wrist. 'You have incredible taste, Mr Murdoch,' she said, giving me another of those big kisses.

'I do try.'

'No, I meant in having Julie buy your presents for you. Excellent move.'

'I probably would have chosen something Dutch and Delftware-ish and more traditional.'

Gudrun gave me a warning look. 'If you're heading in the direction of a comment about a ceramic statuette featuring someone putting their finger in a dyke I'd be very careful.'

'Don't worry, Goods, I know better than to punch above my weight. And I've got another present for you – you didn't hear it from me, but keep an eye on Gwenda the Blenda.'

Gwenda had earned her nickname from a jibe in one of Gudrun's articles. She'd suggested that if the 'Minister for Cock-ups' thought there were votes in putting kittens in blenders then you wouldn't want to be standing between her, a kitchen-appliance store and the local pet shop.

'I thought old Gwen was permanently out to pasture after that last debacle?'

'It seems that, like the proverbial phoenix, the Honourable Ms Felton is rising from the ashes.'

'God, Alby, what have they given her to fuck up now?'

'That would be me. Hall-Smith has just made her the new head of D-E-D.'

'Jesus, mate, not even you deserve that.'

There was a sudden ruckus from the direction of the restaurant.

'We should head back inside,' Gudrun suggested. 'Sounds like the food's started hitting the tables. Mum put together a special sausage platter when I said you were coming. Maybe that'll cheer you up.'

Marta's smoked-sausage platter was something to behold. If we were to get snowed in over dinner with no means of escape for a week, I'd think I was in heaven. Like a lot of her generation in Europe, Marta had endured terrible food shortages in the last years of the war. Now she believed in serving plates heaped with food and expecting said plates to be handed back licked clean. Sometimes this was a bit of a challenge, but Marta Arkell was someone who didn't like to be disappointed.

She had gone all out with her sausage platter, and being well brought up, I tried to do it justice. This might have been possible if the platter had been limited to snags, but along with an assortment of a dozen different sausages, ranging from Bierwurst to Schinkenwurst and Knackwurst and beyond, there was a smoked pork chop, a mountain of German potato salad, winekraut, red cabbage, dill pickles, and dark rye bread. Thank God Gudrun, Amy and Morris were nice enough to help me out when Marta wasn't looking.

Around eleven I decided to call it a night. Since I'd probably had one beer too many and my rental car had a flat, I took Gudrun up on her offer of a ride back to the hotel on the pillion seat of the Indian. By the time we hit the Hyatt's driveway, my face was frozen, my testicles were numb, and I was stone cold sober. You could tell by the expression on the doorman's face that a spectacular six-foot redhead in white leathers straddling a vintage Indian wasn't something he saw every day.

Gudrun killed the engine and the silence was deafening. I climbed awkwardly off the bike, removed my helmet and gave it to her, along with a quick goodnight kiss. She hooked the helmet over the handlebars.

I took a business card from my pocket. 'My new mobile number is on the back. Call me if anything interesting comes up.'

She slipped the card into her jacket pocket, then studied the bracelet on her wrist.

'Thanks again for this,' she said. And after a pause, 'Julie still straight, then?'

'As far as I know.'

'Pity,' she said. 'She still playing hard to get?'

I stared at her. 'What?'

Gudrun grinned, slowly shaking her head. She kicked the Indian's engine into life.

'Jesus, Alby,' she yelled over the roar, 'sometimes you can be so fucking thick.'

The doorman let me open the Hyatt's front door all by myself while he stood and watched Gudrun ride away.

Chapter Thirteen

The Canberra Park Hyatt was built around the original, 1920s, heritage-listed art deco Hotel Canberra, and they actually did a good job of it – the joint oozes style and elegance. The only jarring note is the fact that currently the doorman and bellboys wear cloth caps, green waistcoats and plus-fours with long socks. They look like they should be out on an Irish golf course somewhere, caddying for leprechauns.

In Canberra, I like to stay at the Hyatt, especially when the government is picking up the tab. In Melbourne my favourite hotels are the Adelphi or the Como. The Como made a name for itself in the nineteen eighties with huge rooms, excellent service, and cute little rubber duckies in the bathtubs. Tonight, however, the Canberra Hyatt had gone one better. When I let myself into my room just after eleven my bathtub had a naked girl in it.

After Gudrun took off, I passed on the idea of a nice glass of port and a Monte Christo in the cigar bar, hung a left at the concierge's desk and headed down the corridor to my room to warm up. The Scullin suite was elegant and welcoming, and around twice the size of my Bondi apartment. There was no sign of a mint on my pillow in the bedroom which was disappointing.

In the living room a pair of jeans and a fluffy sweater were draped over the end of the couch, Tierney Sutton was on the stereo, gently toying with the Patsy Cline hit 'Crazy' and somebody in the bathroom was singing along. I poured myself a glass of Glen Fiddich, picked up the jeans and sweater and wandered in to see if my visitor wanted a drink.

The grey marble bathroom had a black marble vanity and a very large bath set atop a row of marble steps. Flickering candles lined the steps and continued around the bath, which was big enough to accommodate two. Right now, though, it had only one occupant. In my tub, with her hair pinned up and immersed in a sea of bubbles, was the lovely Cristobel Priday. A crumpled foil wrapper by her head explained what had happed to the mint on my pillow. Whatever bubble-bath the Hyatt used had been whipped into a froth that threatened to overtop the tub. Cristobel was buried in bubbles up to her chin.

'Good evening, Ms Priday,' I said, 'can I perhaps offer you something to drink?'

She shook her head. 'No thank you, I never touch alcohol.'

'Concerned you might wind up naked in a strange man's bathtub?'

'But you're not a stranger, Mr Murdoch. And you can call me Cristobel.'

She smiled at me. Perhaps it was meant to be a seductive smile but her eyes held a look I recognised. Whatever her original plan for this moment might have been Cristobel Priday was only now realising she was in the middle of making a huge mistake and right now she had no next move.

'I was wondering if perhaps you might like to join me in the tub, Mr Murdoch?'

I couldn't see through all the bubbles but I was pretty certain she had all her fingers and toes crossed hoping I'd say no.

'It's a very tempting offer, Ms Priday, and very Christian of you. And I could do with warming up, but I'm more of a morning-shower kind of bloke.'

Something in her smile told me she was relieved I wouldn't be joining her.

I've got a couple of rules I try to live by. One is not to drink supermarket scotch with names like Clan McBudget, and the other is not to get into a bath or a bed with a woman under twenty – both will leave you with nothing but regrets.

I took a pile of very plush hotel towels and put them on the end of the bath.

'Why don't you dry off and put your clothes on. Should I rustle us up something from room service?'

'That would be very nice, Mr Murdoch. Cocoa perhaps?'

'Right,' I said. 'I'll order some cocoa.'

If this got out amongst the press or the Dedheads my reputation would be toast.

Cristobel came out of the bathroom wearing her jeans and the big fluffy jumper. Her hair was in a ponytail now and she was back to being wholesome and I was kind of glad about that. I was about to ask how she'd managed to get into my room when her face lit up with that amazing smile at the sight of the cocoa and the plate of biscotti. I skipped the question. The Lord and beautiful nineteen-year-old girls both work in mysterious ways.

She made herself comfortable in an armchair, feet tucked up snugly under her.

I handed her a mug of cocoa. 'How did you know I was in Canberra?'

'Miss Gaarg said you were coming.'

In theory Gudrun and Jules were the only people who knew I was spending the night in Canberra. But Chapman Pergo had been waiting at the airport and now Cristobel was soaking in my bathtub.

'And of course, Mr Murdoch, I saw you earlier this evening outside the hotel.'

'Ah, yes, the red paint-hurling incident in the driveway. Is that why you're in Canberra Ms Priday? Helping to redecorate the wife of the Japanese ambassador?'

'That was a coincidence but Miss Gaarg said it was an opportunity we couldn't miss. But we've actually been here to continue lobbying the federal government on the establishment of our vitally needed whale sanctuary in Antarctica. Miss Gaarg is totally committed to the wellbeing of the world's sea creatures, in particular the whales. Whales are truly amazing creatures, Mr Murdoch. They communicate with each other over hundreds of miles of ocean, singing their beautiful songs. It's how they keep track of their families and friends, and let other whales know where to find food.'

'Sort of like their own sonar *Good Food Guide* for krill?'

'Exactly. Did you know, Mr Murdoch, that different whale species converse in different dialects, depending on where they're from? The blue whales from the American Pacific North-west and blue whales in the western Pacific Ocean sound different to each other, and both sound different to those living off Antarctica, and different again to the blue whales living near Chile.'

'You mean like street gangs, with their own 'hoods and homeboys and jive talk?'

Cristobel smiled politely, making me feel about four years old.

'But seriously, Mr Murdoch, the need for a whale sanctuary is vital and our government must get behind it and convince other nations to join with us. The whale is one of God's most magnificent creatures. Time is short and right now it has so few friends.'

After my meeting with the Defence Minister and Pergo, I was beginning to understand how the poor bloody whales must be feeling.

'But enough about me and the whales, Mr Murdoch, what brings you to Canberra?'

'Police business, Ms Priday.'

'Please call me Cristobel. And it's alright, I know you aren't really a police officer, Mister Murdoch.'

'Okay,' I said, 'I admit it, I'm actually a photographer.'

'You're a spy, Mr Murdoch. I don't think you should be ashamed to admit it.'

Shit. How did Miss Born Again know that? And what else did she know?

'There's nothing wrong with being a spy, Mr Murdoch, it's an honourable profession. The bible tells us, "*The Lord spoke to Moses, saying: Send men that they may spy out the land of Caanen which I give to the children of Israel; of every tribe of their fathers shall you send a man, every one a prince among them*".'

Jesus, not only was I a spy, but now I was a prince with it.

'The Book of Numbers, Mr Murdoch, chapter thirteen, verses one and two.

'Who gave you the idea I'm a spy, Ms Priday? Was it Miss Gaarg?'

She paused before answering. 'I overheard something earlier tonight. It was an accident – I don't usually eavesdrop.'

That had to be a first for Canberra.

'I was on my bed in the second bedroom of our suite and Miss Gaarg must have thought I was asleep. She was talking to someone on the phone and said you were with the government security services and poking your nose in places it didn't belong. She said you could ruin everything just when we were so close.'

So close to what was the question? And who had Artemisia been talking to?

'The whale sanctuary really is vital, Mr Murdoch. Miss Gaargs vision has a sanctuary encompassing the entire coast of Antarctica I'm hoping you can see it in your heart not to interfere. Or perhaps you might even join us in this vital work.'

How the hell had my name turned up as an opponent of their planned sanctuary? I had nothing against whales. I'd signed a petition of two on their behalf and donated photographs for fund raising auctions but that was as far as it went.

'Did Miss Gaarg ask you to come and see me and . . . persuade me to help?'

Cristobel turned red. 'Oh heavens no, Miss Gaarg would never do anything like that. I took it upon myself once she went to sleep to come to your room. Perhaps I went too far. I was stupid and I don't know what I was thinking. Fortunately it seems you are a good man.'

A whole lot of people would dispute that, and right now Cristobel and Gudrun were probably the only two people in Canberra who might be happy to write me a reference. And I just might need one.

'Ms Priday, I was wondering why you chose the bathtub.'

She studied the cocoa in her mug intently before answering. 'My mother Louise, often has friends over on sunny days. They lie by the pool and talk about men. Sometimes I find it hard not to overhear their conversations.'

I could visualise Louise Priday's friends by the pool and I could also imagine those conversations.

'According to Louise's friends, Mr Murdoch, a man will do anything you want if he walks in and finds you...'

I think she was struggling with using the word *naked.*

'...undressed in a bubble-bath.'

'Perhaps Ms Priday, Cristobel, you could buy some headphones and listen to music next time your mum has her friends over for a pool party.'

Cristobel nodded. 'I think that's very good advice Mr Murdoch.'

She finished her cocoa and stood up.

'I really should be off to bed now. We have an early start tomorrow and I've disturbed you enough for one evening.'

She had that right.

'Can I have the concierge arrange for a taxi?' I said as I walked her to the door.

She shook her head. 'We're staying in the hotel, but thank you for your concern. And please, whatever you can do to help us in our fight for the whale would be really appreciated.'

She stopped by the door and turned back.

God she was beautiful, but I guess God knew already.

'Mr Murdoch, I was wondering . . . may I take the rest of the biscotti?'

After she left I poured myself another whisky. I'd been in the national capital less than eight hours and already I'd been threatened by a government minister, bumped from a high-level, high-paying job, partied with a bunch of lesbians at a wine and sausage-fest, ridden pillion on a vintage motorcycle behind a six foot red-headed Amazon, been propositioned in my five star hotel bathroom by a beautiful, naked, nineteen year old, whale-loving, scripture-quoting committed Christian and finished my evening with her drinking cocoa. And there are still people who will try to tell you Canberra is a dull town.

Just after midnight, I was thumbing through the hotel's Gideon Bible while contemplating another whisky when my new mobile rang. It was Julie.

'Just checking in, nothing to report,' she said.

We kept the call brief. I asked Julie to sniff around for anything she could find on Operation Chester, then hung up and tried to get some sleep. But my mind was racing. The Canberra trip hadn't exactly been a roaring success. I now had even more questions than answers, and I'd been demoted, which would limit my access to vital information. And they were certainly circling the wagons in Defence. Was it just because the two nuclear warheads had been stolen from an American cruiser on a goodwill visit? Yes, it was embarrassing it happened on our turf, but the responsibility for their safe keeping lay squarely in the hands of the Americans so we shouldn't be getting the flak for that.

There had to be something else making them so jumpy. And though it was great to see Gudrun, she had been a dead end as far as inside info went. Then of course there was Cristobel. That vision alone was enough to keep a bloke awake in the wee hours. And Artemisia Gaarg was close to something that she was concerned I might screw up but I had no idea what it was. Around six I gave up on getting any sleep, took a shower and packed my bag. I was heading across the lobby when I spotted Cristobel and Artemisia Gaarg holding hands over coffee. I decided to say hello.

Cristobel gave me that wonderful high-wattage smile and introduced me as 'the nice Mr Murdoch.' God, that made me feel old.

Artemisia smiled and nodded. 'It's very nice to meet you Mr Murdoch.'

Even seated she was an imposing woman. Her face had the slightly weathered look of a sailor and her long white hair was pulled back in a ponytail. She was wearing a simple, ankle-length cotton skirt and a loosely fitted blouse of raw silk. Around her neck was a string of tiny, multi-coloured carved animals.

'That's a very nice necklace,' I said. I knew I'd seen it somewhere before.

'It's a fetish necklace, Mr Murdoch, made by Zuni Indians. The animals are carved from turquoise, coral and alabaster. Native Americans have always understood the link between ourselves and the animal world, the fact that we are all one upon this planet and all our destinies are linked.'

'Indeed,' I said.

Artemisia might have come across as someone's middle-aged hippie aunt if it weren't for the unsettling gleam of the true believer in her eyes.

'My dear young friend Cristobel tells me you discussed at some length our proposed Antarctic whale sanctuary.'

'Thanks to Cristobel I'm a lot better informed on the subject and I'll definitely be investigating it further.'

They both smiled at me. It was obvious only one of them was wishing me dead.

'Well, ladies, have a good morning, and very best of luck with the whales.'

I was forced to take a taxi to the airport since Chapman Pergo wasn't waiting outside the Hyatt to drive me.

Chapter Fourteen

There were long queues for security at Canberra airport. When I reached the front of the line and emptied my pockets for the metal detector I found the keys for the rented Toyota. I was cutting it fine for the flight so there wasn't time to return them to the desk. I called Julie's mobile and left a message with the rego number of the car and its location and asked her to sort it out with the rental company for me.

I got a bright 'Welcome back' from Chloe at the reception desk. Chloe Ransome answers the phones and does photo retouching for WorldPix. She can make almost anyone look good and she's not too hard on the eye herself – sort of a six-foot Jean Seberg, if Jean Seberg was part-Cambodian. She also had a good eye behind a camera. Julie and I had been recently discussing whether she was a candidate for an invitation to join the other side of the operation.

The office was quiet and the assignment board on the wall showed that most of the team were out shooting. I felt a momentary pang of regret that I wasn't out on assignment like the rest of the team, preferably out of the country, photographing endangered orang-utans or even a spunky young Hollywood starlet with pumped-up lips, unbelievably perfect tits and teeth, and only the vaguest understanding that the earth wasn't flat and Australia wasn't the place that Adolph Hitler, Arnie Schwarzenegger and Sacher torte came from.

I ran some beans through the grinder to make myself a cappuccino, and tried to figure out what my next move would be.

Diego Vega wandered in just after ten, flirted outrageously with Chloe and then dumped his camera bag at a workstation. Diego's family had swapped Chile for Australia when he was a kid and he'd thrived with the change. He was now a deadly combination of the laconic, laid-back Aussie sporting type blended with rugged, Chilean good looks and Latin charm, and the women didn't stand a chance. When he and my mate Byron Oxenbould hit the clubs on a Sunday night, it was like a feeding frenzy. I went out with them once and found the whole business way too depressing, especially when a curvy twenty-year-old told Byron it was nice of him to bring his father along.

'G'day, Alby,' Diego said, hauling a Nikon from his bag and taking out the memory card. 'How was Canberra? Still boring as?'

'Mate, you've got no idea.'

Diego pushed the card into the reader on the computer and downloaded his images. I logged onto another screen to have a look. His work was shaping up nicely. The series of photographs on the screen featured the LNG tanker, but now it was facing the other way up the harbour and a couple of tugs were giving it a nudge towards the heads.

'They're taking her round to Port Botany to repair the engines,' Diego explained. 'Bit embarrassing, eh, breaking down off the Opera House and then getting mixed up in the middle of a major security stuff-up like that.'

'What sort of shots did you get of the trouble on the cruiser?' I said.

'Not as bloody good as yours, I'll bet.'

He opened another file. There were long-lens images of bodies on the wharf, and the paramedics and sailors working on the wounded. There was also a shot of me, Julie, Carter Lonergan and the good-looking lieutenant having our little tête-à-tête.

'How the hell do you always manage to get on the inside, Alby, right where the action is? You must have some amazing connections. Friends in high places, eh?'

'Something like that, mate.' If he only knew – but right now it was more like enemies in high places.

I studied the shot of our group talking on the chopper deck. It was taken from a higher angle than the others.

'Where'd you shoot this one from?' I asked.

He shrugged. 'There was a van parked on the road outside the base gates so I climbed on top. I just managed to get off a couple of shots before some doofus stuck a gun in my face and told me to piss off. Prick.'

'That's a bit heavy. You get any pictures of the van?'

Diego scrolled through the images and clicked on a wide-angle shot of an ambulance leaving the dock. He pointed to a vehicle in the background. But it wasn't really a van – it was a squat grey armoured truck parked with its wheels up on the curb. There was no security company name or logo that I could see and no number plate. On the right side of the photograph I could just see the entrance to the Navy's Cowper Road car park. Was Max already dead on the concrete on level three when Diego snapped this shot I wondered?

My mobile buzzed. A text message from Julie.

'Turn on the ABC news now!' it said.

I picked up the remote and turned on the plasma TV. The tagline on the bottom of the screen read CANBERRA LIVE and the picture showed a car hooked up to a tow truck. There were cops all over the place. The car had an odd outward bulge in the roof and the side windows had shattered into a million pebble-sized pieces.

According to the person at the news desk, the towie had just lifted the car's front wheels off the ground when *ka-bang!* A spokesman for the local police said they suspected a gangland hit gone wrong, and the towie from the car rental company considered himself lucky to be alive. He wasn't the only one.

The bulge in the roof favoured the right-hand side, so it would have been a charge under the driver's seat. Nothing too huge, just enough plastic explosive to turn the occupant into eighty-some kilograms of chopped beef. I pulled the rental car keys from my pocket and checked the rego number on the tag against the licence plate on the screen. No point in posting the keys back now, I decided.

This really upped the stakes. I knew they wanted me off the case, but now it looked like somebody really wanted me dead.

There was a sudden piercing shriek from Chloe.

Diego looked up and gasped. 'What the hell is that?'

I swung round in my chair. Jesus, first the rental car, now this. What immediately came to mind was the closing lines from *Apocalypse Now* – The horror, the horror …'

Chloe had pushed her chair back from the reception desk and was frantically trying to fend off the small brown dog that was enthusiastically humping her leg.

'Leave the girl alone Fritzy. Heel, damn you. Ah, Murdoch, just the man I need to see.'

Fritzy was a miniature dachshund and as usual he was connected by a leash to the Honourable Gwenda Felton AO. Gudrun referred to this combination as the rat on the rope, leaving it open as to which end of the rope the rat was on. Apparently there was a Mr Honourable Gwenda Felton AO out there somewhere but no one had ever seen him. At parliamentary functions, tree plantings, building dedications, and the ritual breaking of recalcitrant public servants on the rack, it was always just Gwenda and Fritzy.

She marched through the office towards me, a swirling kaleidoscope of brightly coloured fabric, crimson lipstick, blue eye shadow, too much rouge, and hair bleached and teased to breaking point. Diego was left choking in a wash of perfume and hairspray. As an Officer of the Order of Australia Gwenda Felton was entitled to have AO after her name, which was entirely appropriate because if this woman was a movie she'd have to be rated Adults Only – way too scary for anyone under sixteen. And she made a lot of people over sixteen pretty nervous as well. She could suck all the oxygen out of a room in just one breath and proceeded to give us a demonstration.

'I think you should have an armed security guard outside that door 24/7 and perhaps we could make the glass bulletproof and I don't think it would kill either you or that boy to wear a suit and tie or get a haircut.'

She handed me Fritzy's leash. I looked down into the dog's beady little eyes and I knew two things. One was that Fritzy was pure evil and the second was that Dougal could have him for breakfast. I handed the leash to Diego, who was looking very confused at this talk of armed guards, bulletproof glass, and people wearing suits and ties.

'Why don't you and Chloe take Ms Felton's doggie for a bit of a stroll, mate,' I said. 'She and I need to have a chat.'

I locked the front door after they left and smiled at my new boss.

'First things first,' I said. 'this is the office of WorldPix, a commercial photo-agency, not D-E-D so you showing up here doesn't do much for maintaining our cover. And having a marked car and an armed guard from the Australian Protective Service out front would be a great way of advertising that something else besides photography is going on here. Secondly, Diego and Chloe work for WorldPix, and like most of the people here, they've got no idea what D-E-D is and I'd like to keep it that way. Thirdly, wearing a suit and tie *could* very well kill me. If I'm under cover as a photographer then I need to be damn sure I look like one.'

'Rupert said you were difficult, Murdoch, but I've handled difficult people before.'

This was true. Gwenda Felton AO had left a long trail of shattered underlings in her wake. Her motto was 'my way or the highway', and out on that particular highway Gwenda Felton AO was a B-Double with very dickey brakes.

'As to my showing up here, Murdoch,' she went on, 'I'm not a complete idiot.'

That was the kind of admission you rarely got from politicians these days. But having the fate of the nation in the hands of almost complete idiots wasn't much consolation.

'The official reason for my visit is that I need to update my PR photographs. So coming here allows me to kill two birds with one stone. We can talk about the new rules for D-E-D operatives while you take my picture.'

What the hell did she need PR shots for? Did she think she was going to get a profile in *Spy Weekly*?

While I set up the lights in the studio, Gwenda Felton laid down the law. There would be a lot more in the way of paperwork and a lot less in the way of operatives acting on initiative. My investigation of the business on the *Altoona* was now closed, shut down, *finito*, put to bed, never to be mentioned again.

'And just so we're clear, Murdoch, I'm contemplating setting up a branch office of WorldPix somewhere in the far north of Finland, and people who mess with me could find themselves up to their ears in snow and caribou.'

I think she meant reindeer, but I got the point.

'Perhaps we should also think about changing the name of D-E-D,' she continued. 'It makes for a rather depressing acronym, don't you think?'

The Directorate for Extra-Territorial Defence had been the cover name for a military-support section for Coastwatchers on enemy-occupied islands in the Pacific in World War II. The officer in charge had covertly and unofficially turned it into a visual-surveillance operation, with his eye on setting up a secure government job for himself after the war. The plan had worked and D-E-D was now one of the oldest security operations going. We had a long and proud, if totally secret and deniable, history, and now this bureaucratic blow-in wanted to change the name on her first day on the job. How typical was that?

Through the camera lens, Gwenda Felton was a riot of colour and movement. Her outfit made Carter Lonergan's Hawaiian shirt collection look sedate. I suggested we postpone the shoot and get a wardrobe stylist and makeup artist in and she asked if I'd ever eaten caribou meat, so I let it go and figured I'd get Chloe to work her magic in Photoshop. The girl would be up for a major pay rise if she could pull this one off.

Thank God for auto-focus cameras. I turned the music up, closed my eyes and tried to think about Saturday lunch at Buon Ricordo, the Italian place run by my friend Armando. The image I actually conjured up was Cristobel Priday naked in my bathtub, but that was okay too.

Chapter Fifteen

When Gwenda and Fritzy had gone I made a few phone calls. The first was to a computer boffin mate of Harry's, the second to Byron Oxenbould's agent, the third was to Carter Lonergan.

Carter and I had been talking about getting together for lunch since he took up his post. He was wary of my invitation at first, so I mentioned that Julie would be joining us and he was suddenly able to rearrange his busy schedule and make himself available around noon the next day.

I was now well and truly out of the loop on the non-missing, non-existent nukes. I knew Carter would be right in the middle of the action, and if my plan worked I should be able get some useful information.

I headed into the city down Hickson Road. I figured a walk along the harbour front and through the Rocks might clear my head and get the image of Gwenda Felton smiling like a rouged piranha out of my brain. The other image I was trying to lose was the rented Toyota bulging outwards from the explosive charge that someone hoped I'd be sitting on. I must admit that made me a bit jumpy.

Up towards the casino I picked up a tail: a young bloke in lycra on a Bianchi Cross Veloce with a courier satchel over his shoulder. Probably just one of Gwenda's minions making sure I was obeying her directive to drop the case, but I wasn't taking any chances. I ditched him by detouring through the casino, ducking out the staff entrance and grabbing a passing taxi. It was all a bit too easy, so I figured he must have been one of Gwenda's boys.

At Circular Quay a kilted busker with bagpipes was competing with an Aboriginal bloke on a didgeridoo. It was hard to say who was winning, but it definitely wasn't the ferry passengers. There were a number of large trucks parked outside one of the burger chains on Pitt Street, and the presence of movie lights, muscular blokes in T-shirts and tool belts, and hyperactive young production assistants rushing about with clipboards and walkie-talkies indicated the presence of a film crew.

Byron Oxenbould, or Boxer to his friends, was sitting on a folding chair with his feet up on a trolley full of audio recorders, microphones, boom poles, and headphones. He was reading an electronics magazine and looking bored. When my shadow fell across his magazine he glanced up.

'What a fucking debacle this is,' he said. 'It's a one-day shoot and I reckon we'll be here till bloody Christmas. Plus every time we do a take I've got to get an assistant director to slip Mr Didgeridoo and Bonnie Prince Charlie over there ten bucks each to pack it in for five minutes so we can hear what the actors are saying. Noisy buggers are making more out of this job than I am.'

One of the top motion-picture sound recordists in the country, Boxer did the odd TV commercial between feature films, and occasionally some clandestine sound stealing for D-E-D He was very good at his job and he hated working with people who weren't good at theirs. Boxer was a handsome bastard in his own dishevelled way, and a couple of very famous actresses insisted he was the only man they'd let tape those tiny radio mikes inside their cleavage. As Boxer liked to say, 'It's a dirty job but someone has to do it.'

The director started screaming at a young PA with a bum bag round her waist that looked like it held everything including the kitchen sink.

Boxer shook his head. 'That bloke couldn't direct traffic on an escalator.'

'But you're getting all the fast food you can eat, right?'

He gave a sardonic laugh. 'Eighteen hours out of my life and forty thousand feet of film for thirty seconds on air extolling the delights of the triple-cheese, double-crumbed, ham-steak, barbecued-bacon chilli burger with pineapple – and would you like extra fat with that, Sir?'

Boxer tilted his head towards the street, where the film crew vehicles were parked between rows of orange witches hats. 'You could stuff one of those damned burgers into a grease gun and do a decent lube job on half those trucks out there. If I had higher ethical standards and a lower mortgage I'd tell 'em to stick it.'

He tossed the magazine onto his chair and looked at me. 'And speaking of dubious ethical standards, to what do I owe the pleasure of your company?'

'I've just been photographing Gwenda Felton, so I needed some fresh air.'

Boxer shivered. 'I reckon you'd need more than fresh air after something like that, mate. Maybe an eyeball transplant.'

'Your agent told me you were working down here for the day. I might have a job for you, if you're interested.'

Boxer glanced over to where the bulk of the film crew were now milling around the director, who looked like he might be about to have a stroke.

'Let's go grab a coffee. It's gonna be at least an hour before this dill works out that he's never going to be able to make this little burger epic look like the opening shot from *Goodfellas*.'

We found a café with tables upstairs where I could keep an eye on the street. The waitresses were a couple of young and beautiful Scandinavian backpackers and they fell on our table like the Mongol hordes when they spotted Boxer. In Sydney, good-looking gets good service, and we had frothy cappuccinos and a couple of apple Danish in front of us in no time flat.

When the waitresses finally left us alone I ran a couple of questions past Boxer. He nibbled at his pastry and thought about his answer for a good five minutes, eventually nodded and said yes, it was probably possible. I explained who the target was and he said no, it was totally impossible, adding that I must be out of my tiny mind.

'Okay,' I said, 'if you don't think you can do it, I understand. I'll find somebody else.'

'Gee, Alby, reverse psychology? That'll work on me every time.'

'Sorry mate. I can't explain why I need this done, but you know I wouldn't ask you if it wasn't important.'

He looked at me for a minute. 'Yeah, okay, I'm in. But you owe me big time.'

I called for the bill, which arrived at the speed of light. 'I'll get this,' I said.

'You got that right, pal.'

The waitress brought back the change and handed Boxer one of the café's business cards, which had two phone numbers written on the back. It looked like Mr Good-looking would be getting more than just great table service.

I left Boxer at the film shoot and walked back to the Quay, trying to decide between taking a bus or train to Bondi. Cabs were out – I'd heard enough rant-back radio on the ride over from the casino. I opted for the train to Bondi Junction and a bus down the hill.

Julie's board was outside the front door and she was still in her wetsuit, towelling her hair dry. Julie in skin-tight, glistening black neoprene was quite a sight.

'How's the surf?'

'Great. That northerly's perfect for the south swell. Just magic.'

I tossed the rental car keys onto the dining-room table

'That was meant for you, wasn't it? she said. 'What's going on?'

Whoever planted the bomb probably didn't notice the flat in the dark. A puncture, one beer too many, and freezing my nuts off on the back of Gudrun's Indian saved me from getting them blown off in a rented Toyota. 'I guess someone really does want me off this case.'

'Half a kilo of C4 triggered by a mercury switch would definitely achieve that,' Julie said. 'And then some. But apart from that, how was Canberra?'

I gave her the good news about my demotion and the bad news about our new boss and she took it rather well. After two minutes at the computer her printed out resignation letter was a masterpiece of tact and brevity. There were only two problems that I could see.

'First of all I've got no idea what a funking bitch is,' I said, 'and secondly, who's going to watch my back if you leave?'

She took the letter from me, tore it up and threw it in the bin.

'Got that out of your system?' I asked.

'Yep.'

'Good. Now, I ran into Cristobel Priday with Artemisia Gaarg in Canberra this morning. Any idea what the connection there is?'

'I know Cristobel is part of Artemisia's save-the-whale crusade.'

'Yeah, I know, but I sprung them holding hands over toast and Vegemite. Are you sure there's nothing more to it than whales?'

'For fuck's sake, Alby, what is it with you men?' She reached around to unzip her wetsuit. ' Two women just have to look like they're having a good time together and instantly you see girl-on-girl action. One bloody night in Canberra with Gudrun and you think everyone's gay.'

'We are strange and mysterious creatures.'

'You can say that again. Anyway, I think the Cristobel–Artemisia relationship is more of a mother–daughter thing. They met when Cristobel was visiting her dad in prison and Artemisia was setting up some kind of prisoner support program. When Priday was paroled and started his ministry, Artemisia was an early supporter. She signed the deeds of Jindivick, her family home, over to his church.'

'That's right, Cristobel said they had a benefactor.'

'I'll see what else I can dig up. Just don't go get your hopes up for any kind of a lesbian love nest.'

She turned her back to me. 'My zipper's stuck, can you get it for me?'

I was happy to oblige. I freed the zip and ran it down the curve of her back revealing smooth tanned skin.

'I'm going to hit the shower,' she said, heading for the bathroom.

I could do with a cold one myself, I decided.

'Find anything on Operation Chester yet?' I called after her.

'Zilch. Absolutely nothing. Everyone clams up as soon as I mention the name.'

'That's exactly what Gudrun said. She sends her regards, by the way. She thinks I have exquisite taste in choosing people to choose my gifts for me.'

I heard the water running in the shower.

'She also wanted to know if you were still straight.'

'Well,' Julie said, popping her head round the bathroom door, 'if I have to keep hanging round with blokes like you and the rest of the Dedheads, I might be tempted to reconsider.'

That was a very low blow.

'A cappuccino would be nice,' she called out as she closed the door.

While the espresso machine warmed up I logged onto the Bondi Beach Surf Cam. With a click of the mouse you can pan right along the beach to check the surf. You can also check out the people on the beach, walking along the promenade or loitering in the park. I zoomed in on a black Astra nose-in to the curb, facing Campbell Parade. The passenger was using binoculars and they were pointed at the front of my building.

Julie came out of the bathroom in a tight white T-shirt and lean hipster jeans. She was fresh-faced and glowing, her wet hair slicked back in a ponytail.

I handed her a cappuccino. 'Have a look at this,' I said, showing her the webcam. 'Recognise either of them?'

Julie shook her head. 'Gwenda's people?'

'I reckon they might be. They're about as subtle as she is.'

'You worried about them?'

'No, I'll lose them on the way to dinner. But I don't think they're dangerous. It's the ones you can't see that you have to keep an eye on.'

I shook off the bozos in the Astra by doubling back through a couple of one-way streets in Tamarama. By seven-fifteen I was in a private room at Tetsuya's waiting for my date.

Tetsuya Wakuda is a lovely Japanese bloke who got off a plane from Tokyo one day in the early 1980s, took a bus to Darlinghurst, and using the few words of English he knew, got himself a job washing dishes in a fish restaurant. Twenty-five years on, Tetsuya's is consistently rated one of the top five restaurants in the world, and people fly in from all sorts of places to marvel at a twelve-course degustation menu that changes subtly from visit to visit but which is always sublime.

The private rooms looking out over the immaculately groomed traditional Japanese garden are always great for impressing women. But not tonight. My dinner companion arrived sporting a walking stick, a newly installed titanium hip and a pensioner-discount card. He smiled and stuck out his hand.

'Fell off the fucking massage table, Alby, can you believe it?'

Charlie Somersby was a former World War II bomber pilot who now enjoyed a very pleasant retirement to Byron Bay thanks to an inheritance. The last time I'd seen him he'd been naked on his living-room floor, getting a rubdown from three beautiful young ladies wearing frangipani leis and nothing else. They traded, according to the sign on their Kombi van, as Lovely Hula Hands and provided holistic massage, involving coconut oil, incense and ukulele music. They offered a pensioner discount to boot, which put Byron Bay well up on my list of retirement possibilities.

'Been meaning to try this place for years,' Charlie said, looking around the room approvingly. He patted his new hip. 'I was a bit worried I'd have to sit on the floor, though, and then we'd be buggered.'

Charlie had been piloting RAF Halifax bombers on secret missions over occupied Europe before he turned twenty, and he'd survived more than thirty missions without a scratch. On his eighty-fifth birthday, the hula girls had thoughtfully suggested using the massage table rather than the floor and the poor bastard had fallen less than a metre and fractured his hip.

'Didn't have my bloody parachute on, did I Alby? Didn't have any bloody thing on. When the ambulance arrived they took one look at the girls and sent out a radio call. Ten minutes later every emergency vehicle from Ballina to Southport was parked in my driveway. Fire engines, police cars, State Emergency Services, the lot.'

He ordered champagne. 'Seeing I'm on the government's expense account down here, Alby, I reckon we should go the whole hog.'

'No argument from me there, mate,' I said.

We drank a toast to absent friends, which of course meant Harry. I'd first met Charlie through my mate Harry Wardell, a fellow Dedhead who'd stuck his nose in someplace it wasn't welcome and paid the ultimate price. I missed Harry and I know Charlie did too.

As we worked our way through the snow egg and caviar sandwich, the tartare of tuna on sushi rice and avocado, and the Spring Bay scallops with wakame and lemon, Charlie described his adventures in orthopaedic surgery in gruesome detail. When we got to the confit of Tasmanian ocean trout with konbu, daikon and fennel, I figured it was time to get down to tin tacks and find out what he'd been able to come up with on Operation Chester.

'You called at just the right time, old chap. I was in the bowels of one of the Defence Department servers so I had a quick poke about using the Minister's access code.'

'You can do that?' I asked.

'Piece of piss, as my great-grandson likes to say.'

Charlie was an early adopter of computers in the seventies and he was an expert in IT before anyone knew what IT was. He set up the first systems used by the Defence Department and still did occasional consulting work for them, so he had retained his high-level security clearance.

'This trout is spectacular, Alby. Are you going to finish yours?'

'You better believe it, mate. But getting back to Operation Chester, Charlie, what did you find?'

'In a nutshell, old chap, in late 1991, post Gulf War One, the US Defence Department proposed that Australia should be secretly provided with a couple of tactical nuclear warheads. The weapons would be a last-resort option should our region become unstable at a time when the US military might be overstretched – say, in the Middle East – and unable to provide support to Australia as required under the ANZUS treaty. The plan was code-named Operation Chester.'

'Fuck me drunk.'

'Exactly. But the plan was quickly rejected,' he continued, 'on the grounds that the revelation of an Australian nuclear capability would of itself destabilise the region with unforeseeable political, economic and social consequences in our sphere of influence.

'They had that right.'

He nodded. 'However it seems that when Iraq went wobbly and with this business with Iran some bright spark in the Pentagon turned up the Chester plan and figured it might be time to reactivate it. Canberra agreed, and now it looks like Defence is about to sign for a couple of special delivery nukes. Bloody idiots. All very hush hush, of course Alby. And you didn't hear it from me. If word of this arrangement got out the shit would hit the fan.'

He turned his attention back to his plate and that delicious fish.

I didn't want to put an old digger off his dinner but the shit had already well and truly hit the fan and it was worse than Charlie could imagine. No wonder Hall-Smith was apoplectic -- they were our nukes that had been nicked. Just how far would they be prepared go to keep something like this quiet? My mind flashed back to the rented Toyota with the bulging roof and I had a pretty fair idea.

Chapter Sixteen

JULIE TURNED UP AT BONDI JUST AFTER NINE THE NEXT MORNING. I WAS on my second coffee and she'd brought a large orange, apple and carrot Goodie, and we headed up to the roof for some sea air, a bit of vitamin D and a debrief. I filled her in on Charlie's revelations.

'Two tactical nukes on loan? They must be out of their minds. That's taking the deputy-sheriff business way too far. The whole region would go apeshit if word of that got out.'

'Just imagine what will happen if word gets out they've been nicked.'

'Holy shit, Alby, no wonder people want to shut us down. Everyone in Canberra must be running for cover.'

Back downstairs in my apartment, Julie got out a big sheet of paper and coloured markers and we sat down and tried to figure out what we knew so far.

After fifteen minutes we sat back and looked at what we had. Which wasn't all that much: in a top secret operation, the USS *Altoona* was delivering a couple of nukes to the Australian government, and the ship's choir had done a runner with them. But why? There had been no ransom demands, no links to terror organisations, no threats about setting them off. They'd just vanished.

The only local link to the choir was the Reverend Priday and the soiree at Jindivick. Young Max Gallagher had photographed the occasion and then turned up dead at a vantage point overlooking the scene of the heist. And someone had pulled the memory card out of his camera. Plus Priday's daughter Cristobel knew I was a spy – if it was her old man on the other end of that phone call to Artemesia who had told him?

And what had Chapman Pergo been arguing with Carter Lonergan about on the decoy tanker? Lonergan would have known about the delivery of the nukes, which would explain why he'd been on deck at sparrow's fart on Monday. And why, when Pergo came to the D-E-D office, had they acted like they'd never met?

In the end, we had more questions than answers.

'By the way, I got some info on the Gaarg family for you,' Julie said, tossing a folder on the table. 'That Artemisia's a pretty amazing woman – no wonder Cristobel's a disciple.' She held up the half-empty Goodie she was drinking.

'She owns the Wake Up to Goodness company that makes these – fresh-squeezed juice every day. I couldn't live without them.'

I flicked through the pages. It was quite a family saga. Artemisia's father, Sir Linus Gaarg was a tinkerer and inventor. He built the family fortune from his inventions, including a national chain of automated tearooms. These were converted into malt shops for GI's in WW2, making him an absolute motza. Post-war Gaarg had gone into the aerospace industry, once again making a fortune. He married a well known artist and bought Jindivick for her as a wedding present

Artemisia was an only child. At age ten she had seen her mother taken by a shark while swimming off the Jindivick jetty. Her hair turned white overnight. Later, while studying arts at Melbourne University, she developed an interest in sailing, representing Australia twice at the Olympics, crewing on 5.5 metre yachts.

In 1994, Gaarg Aerospace Group International took over Genki Heavy Industries of Japan to become one of the world's largest companies. Sir Linus died unexpectedly from fugu poisoning in a top Tokyo seafood restaurant where the merger was being celebrated. Artemisia, an avowed vegetarian, had refused to touch any seafood at the dinner, including the fatal Puffer Fish sushi.

As her father's sole heir, she became the major shareholder in Gaarg/

Genki International, appointing herself chairwoman and CEO. Within months she had sold off almost all of the Gaarg empire's companies and assets. Her only business interest now was the wildly successful Goodie juice line, whose profits, along with the rest of her wealth, were consolidated into the Gaarg Foundation.

The foundation's stated aim was 'to do good works', and Artemisia had certainly achieved that in the past ten years. Gaarg Mobile Clinics had been established in remote areas to improve the health and living standards of indigenous Australians; every large city in Australia now had a Gaarg Fresh Start Centre, which provided meals, accommodation and a helping hand for the homeless to get back on their feet; the children's hospitals in Sydney, Melbourne and Darwin had a Gaarg Wing, with more planned for Brisbane, Perth and Adelaide.

There was also the Gaarg Oceanic Institute, working to preserve the marine environment and improve the wellbeing of the world's sea creatures, most specifically the whale. Why anyone who had lost her parents to sharks and toxic fish liver was so dedicated to our finned friends was a mystery.

I tossed the file back on the desk. Julie was right. Artemisia did sound like an amazing woman and I could understand why Cristobel was taken with her. Plus the woman was a great shot with a four-litre can of Dulux Federation Crimson.

Around eleven, I picked up my mobile, announcing I was off to lunch. Julie was all in favour of joining me but I explained there was a little job I needed her for.

The bozos from the Astra were easy to lose in the confusion of Chinatown, but I doubled back through Paddy's Markets using the rear elevators in Market City just to make sure.

The Dragon Star was buzzing. All of its eight hundred seats were filled, with another hundred or so hungry customers lined up outside, waiting for their number to be called by a Cheongsam-clad hostess.

I spotted Carter wearing one of his appalling Hawaiian shirts and steered him inside, past the display of giant dried shark's fin and glass tanks full of live fish, crabs and abalone. Diners at the packed tables were waving and shouting to waitresses pushing trolleys stacked high with bamboo baskets of steamed dumplings, or laden with plates of spring rolls, and noodles, or bunches of shiny green bok choy waiting to be plunged into steaming vats of boiling water before being chopped up and doused with oyster sauce.

I waved to Sam, one of the managers, and smiled at the elegant hostess. She spoke into a walkie-talkie and scrawled a number on a ticket before pointing towards a table at the back of the room.

After ordering a pot of Bo Lai tea and some chopped chilli in soy sauce, I started looking around for lunch.

'Is there anything you don't eat, Carter?'

'I drew the line at a sheep's eyeball in Afghanistan,' he said, 'but other than that I'm willing to trust you.'

That was what I liked to hear. I flagged down a passing trolley and chose a variety of steamed dumplings to get us started – su mai, har gow, wor tip, and the delicious barbecued pork in a steamed bun called cha siu bow. I picked up a prawn dumpling with my chopsticks and dipped it into the soy and chilli mixture.

'Shouldn't we wait for Julie?'

I shook my head. 'Three rules of yum cha in my circle, Carter – get there, get a table and get stuck in. Latecomers are on their own.'

To give Lonergan his due, he did just that. He seemed to be enjoying himself up to the moment I ordered a plate of chicken's feet, and then my mobile rang. It was Julie and she was right on time. Exactly thirty seconds into the conversation the phone gave a loud beep and died.

'Bugger,' I said. 'forgot to charge the damn thing.' I dropped it into my pocket. 'Julie can't make it. She sounded a bit stressed. Can I borrow your phone to make sure she's okay?'

He handed me his mobile and I dialled Julie's number. When she answered I made a big show of not being able to hear. I stood up and indicated that I was heading for the side exit to get a better signal. Carter nodded distractedly and was jabbing at the chicken's feet with his chopsticks as I walked away.

I ducked into the men's toilets. The first stall was occupied and the door to the second carried a hand-written notice in English and Chinese characters saying the toilet was blocked and shouldn't be used. I took the sign off, walked in, locked the door, lowered the seat and sat down. After a quiet goodbye to Julie I handed both phones, mine and Lonergan's, under the partition to the adjoining cubicle where Boxer was waiting.

I continued my conversation with a non-existent Julie, raising my voice just loud enough to carry out to the main area of the toilets in case Lonergan decided to check up on me. Three minutes later, Boxer handed the phones back under the partition. I screwed up the handwritten sign from the door and flushed it down the toilet.

Back at the table, I handed Lonergan his phone. 'Julie sends her apologies.'

'Is she all right?'

'Yep. But she's got a photographer in trouble in Iraq and she's trying to arrange his evacuation.'

'Anyone I know?'

'Tas Johnson.'

'Oh, is he one of yours? I met him in Kabul.'

'Yeah, he's a good operator. It's unusual for him to get himself in a jam.'

'Happens to the best of us,' Lonergan said. 'Sometimes a man can open up a can of worms and find himself knee-deep in snakes in the grass.'

Suddenly I had the feeling we weren't talking about Tas any more. I prefer my mixed metaphors shaken, not stirred, but there was no doubt Carter was making a point.

'Found those pesky nukes yet?'

'You know I can't discuss that with you, Alby. You're off the investigation.'

'Yeah. Why is that? You'd think with two nukes on the loose in these dangerous times, they'd want every man and his dog on the case. Instead they're shutting people down.'

Lonergan considered this. 'Okay,' he said after a pause, 'totally off the record, we believe what we have here is a hijacking for ransom – that the crewmen from the *Altoona* have the warheads stashed somewhere, and when we pay up they'll head for Brazil with the cash, then tell us how to find them.'

'You sure about that?'

Carter took a sip of tea. 'It's happened before.'

Jesus. This was something I hadn't heard about.

'In 1996, a Russian mobile ICBM launcher disappeared while on exercises in Georgia in the former USSR. It was carrying an SS-25 Sickle missile armed with a nuclear warhead. A week later, the transporter vehicle was located on the bottom of a lake with the crew still inside. The warhead from the ICBM was missing. A week after that, a spokesman for a dozen Russian ex-Spatnez commandos contacted the US embassy in Moscow and announced they could tell us where the warhead was – for a fee, naturally. The asking price was thirty-six million dollars, twelve US green cards and total immunity. If the offer was rejected, the spokesman hinted that the warhead would find its way onto the open market and go to the highest bidder.'

'But the US government doesn't negotiate with terrorists,' I said.

'No, of course it doesn't,' Carter agreed. 'However, a private company did transfer funds into a number of Swiss bank accounts, a series of visas were issued, and the warhead was recovered from a warehouse in Tirana.'

'And you think you've got a similar scenario here?'

He nodded. 'We've been informed there will be an offer on the table by Monday at the latest, and the matter will be resolved by the end of the week.'

'So you're absolutely sure there's no terrorist angle?'

'There's still been no demands, no chatter. We'd have had a whiff of something by now.'

'So you're suggesting it's just that good old American entrepreneurial spirit at work?'

'It would seem so.'

I decided it was time to throw a cat among the pigeons. 'So with all this going on, do you think you'll still be able to keep the lid on Operation Chester?'

Lonergan was good. I saw him flinch but he didn't take the bait.

'A word of advice, Alby,' he said, 'keep your head down and stay well clear of all this. The situation will work itself out, trust me on that.'

'Right. If you can't trust the CIA, Carter, who can you trust?'

He checked his watch. 'I have to be somewhere,' he said, reaching for his wallet.

'I'll get lunch. But tell me, those Russians who nicked the nuke, did they wind up living happily ever after in the US of A?'

Lonergan folded his napkin beside his plate. 'A very sad story. They arrived in Portland, Oregon to start their new lives and apparently all fell asleep in a rented minivan on their way from the airport. Jetlag, I suppose. The van had broken down in the middle of a railway crossing at the time and a freight train hit it before the engineer could put the brakes on. There were no survivors, apart from the driver.'

'Too bad,' I said.

'Yeah. Shit happens.'

'Certainly does. They've got trains in Brazil too, right?'

Carter smiled. 'I believe so, Alby.'

He stood up. 'Thanks for lunch. Always a pleasure, and regards to Julie. I hope she gets Tas out okay – we can't afford to lose good guys.'

A couple of minutes after Lonergan had left, Boxer dumped his backpack on a spare chair and reached for the chopsticks. Just then my phone, now fitted with a fully charged battery, played the opening bars of 'The Star Spangled Banner'.

'Very subtle,' I said.

Boxer grinned. 'Press *1984#,' he said. 'That code disconnects the microphone in your handset when you connect,' he said, 'so you can listen in and nobody knows you're eavesdropping.'

I held the phone to my ear. Boxer does good work and the connection was clear as a bell. I could hear both ends of the conversation and Lonergan wasn't wasting any time. He was on to his office and wanted a complete rundown on anyone who'd had access to the Chester file in the past week.

When the call finished I pressed END, put the phone on the table and poured some more tea.

Boxer picked up my phone and fiddled with it for a couple of minutes. 'Okay, I've dumped "The Star Spangled Banner" for you. When Lonergan turns his phone on or makes a call, you'll get a single tone and the display will read OUT. When he gets a call it's a double tone and it reads IN. Plus you'll get exact copies of every text message he sends or receives, and notification if he changes Sim cards, including the new number. I've also beefed up the memory so you can record the conversations if it's not convenient to eavesdrop. Just Bluetooth the info across to your computer to archive it.'

This was all very impressive. 'Any chance he'll spot the bug in his phone?'

Boxer took another dumpling. 'Nah, nothing to spot, it's all done with software. Whenever he uses that phone he's actually making a conference call, only he doesn't know it. I cloned his Sim card, by the way, so I can give you a copy of his private phone book if you want.'

Who wouldn't want a copy of a CIA station head's private phone book? I knew Chapman Pergo's number would be in there for sure.

A trolley laden with plates of barbecued pork and roast duck was passing and Boxer flagged it down.

'Since I've just broken every telecommunications law in the country and hacked in to the private conversations of the world's most powerful spy agency, I think the condemned man deserves a hearty lunch,' he said. 'And you're paying.'

'Work up a bit of an appetite with one of those Scandawegian waitresses, did you?'

Boxer grinned as he dipped a sliver of crispy-skinned roast duck into a small dish of plum sauce. 'What makes you think it was just the one?'

Chapter Seventeen

My afternoon spent eavesdropping on Carter Lonergan's phone revealed that the day-to-day life of a CIA station chief was pretty routine, even with two nuclear warheads on the loose. Perhaps it was just the life of a station chief in Australia, or maybe Lonergan was much too smart to spill his guts on a mobile phone and all the serious chat would be over an ultra-secure satellite link routed back through Langley.

I was studying the flowchart, trying to make sense of a dozen different possible scenarios, when Julie burst in the front door, pulled her laptop from her Crumpler bag and fired it up.

'I think I've got something,' she said. 'I just had lunch with Damien Rothwell.'

'From the *Fin Review*?'

'Yep. It seems that over the past few months the good Reverend Priday has been quietly liquidating the assets of the Church of the Lord's Bounty and using the cash to buy gold. It seems the vaults of the old Rural Colonial Bank are stacked to the ceiling with bullion.'

'Sounds like the Reverend is preparing for a bit of a downturn in the stock market,' I said.

'That's what Damien reckons. But if Priday's buying gold hand over fist, he's got to be expecting more than just your average cyclical dip in the market, right?'

She had that right. 'I wonder what might have the potential to cause an economic downturn serious enough for someone to want to dump their property and share portfolio and buy up big on gold?'

'The news that a couple of nuclear warheads are on the loose could do it,' Julie said.

I nodded. 'That would definitely do it. But how the hell could someone like the Reverend Priday be involved in all this? There has to be a connection here we're missing. What the hell is it?'

When you've run out of answers the rule is to go back to the beginning and start digging again. I walked to my office computer and opened the file of Max's pictures from the Jindivick soiree.

'Let's take another look at this happy band of Christian soldiers.'

Julie was looking over my shoulder as I clicked through the images.

'No surprises there,' I said. 'The Reverend and Mrs Priday, Cristobel, the choirboys.' I spotted a fetish necklace. 'That's Artemisia Gaarg talking to Priday. I didn't recognise her before.'

I kept clicking through the shots. Just more of the same – party guests, waiters, and those close-ups of the canapés. Then something caught my eye. One of the close-ups showed a man's hand reaching for a thin slice of beef fillet nestling on a toasted ciabatta square topped with beetroot relish. I couldn't blame him –it looked like Wagyu beef, nice and rare and exactly the piece I'd have gone for.

But the canapé wasn't what had got my attention. What caught my eye was a familiar-looking cufflink in a French cuff – diamonds set in gold in the shape of the letters CFP.

'Well, well, well,' I said to Julie, 'our old pal Chapman Fucking Pergo.'

All roads might lead to Rome but right now all the evidence was pointing towards Chapman Pergo and the Reverend Priday being in this up to their necks and that particular road led directly to a church in Sydney's CBD.

I headed downstairs and made a big show of hailing a cab on the beach side of the Parade. By the time we stopped at the lights at the top of Bondi Road, the Astra had dropped in behind us, two cars clear.

I gave the taxi driver ten bucks, walked back to the Astra and climbed into the rear seat. The driver and passenger turned round and stared at me.

'Sorry about losing you guys all the time,' I said. 'I'm heading for the city, and you know what Thursday afternoon traffic is like. If we car-pool you won't have any trouble keeping up. Martin Place is good for me, I'm off to church.'

The driver and passenger looked at each other. There was a long blast on a horn from somewhere behind us.

'Light's green,' I said. 'My bet's the expressway, down Ocean Avenue and then New South Head Road and William Street.'

'What about we take the Cross City Tunnel and get off at Macquarie Street?' the passenger suggested, and the driver glared at him.

'I'm easy,' I said, fastening my seat belt. 'Gwenda got you boys on eight or twelve-hour shifts?'

The passenger turned round. 'Sixteen,' he said, and the driver glared at him again.

'You poor bastards.' So they were definitely Gwenda's boys. 'Next turn on the right'll get us down to the tunnel.'

It took us twenty-five minutes to get to Martin Place, which was a pretty good run, all things considered, and the conversation for the rest of the trip was minimal, to say the least. The last I saw of the Astra was the driver trying to talk his way out of a ticket for stopping on a clearway to drop me off.

The First Church of The Lord's Bounty is a well-built and imposing edifice, as were the two men in suits standing guard outside. One of them quickly sized me up and said he would need to take my gun. I sized him up and asked him how he intended to hold it with ten broken fingers. It was a bit of a stand-off till the other bloke murmured briefly into his cuff, tilted his head to listen to a response that crackled in his earpiece, then indicated I could enter the building un-frisked.

The bank was built around a three-storey atrium with massive stone columns, marble facings, and wrought-iron and polished-oak railings running around the walkways on the upper levels. There was a pulpit on the mezzanine and underneath it a string quartet was setting up on a small stage. Several women were lining up chairs in neat rows in front of the pulpit. Name any religion and women always seem to get stuck with the grunt work.

The Reverend Priday was waiting for me and having the Sauer wasn't much joy since I realised I was heavily out-gunned. Half a dozen goons were standing with the Reverend, as was my old pal Lothar.

Lothar owned and ran the Double-D-Luxe Motel, a decrepit flea-pit down a dismal back alley in Kings Cross. He rented rooms and girls or boys by the hour, sold pills by the handful, and did a nice little sideline in side arms. Lothar was so sleazy that the local junkies, pimps, dealers and brothel owners regularly complained to the Kings Cross Chamber of Commerce that he was lowering the tone of the neighbourhood.

I hadn't seen Lothar since last March, when I'd needed to get a gun and some money in a hurry and he'd handed over a geriatric Beretta and fifty bucks, but only after demanding my watch as collateral. Fifteen minutes later the bastard tried to sell me out to the highest bidder. A week later I picked up my watch and gave him back his gun and his money, along with a knuckle sandwich for interest.

Lothar smiled nervously, all bad teeth, sallow skin and what looked like a pathetic attempt to grow a moustache. Always scrawny, he'd lost weight since I'd last seen him and right now he'd make a medical school skeleton look positively obese.

'Hello Mr Murdoch,' he said, 'How are you keeping? Good?'

'Excuse me for not shaking hands, Lothar,' I said, 'but I don't have any disinfectant wipes on me.'

'Gentlemen,' the Reverend said, 'This is a house of peace and goodwill. My friends are simply gathered together here in preparation for our evening service.'

I looked down at the two bulging sports bags on the floor at Lothar's feet.

'I'm a big fan of peace and goodwill Reverend, but I've got a feeling if I unzip one of those bags I'm not going to find any hymn books. My money would be on something that delivers a nine millimetre sermon at five hundred rounds a minute.'

'Six hundred,' Lothar said defensively, and then he slammed his mouth shut with a snap that echoed around the marble-clad walls.

'*Si vis Pacem, Para bellum*, Inspector Murdoch,' Priday said.

Lothar looked confused.

'It means, those who desire peace should prepare for war,' I explained. 'You could put it on your business cards, Lothar.'

'Perhaps we need to go some place where we can speak privately,' the Reverend said, and ushered me across to a set of stairs leading to the first-floor walkway that surrounded the former banking chamber. Well-heeled worshippers of the Lord's Bounty were starting to arrive and the string quartet was tuning up.

'No electric guitars, Reverend? Or choirs of blonde, blue-eyed maidens who've pledged to save their virginity for the marriage bed?

He smiled. 'We leave that to the more populist evangelicals.'

Priday's office was on the mezzanine, just behind the pulpit, which jutted out over the stage and dominated the cavernous hall. The pulpit reminded me of Father Mapple's in the Whaleman's Chapel in *Moby Dick*. While Mapple climbed up to his pulpit via a rope ladder, I was sure that if he wanted to the Reverend Priday could pop down to the vaults in the cellar and build ~~a~~ himself a stairway to heaven out of gold ingots. And there wasn't a doubt in my mind that his congregation would bloody love it.

The Reverend must have been an old romantic, since there was a framed photograph of his wife on his desk. Sure, Louise was naked, and it was what some of my less-than-couth work colleagues might have called a beaver shot, but you have to admire the sentiment. It made me a touch uncomfortable knowing I'd now seen both the Reverend's wife and his daughter as naked as the Lord had made them, but I decided if there was a prize for God's handiwork it would have to go to Cristobel.

Priday took a bottle of whisky and two glasses from the impressively stocked bar. Glenfarclas again, but this time it was the twenty-five-year-old stuff.

'Can I offer you a drink, Inspector Murdoch?'

'Thanks, but I'm getting a bit choosey about who I drink with,' I said.

The Glenfarclas was seriously tempting, but right now I figured I needed my wits about me.

As the Reverend poured himself a very stiff drink, his hand shook slightly. Something was definitely putting the wind up him, judging by the firepower he was acquiring from Lothar.

'That's a lot of muscle you've got standing around downstairs,' I said. 'You worried someone might do a runner with the collection plate?'

Priday smiled. 'You're a little behind the times Inspector, we provide a direct debit system for our parishioners to donate to the church.'

'Of course you do. So, it must be all that gold bullion stacked up next to the cases of sacramental Grange in the cellar that you're worried about?'

Priday's smile froze for a brief moment, then he recovered. 'I've found both the Grange and the gold to be excellent long term investments for the church, Inspector Murdoch.'

Bugger me, I'd only been joking about the Grange.

'But, yes, we do have some security concerns in that area,' the Reverend continued, 'and Lothar, as a recent member of my flock, is assisting us with resources.'

I figured that the church must have had one hell of a community outreach programme to turn up a bottom-feeder like Lothar. Or maybe they'd met when the Reverend had been detained at Her Majesty's pleasure – Lothar had done more than a few stretches himself.

'Surely you're not here to scrutinise the investment strategy of the church, Inspector Murdoch. There's nothing illegal about buying gold.'

'It's the timing of your gold acquisition that interests me, Reverend. Almost as if you're expecting a sudden downturn in the stock market – one might even say banking on it.'

The Reverend finished his whisky and poured another. His hand was shaking again and the neck of the bottle rattled against the lip of his glass. I decided to ramp up the pressure. 'Is Chapman Pergo also a member of your flock?' I asked.

I saw the flicker of fear in his eyes before he turned away from me and said calmly, 'I'm afraid I don't know any Chapman Pergo, Inspector Murdoch.'

The Reverend was obviously shit scared of Pergo and the only way I was going to get anywhere with him was to make him more scared of me. I lunged at him, spun him around and pushed him hard up against the wall with my arm across his throat. His glass, still holding about a hundred bucks worth of single malt, shattered on the polished wood floor.

'Listen, you sanctimonious prick, I know you and Pergo are up to your eyeballs in this and you're going to tell me all about it right now!'

His eyes bulged and beads of sweat glistened on his face. I kept my arm across his throat until he gasped for breath and then I pressed harder just to let him know I was serious. 'Do we understand each other?' I asked.

Priday nodded furiously and I released the pressure and backed away.

He rubbed his throat as he caught his breath, then straightened his collar and tried to compose himself.

I poured another glass of whisky and handed it to him. 'Let's try that again. Is Chapman Pergo also a member of your flock?'

He took the glass with both hands. 'No, alas, Mr Pergo is not a believer, Inspector Murdoch.'

'So what's your connection with him?'

Priday sank into the leather Chesterfield. 'Mr Pergo and I met when the Defence Minister decided a bit of high-profile church-going might improve his chances for a run at the top job, should the PM ever decide to abdicate.'

That sounded about right. Every so often there was a rush of prime-ministerial wanna-be's sitting piously in church pews on Sunday mornings, trying to out-God each other for the Christian vote. Most career politicians would be right into burning non-believers at the stake at half-time in the AFL grand final if they thought it would swing them some extra votes from the evangelicals.

'Mr Pergo accompanied the Minister and we found we had similar interests.'

The only similar interests these two arseholes were likely to have was self-interest. 'Go on.'

Priday took a large swig of whisky. 'Some months back, during a casual discussion on the price of gold, I mentioned to Mr Pergo that after the Viet Cong's Tet offensive in Vietnam in '67 there was a crisis in confidence and the world stock markets panicked. The price of gold went so high that trading was temporarily suspended on the London bullion exchange. It was a disaster for many investors, but for those with the foresight and the resources to have stocks of gold on hand it was —'

'A goldmine?' I suggested.

'Exactly.'

'And that piqued his interest?'

'Mr Pergo revealed that a special delivery was to be made by an American warship, and that if details of that delivery became public it would most certainly create instability in the region.'

He was talking like this was just another business opportunity which a man would be a fool to pass up.

'So you and Pergo got into bed together and you were going to leak Max's happy snaps of the delivery of the nukes to the media and make a killing on the gold market?'

Priday was looking decidedly uncomfortable. 'That was the plan, yes.'

'And how's it working out so far?'

The Reverend finished off his drink in one gulp and stared at the floor.

'Okay, let me lay it out for you,' I said. 'Four innocent people are dead and two nuclear warheads have gone missing.'

'The warheads are missing?'

Priday's shock was genuine.

'You don't want to believe everything you see on TV, Reverend. That wasn't an accidental explosion on the *Altoona*. It was two nukes being hijacked by your friends in the ship's choir.'

'But what would the members of a choir want with two warheads?'

'I've got not idea, but I've a feeling your partner-in-crime Mr Pergo could tell us, and I reckon it involves a larger return on his investment than you were offering. And, unless I miss my guess, suddenly Pergo isn't taking your phone calls.'

I could tell by the look on his face that I hadn't missed my guess and that Pergo had screwed the Reverend over.

'Who else knew that Max would be in the car park at that time?' I asked.

'Pergo gave him the date and time of the handover. And he suggested the vantage point.'

Son of a bitch! No wonder Priday was so tooled up. He must have been wondering if he was now also *surplus to requirements* and in line to meet the same fate as Max.

'So what was the tanker business all about?'

'Pergo told me it was a government operation to distract attention from the docks during the delivery of the weapons.'

'And you believed that?'

'Given the transaction that was taking place, I was ready to believe anything.'

He stood up. 'I'm telling you the truth, Inspector Murdoch, I had no knowledge of any of this and absolutely nothing to do with that young man's death. Max was just going to take photographs of the handover, that was all. Nobody was supposed to get hurt.'

'Nobody ever is,' I said. 'And the thing that really pisses me off, Reverend, is that even though your greedy little scheme has gone pear-shaped, you still stand to benefit. If word of this gets out the effect on the stock market will be disastrous and your profits will be fucking astronomical.'

It was as if he took comfort from this and that smug self-confidence was back.

'Perhaps I may benefit financially whatever the outcome of this situation, but that is in the hands of the Lord.'

'And the Stock Exchange.'

'Religion and the stock market have a lot in common, Inspector. Both are very much faith-based.'

He was right on that point but I wasn't willing to leave this situation in the Lord's hands.

'I ran into Cristobel in Canberra a couple of days ago.'

Priday nodded. 'I understand she was there with Miss Gaarg to lobby for the whale sanctuary. Cristobel has absolutely nothing to do with any of this, Inspector Murdoch. My daughter is driven by only the purest motives.'

The reverend seemed to still be buying my cop routine, so who had Cristobel overheard telling Artemesia I was a spy?

'Is she here this afternoon?' I asked.

'No, she's spending some time whale-watching in Tasmania with Artemisia. My daughter has quite a passion for Miss Gaarg's cause.'

Downstairs, the string quartet launched into Onward Christian Soldiers.

'And now if you'll excuse me,' Priday said, 'I'm afraid it's show time.'

I followed him out to the pulpit. There were about a hundred and fifty people in the banking chamber, a late-twenties crowd, mostly men in expensive suits with a smattering of women dressed for success. No doubt about it, Priday was aiming right for Sydney's money jugular.

'Nice turnout for a Thursday afternoon,' I said.

'We don't believe in numbers in the Church of the Lord's Bounty, Inspector Murdoch,' Priday said, 'we believe in net worth.'

I got to the main door just as the hymn finished. A few latecomers were scurrying in, so I moved to one side. The Reverend Priday stepped up to the microphone and raised his arms skyward.

'Welcome, fellow shareholders in the Almighty's bounty,' he said, his amplified voice echoing around the stone walls. 'It's a fine Thursday afternoon, the Stock Exchange is closed for the day, and the All Ordinaries is up forty-nine points. Praise the Lord!'

The congregation seemed to like that. With one voice they shouted out, 'Praise the Lord,' in response.

As I grabbed the brass handle of the main door, Priday called from the pulpit, 'Go with God, Inspector.'

'Buy low, sell high,' I shouted back, and there was an approving murmur from the crowd. Priday's congregation seemed to like that too.

Chapter Eighteen

'Yoo-hoo! Anyone for fish and chips?'

I'd just finished filling Julie in on my encounter with the Reverend Priday and his avaricious flock when Mrs T popped her head round the door. I needed to eat and her suggestion made as much sense as anything else right now, so I grabbed a chilled bottle of white wine and some glasses, and announced I was taking the whole gang out for dinner.

We lined up at Bondi Surf Seafood and I let them order whatever they wanted, except for the deep-fried Mars Bars, of course. Twenty minutes later we were sitting on the grassy slope that runs down to the beach and I opened the wine while Julie and Mrs T unwrapped the food and Dougal set about annoying the crap out of the hovering seagulls.

Late-afternoon light on Bondi Beach, a mild onshore breeze, chilled Semillon, fresh Sydney rock oysters, lightly battered king prawns and Tasmanian scallops, potato cakes and a large serving of chips for Mrs T – if anything could take a man's mind off a couple of missing nukes, a new boss who made Maggie Thatcher look like a sissy, and the fact that I hadn't woken up in bed with a woman for at least six months, this should do it.

I waved to the guys in the Astra and the talkative one waved back. Mrs T waved too.

'They've been there all week, Alby.' she said. 'Friends of yours?'

'Not exactly.'

'Didn't think so.'

God, how bad were these guys? Even Mrs T, an eighty-five year old pensioner with mild cataracts had made them.

She fed Dougal half a potato cake. 'Are you in trouble again, Alby?'

'Nothing I can't handle, Mrs T.'

'Alright, dear, but you'll let me know if I can be of any help, won't you?'

'Sure will.' I raised my glass. 'With you two in my corner I reckon I can take on anything.'

Julie leaned across and clinked her wineglass against mine. 'Here's to fighting the good fight,' she said.

'It would be a lot easier without one hand tied behind my back.'

'I'm sure you can take good care of yourself with just one hand, Alby,' Julie said under her breath.

I stared at her. Now that was just plain rude.

Back at Luxor Mansions, Mrs T and Dougal had hit the sack, Julie was at her laptop, and I was considering my next move when the intercom sounded. The video display showed Lieutenant Clare Kingston standing in the street. I buzzed her in.

Julie stuffed her laptop in her bag. 'I'll leave you to it,' she said. 'I've got to get home and feed the cat.'

'You don't have a cat,' I pointed out.

She was already out the door. 'You're right. I must remember to get one next time I'm at the pet shop.'

Clare was wearing a light summer dress. It was either a very short dress or she had really long legs, but either way I liked the effect. I asked her if she'd like a drink. She shook her head.

Her shoulder bag hit the floor with the familiar clunk and she kicked off her sandals, staring at me with that same look that had made my hair stand up in the D-E-D offices. An energy force was suddenly crackling back and forth between us. I asked her if she was hungry and she nodded and pulled her dress off over her head. She didn't have anything on underneath.

Those legs *were* really long. Her breasts were even more spectacular than I'd imagined, and by golly, she was a natural blonde to boot. No tattoos of mermaids or tigers or hula girls that I could see, though. What the hell was the modern navy coming to? I thought. And then I stopped thinking.

Clare was asleep on her stomach. Through a gap in the blinds a shaft of street light from out on the Parade cut across the bed and over her firm little butt. I glanced at my watch on the bedside table. Just after three. I could feel the scratches on my shoulders and I knew they were going to sting later in the shower. When I looked back at her she was smiling.

'Been at sea a long time then, sailor?'

She laughed. 'I hope I haven't made you feel used.'

I shook my head. 'I like to do what I can for the girls in blue. I'm nothing if not patriotic.'

'But I'm not in your navy,' she pointed out. 'And I was wearing my khakis when we met.'

I shrugged. 'I'm a big fan of the coalition of the willing.'

'Really?'

'No, not really, but let's just say this particular coalition has a lot going for it.'

She laughed again. It was a nice laugh. I'm a sucker for women who laugh at my jokes.

'I was a bit surprised to see you here,' I said. 'Not that I'm complaining.'

'I was confined to quarters for the duration, and then all of a sudden last night word came down from the top that I had eighteen hours' shore leave. I don't know what's going on but I thought I'd make the most of it.'

'You certainly did. I'm thinking of sending the top brass a thank you note.'

'Happy to do my bit for the ANZUS alliance.'

'What's a nice girl like you doing in a sailor suit, anyway?'

'Military family. My dad served two tours in Vietnam, humping an M60 through Indian country, and my uncle Bob flew Navy F4s up in the wild blue yonder.'

'The old Phantom was a pretty rugged plane.'

'Not rugged enough. Uncle Bob's was hit by a SAM on a mission over Haiphong. His wingman saw Bob and his Radar Intercept Officer eject and two parachutes were spotted, but that's the last that was ever heard of either of them.'

'What about your dad?'

'Apart from the Purple Heart he got when he fell off a bar stool and broke his ankle during a mortar attack, he came home pretty much unscathed.

'But why the Navy?' I asked.

'Uncle Bob's service smoothed my way into Annapolis and a degree in electrical engineering from MIT, then a Weapons Systems Engineering major at the Naval Academy ensured I'd get sea duty, which was what I really wanted.'

She reached up and touched the scar on my left shoulder. 'This looks recent, what happened?'

'I stuck my nose in where it wasn't welcome.'

'Looks like you're still doing that, Alby.'

'Can't seem to help myself.'

'You know, I had another reason for coming here tonight.'

The first reason was good enough for me, but her tone was serious so she had my full attention.

'The *Altoona* is locked down tight, no one is talking to anyone about anything, and the decks are awash with CIA and NCIS heavies, and guys with IDs from departments I've never even heard of.'

'A couple of missing W80s would tend to bring out the problem-solvers,' I said.

'That's the strange thing. I ran the weapons inventory when I got back on board so I could get the serial numbers for my report, and I got shut out of the system after about fifteen seconds. Two minutes later, a NCIS heavy turned up at my station and removed my computer. I tried to log on from another station when he'd left but my ID code was suddenly invalid.'

'Probably just someone displaying a healthy level of paranoia until they have a board of inquiry.'

She shook her head. 'If anyone should have a high level of paranoia it'd be me. The fifteen seconds I had on the system were enough to see that the *Altoona* is showing a full weapons inventory. Everything is accounted for.'

I looked at her across the bed.

'I was aiming at that Seahawk when it lifted off,' she continued, 'and I know I was doing my best to avoid pointing my M16 at two warheads. I could see them sitting on her cargo deck. It doesn't make sense.'

'Nothing about this whole business makes a lot of sense. Who'd have put money on the ship's choir being the bad guys?'

'Not me, that's for sure. But I went back through the *Altoona*'s personnel files and I discovered that most of our choirboys weren't exactly, well, choirboys. They'd all been in some sort of trouble over the years, but when Chief Warrant Officer Brames formed the *Altoona*'s choir, all that suddenly stopped.'

'What's Brames's story, then?'

'He did a tour in Iraq in 2004, detached from the Navy, flying support for ground troops, and while off-duty found his way into trouble on a regular basis. Apparently he was involved in some pretty shady stuff, and being transferred back to sea was the only thing that saved him from a court martial and serious jail time in Leavenworth. Then he suddenly found God in San Diego and cleaned up his act.'

I knew Pergo had been in Iraq around that time. Iraq was a big country, but the bad boys do tend to find each other.

Clare rolled over and sat up. She was bloody stunning.

'You're looking perplexed,' she said.

'Too many loose ends and too many players. I don't like a situation I can't get on top of.'

'Well, we have that in common,' she said. 'And since we're talking about getting on top of things …' and then she did.

When I woke up, the streetlights had been replaced by another sunny Sydney morning. While the espresso machine was warming up, I checked my emails. There was one from Julie saying she'd be over mid-morning, and a couple from people who wanted to sell me some pills that would apparently do extraordinary things to my penis. Clare wandered out for coffee wearing one of my old T-shirts that had shrunk fairly dramatically in the drier and instantly I knew that the pill sellers wouldn't be getting any of my money.

An hour or so later, we finally made it into the shower. While Clare was drying her hair, I made the grim discovery that the fridge offered extremely limited breakfast options. After the night I'd just had some hearty food was essential, so twenty minutes later we were heading into my favourite beachside breakfast spot.

Tucked away in a huddle of shops opposite the north end of the beach, Soggy Togs has panoramic views of the sweep of the beach, right across to the Bondi Icebergs and its ocean pool. More importantly, Soggy Togs serves a great cup of coffee. When we arrived a Goodie juice delivery van was parked outside and Alex, the owner of the joint, was paying some blokes who'd just finished installing a big new illuminated sign above the café's entrance.

Inside, the place was jumping – packed with local mums and kids and teenagers from the surfing school – and we just managed to grab the last empty table at the back. Alex handed us menus, smiled at Clare and gave me a warning look. It was a little over six months since his espresso machine had been shot to death by an assassin with a silenced nine millimetre pistol who was after yours truly. The insurance company gave him a hard time over his claim and he'd been giving me grief ever since. But his new machine produced an even better coffee than before, and since he made a breakfast to die for, which I literally almost had, I was trying to stay on his good side.

I persuaded Clare that she needed to discover the majesty of a real Aussie hamburger with the works. Alex's Big Bloke's Burger is an excellent test of a woman's character. Prime ground topside beef seared on a red-hot grill for a crunchy crust, smoky bacon, melted cheddar, tomato sauce, fried onions, sliced tomato, and shredded white cabbage mixed with the iceberg lettuce for extra snap. And beetroot, of course. I could see the concept of beetroot on a burger was causing her some concern.

'Not convinced about the beetroot?'

'Not totally.'

'Trust me. You'll love it.'

'I don't know who to trust right now,' she said, 'even about a burger.'

She was right about that. I wasn't even sure how much I should trust her. Turning up out of the blue, suddenly on shore leave after being told she was confined to the ship, and giving me inside info on the ship's arsenal. My gut told me she was genuine, but you could never be too careful.

I lowered my voice. 'Was there anything else about the *Altoona's* voyage that was unusual? Anything at all?'

'Nothing. Well, just the passengers.'

'Passengers? On a cruiser?'

'We had a couple of VIPs onboard for the San Diego–Sydney leg.

'What sort of VIPs?'

'Don't know, but they must have been important because there was an armed guard outside their door twenty-four hours a day. They stayed in their cabin for the entire voyage, didn't even come out for meals.'

'And you've no idea who they were?'

'Not unless the name Chester means anything to you?'

'Chester?'

'That was the name on the manifest: Chester, initial A. and Chester, initial B.'

'Well, that explains why you were showing a full weapons inventory. I think you'll find the *Altoona* had a couple of surplus-to-requirements nukes tucked under the bunks in the guest bedroom.'

'Shit!' Clare said, but not because of what I'd just told her.

She was staring in the direction of the café's entrance.

As I turned towards the door the Soggy Togs brunch crowd went silent, except for someone who gave a sort of half-gasp, half-scream.

Bugger, I said to myself, was Alex ever going to be pissed off.

Chapter Nineteen

'If nobody moves then nobody gets hurt.'

The MAC 10 in the hands of the man in the doorway near the gelato freezer made a very persuasive argument. The MAC 10 is small as submachine guns go, but the big grey cylindrical silencer on the front added a bit of authority. The bloke holding it was wearing motorcycle leathers and a full-face helmet with a mirrored visor. The visor was raised and I could see he was wearing a black ski mask under the helmet.

I put my hands up, palms out, and stood up. Clare did the same.

'Outside now, you two, and don't dick about.'

'Everyone keep calm and stay exactly where you are,' I said in the loudest and most assertive voice I could muster. 'This gentleman wants to talk to us, so we're going to walk outside and there shouldn't be any problems.'

We moved towards the door with our hands up, and out of the corner of my eye I could see a teenage boy taking pictures on his mobile phone. The MAC 10 isn't terribly accurate but it has a phenomenal rate of fire and at this range the shooter wouldn't even have to aim. It was the collateral damage in the crowded café I was most worried about.

Outside there were two Yamaha motorcycles at the kerb. One, a nice sporty red, had a rider on board, while the second, painted green, was parked. Its rider was on foot, covering the café with a Browning semiautomatic pistol. He had a spare helmet in his left hand which he tossed to Clare, who deftly caught it.

'Get on my bike, Lieutenant Kingston,' he yelled, gesturing with his pistol. You don't often hear a New Jersey accent in this neck of the woods.

'You're in a lot of trouble, Chief O'Reilly,' Clare said. 'Murder, mutiny, desertion, and theft of government property. Do you really want to add kidnapping a superior officer to that list?'

One more charge wasn't going to make too much of a difference to a list like that – Clare was letting me know that this O'Reilly character was one of the choirboys.

'If you need a hostage,' I said, 'why don't you leave the lieutenant alone and take me?'

'And why don't you shut your trap, buddy?' the bloke with the MAC 10 said. 'Before I shut it for you.' He pulled back on the cocking knob. 'Now you get on that bike, lieutenant, or I'm gonna shoot your friend here full of holes.'

O'Reilly shouted, 'Don't hit the lieutenant, for Christ's sake.'

Clare was suddenly moving forward, edging towards O'Reilly, making conciliatory noises. 'Okay, Chief, I'm getting on the bike, why don't we all calm down a little.'

I heard a clicking sound behind me and turned to see the kid from the café walking towards us, still taking pictures with his phone.

'Get back inside, you little fuckwit,' I yelled, and when the bloke with the MAC 10 glanced in his direction I took my chance. The flying tackle knocked him backwards into Clare as she swung the helmet at O'Reilly's head and we all went down in a messy scrum on top of the green bike. There was a confused melee of fists, feet and elbows, and someone was trying to gouge my eyes when we heard a pistol shot.

The bloke from the red Yamaha had the kid round the neck, holding a gun to his temple. 'On my bike, lady,' the gunman yelled. 'Now! Or the next shot doesn't go in the air.'

Clare looked at me and I nodded. I was sitting on my backside on the roadway with a MAC 10 pointed at me. We really didn't have any choice. She scooped up the helmet from where it had fallen, pulled it on and straddled the red bike. The rider shoved the kid away after smashing his mobile on the ground. He stuffed the pistol inside his leathers before grabbing Clare's hands, pulling them round his waist and slipping a pair of handcuffs on to her wrists. She was stuck on that Yamaha until they chose to let her off or someone turned up with a hefty set of bolt-cutters. The rider gunned the engine and the bike roared off towards Campbell Parade.

O'Reilly pulled the heavy green Yamaha back onto its wheels, straddled it and started the engine.

'Do it now,' he yelled to the bloke with the submachine gun, who levelled the muzzle at my chest in a way I really didn't care for.

Suddenly a black-clad figure was flying through the air sideways, both feet connecting with the gunman's elbow, knocking him off balance just as he pulled the trigger. Half a magazine from the MAC 10 blasted the newly-installed Soggy Togs sign into a shower of plexiglass shards and then I was trampled by a screaming mob of mums and kids and student surfers.

When the tidal wave of customers cleared, the green Yamaha was roaring off towards the Parade, the gunman hanging onto O'Reilly for dear life and possibly cursing a broken arm, his MAC 10 abandoned in the gutter. Julie was lying in the middle of the road. She sat up slowly, reached across the bitumen for the submachine gun and pulled the magazine out, making sure the chamber was clear. Julie has a disturbing proficiency with weapons.

When she stood up I saw a huge tear in the back of her steamer, revealing a bloody graze on her left bum cheek. 'Son of a bitch,' she said softly, 'this is a brand new wetsuit.'

'I probably should have a look at that,' I said. 'I'm sure there's some out-of-date mercurochrome in my medicine chest.'

Julie smiled at me. It was one of her 'not in a million years' smiles.

'Don't be like that, Jules. I've got a St John's Ambulance First Aid Certificate and everything.'

'And you might need it,' Julie said, looking at my groin.

I glanced down. A dark red stain was spreading up the front of my trousers and I was aware of a sticky wetness between my legs. I felt my heart stop.

'Jesus, Jules, I must have got shot in the fracas!'

'I think you'll find the "s" is silent, Alby,' she said. 'And I reckon that's apple, ginger and beetroot juice you're sitting in, and your fracas are just fine.'

I looked over my shoulder. Some of the slugs from the MAC 10 had punched holes in the side of the Goodie delivery van and a crimson river of fruit and vegetable juice was running down the roadway.

As I got to my feet I could hear police sirens in the distance and I knew the situation had the potential to get really awkward. And just when you think things can't get any worse, they usually do.

Alex was standing in the middle of the road, a plate with a Big Bloke's Burger in either hand. You could see the crisp green iceberg lettuce and the juicy red tomato slices and the glistening brown of the char grilled meat patty in the toasted bun. There was a heaped serving of golden-brown shoestring fries on each plate. They looked bloody fantastic.

Alex stared at his shattered sign, the empty café and the two burgers he was holding. Then he looked at me.

'Alby,' he said slowly, 'you are fucking barred for life.'

And he didn't even offer me a chip.

Peter Sturdee turned up within minutes of the arrival of the first cop car. The front passenger seat of his van was loaded with plastic shopping bags, and the back was chock-full of baby seats and baby capsules which were chock full of babies.

'I was heading home from Coles at Bondi Junction when I heard a 'Shots Fired, Bondi Beach' radio call on the scanner,' he said. 'Couldn't help myself. How did I know you'd have to be involved, Alby?'

'You've got a scanner in the Tarago?'

He nodded. 'Tragic, isn't it? Anyway, what the hell went down here, mate?'

'They've taken Clare.'

'Lieutenant Kingston? Who's taken her?'

'It was three of the choirboys off the *Altoona*. Clare recognised O'Reilly.'

'Is she hurt?'

'No. They made a point of keeping her in one piece. They had other plans for me.'

'Why would they want Clare?'

'Buggered if I know. But they weren't about to let anyone stop them. Any chance you can keep my name out of this? If upstairs gets wind that I'm involved, I'll be in Helsinki before breakfast tomorrow.'

'I'll give it a shot but I can't promise anything. I'm not exactly flavour of the week at the moment. What were you doing with the lieutenant, anyway? Business or pleasure?'

'A bit of both. She was confined to the ship then suddenly got shore leave late yesterday so we took the opportunity to compare notes.'

'I thought you were off the case?'

'Yeah, I am. But you know how it is, sometimes these things get personal.'

Sturdee nodded then walked across to a detective with a clipboard and shook his hand.

Out of the corner of my eye I could see a tubby uniformed walloper scarfing down my burger and chips while questioning Alex.

After a few minutes of serious conversation, Peter shook the detective's hand again and walked back.

'That's sorted. You were never here. You and Jules had better scarper before the TV cameras turn up.'

'Thanks, mate.'

'Watch your back, Alby. Clare suddenly gets shore leave and then this happens. Whoever these guys are, they're serious, and they've obviously got friends in high places.'

He was right about that. But just how high up did it go?

Chapter Twenty

Mrs T disinfected and dressed the graze on Julie's bum and then brewed her a medicinal pot of Darjeeling, before heading off to finish watching Oprah. Julie swallowed a couple of aspirin with her tea.

'What would those guys want with Clare, Alby?'

'I don't know. But I shouldn't have let my guard down. They must have followed her here and then waited for the right moment to grab her. And I didn't see it coming. Damn. Peter was right, it's no accident she suddenly got shore leave – she was set up.'

My mobile rang. 'Goods,' I said, 'got something for me?'

Gudrun went straight to the point. 'A tuna boat pulled a body out of the drink about 10ks off Eden late yesterday afternoon. Skipper said the bloke looked like he'd been in the water a couple of days and he'd copped a bullet through the chest.'

'Nasty,' I said.

'Tell me about it. Funny thing is, one of our stringers down there said that within thirty minutes of them radioing it in, Eden was swarming with military choppers and men in suits. He emailed me some images and one of those men in suits was your good friend Pergo. Thought that might interest you.'

'It sure does, Goods. Anything else?'

'That's it for now. I'll keep my ears open.'

'Thanks, mate.'

'Alby, be careful with this one. It could get ugly.'

'Thanks,' I said. 'But it already has.'

I booted up the computer in the office and opened the folder containing my pix of the hijacked Seahawk hovering over the tanker.

'What was that about?' Julie called out.

Twenty frames of the chopper popped up on the screen and I dragged them into Photoshop. 'Just a sec,' I said.

I scanned through the previews and clicked on one. The image showed the Seahawk, tilting slightly as it dropped down towards the two men on top of the tanker, the gunman with the M16 clearly visible in the open doorway. In the shadows behind the gunman I could make out a couple of cylindrical shapes on the cargo deck that had to be the W80s. There was something black draped over the weapons that looked like a tarp or a blanket. I clicked a couple of times to magnify the image and then lightened the picture.

No doubt about it – there was a black-clad body slumped on top of the nukes.

'Come and have a look at this,' I yelled, but Julie was already looking over my shoulder. 'Gudrun just told me some fisherman pulled a body out of the water near Eden. One of our choirboys must have copped a bullet during the heist and they dumped him out at sea.'

'Off Eden?'

'About 10ks off the coast. At least that gives us a direction: they've headed south. What's the range on a Seahawk?'

'About 450 nautical miles, probably less with the load she was carrying.'

'Some pretty isolated beaches down that way,' I said. 'They could land and offload the nukes into a truck or van without any trouble.

'They could also rendezvous with a ship out to sea and do a transfer.'

Bugger, they could do pretty much anything and we'd never know. 'But why south?'

'No idea, but while you're thinking about it, go take a shower and get all that juice off. You're starting to smell like a bowl of borscht.'

When I came out of the bathroom ten minutes later, I caught the distinctive aroma of lamb shanks coming from Mrs T's. Julie was on her laptop in the living room, Dougal snoozing at her feet.

'Can you take sleeping beauty here away,' Julie said. 'Little monster keeps dropping the most disgusting farts.'

I took an uncooperative Dougal next door, had a quick taste of the simmering lamb shank broth, got scolded by Mrs T for adding pepper, and grabbed a hot oatmeal biscuit off a tray fresh from the oven.

'I think I'm on to something interesting here,' Julie said as I walked back in. 'I did a little more digging on Artemisia Gaarg. Around six months ago, the Gaarg Foundation set up a series of medical clinics at Aboriginal settlements in Arnhem Land, made a large donation to the National Maritime Museum, gave a new air ambulance to the Royal Flying Doctor Service, and funded an extension for a nursing home in Edinburgh.'

She paused. 'Spot the odd one out.'

'Edinburgh?'

'The new section of the nursing home, currently under construction, will be called the Morag Cullen Wing. The list of Sydney Ports harbour pilots has an Andrew William Cullen. I did some checking and it seems he retired about ten years ago and went back to Scotland. He had a wife named Morag. I rang the nursing home in Edinburgh, but it's about four in the morning there and I got a grumpy night nurse with a Scottish accent you could cut with a knife. I couldn't get anything out of her, mostly because I couldn't understand half of what she said.'

I picked up the cordless phone. 'The call to the nursing home was the last one you made?' I asked, and Julie nodded.

Mrs T was stirring the lamb shank broth when I walked into her kitchen. I handed her the phone.

'I need a favour, Mrs T,' I said. 'Can you press redial and talk to whoever answers? Try to find out everything you can about a Morag Cullen and her husband.'

'Who am I calling, dear?' she said, putting down her ladle.

'It's a nursing home outside Edinburgh, and since it's very early in the morning over there they might be a bit shirty, but it's important we get all the information we can – without being too obvious.'

'It could be an expensive call, dear.'

'I'll be getting reimbursed,' I said.

'You just make certain that you do, Alby.'

Mrs T worried about my finances a good deal. Perhaps she thought that if I were more financially stable Julie might find me a bit more interesting as a marriage prospect. I figured it would take a lot more than that.

'It's Morag Cullen I'm to find out about, is that right? With a wee bit of subtlety.'

'On the money, Mrs T. Just press the redial button when you're ready and see what you can find out.'

She looked at me, looked at the stockpot on the stove, picked up her pepper grinder and walked across to the recliner in the sunroom. Dougal trotted after her.

Back in my apartment, Julie was busy running down more details on the Gaarg family. I got on my Mac in the office and searched the WorldPix image archive for any photographs that might broaden the picture we had of Artemisia.

With WorldPix being a massive financial success from day one, we'd directed some of our profits into buying up collections of historic and contemporary Australian photographs as they came onto the market. It was a way of preserving our unique visual history, but it was also invaluable for research. Good for both sides of our business.

I clicked on a black and white shot in the Gaarg family archive and enlarged it. The caption made interesting reading.

'Did you know that Jindivick had its own twenty-seat cinema?' I called to Julie.

She came in, leaned over my shoulder and studied the photograph. It was part of a series published in *Post* magazine to celebrate the restoration of Jindivick in 1958. Sir Linus and Lady Gaarg, with a very young Artemisia at their feet, were posed awkwardly in the plush seats of a tiny art deco cinema.

Framed movie posters lined the walls of the cinema and I clicked on one to enlarge it. It featured an illustration of a muscular man, stripped to the waist, wielding a heavy wrench, while another bloke loaded a shell into a large cannon aimed towards the harbour bridge. Big bold type screamed, TENSION AT ITS GREATEST! and Aldo Ray never looked so good.

'*The Siege of Pinchgut*,' I said, pointing to the movie's title.

Julie was intrigued. 'What's that all about?'

'It was a nineteen fifties film set in Sydney starring Aldo Ray. An escaped convict holes up on Pinchgut – also known as Fort Denison – and threatens to blow up a freighter full of high explosives moored nearby. The whole city is shut down and they evacuate all the harbour side houses. Sound familiar?'

'Wow,' she said. 'That's a bit of a strange coincidence.'

'And you know what I think about coincidences. Let's keep digging into Miss Artemisia Gaarg.'

'I'm on it,' Julie said, heading back to her laptop. 'But come and have a look at this. I've found some interesting happy snaps from the World Whale Conference in San Diego last year.'

In the living room, I had to put my head right next to Julie's to get a clear view of the laptop's screen. Her hair smelled nice.

'This one's for you, Alby,' she said, clicking on a thumbnail. 'The caption says it's a reception to welcome conference delegates from Australia.'

It's a fact of life that male press photographers will unerringly gravitate towards the best-looking girl in a group and get a shot of her, often ignoring crowned heads of state, famous opera singers and the guest of honour. Our man in San Diego had upheld this noble tradition and the lovely Cristobel Priday looked fantastic.

'She's quite a babe, young Cristobel,' Julie said.

'Can you enlarge it a bit?'

'Which bit? Everything looks in perfect proportion to me.'

'You should see her in the flesh.'

Julie laughed. 'In your dreams, Alby.'

I smiled. Images of Cristobel in that Tiger Lily bikini and in the bubble bath had been invading my dreams lately, I must confess. But there was something else in the photograph that caught my eye.

Cristobel was chatting with two bearded and besotted-looking greenies wearing save-the-whale T-shirts. Behind her I could make out Artemisia deep in conversation with a well-built, crew-cut man in a short-sleeved shirt. Julie brought that section of the image up to fill the screen.

'That face look familiar?' she asked.

I've got an excellent memory for faces, it goes with the job. Names sometimes give me trouble. 'His picture was in the files on the choirboys Clare brought to the meeting, right?'

Julie's good with names. 'It's Chip Brames.'

'So we've got Artemisia Gaarg, friend of the whales and benefactor of the Reverend Priday, deep in conversation with Chief Warrant Officer Chip Brames, until very recently senior helicopter pilot and choir leader on the USS *Altoona*.'

'That's got to be more than coincidence.'

'It gets more interesting. Brames and Pergo were both in Iraq in 2004 and they were both mixed up in shady deals. I'd put money on their paths having crossed there.'

'I'll see what I can find on that. Pergo was working for Black Falcon security back then, right?'

'Yep. Jesus, Jules, I don't know what the hell any of this means yet, but I think we're finally starting to join the dots

Mrs T came in with a tray that held a pot of tea, three bone-china teacups, a plate of fresh oatmeal biscuits, and my phone.

'I hope I wasn't too long, dear,' she said, 'but some of these people do like a natter.'

That was rich. I'd once gone on a two-week assignment to South Africa, waving goodbye to Mrs T while she was on the phone to her friend Kay, and I'm pretty sure the same call was still in progress when I waved hello a fortnight later.

'It looks like you had more success with the nursing home than I did then, Mrs T,' Julie said.

Mrs T put the tray down on the table. 'The night matron is called Jessie and her grandmother came from Skye, just like I did, dear, so we had a nice old chat. I said it was a wrong number when she answered, but after she heard my accent we just got into it. Then I said I was calling from Sydney and she told me one of their patients had lived in Sydney for a long time. Morag Cullen is her name and the poor woman has dementia. Who's for tea?'

I knew we wouldn't get any more out of Mrs T until the tea was poured, so I picked up the pot, filled the cups – milk in first, just the way she liked it – and passed around the biscuits.

'Well, strange as it seems,' she continued, 'a Sydney charity is funding a whole new wing for Morag and all the other old dears with dementia. Apparently Mrs Cullen's husband arranged it. Andy Cullen was a harbour pilot in Sydney for over twenty years, would you believe it? Visits Morag every day, regular as clockwork, even though she doesn't really know he's there, poor wee thing. He hasn't been in for the past month, though. Apparently he came out of retirement to do one last seafaring job.'

Mrs T looked at me. 'Is that of any help?'

'Great,' I said. 'Exactly what we needed to know. There wasn't anything you left out?'

'Just the tarragon.'

'What tarragon?'

'Jessie suggested I might try some tarragon in with my lamb shanks.' She wrinkled up her face and shook her head. 'I don't think so Alby, do you?'

'I'm with you on that one, Mrs T. And I think you were probably right about that extra pepper too.'

My mobile beeped. I excused myself and went into the office, and with the push of a button I was listening in on a conversation between Chapman Pergo and Carter Lonergan.

The exchange was short and to the point. Pergo was his usual insincere, reassuring self. He was on the case, his leads were good, and his people were closing in on the culprits. He was so damned convincing that for a minute I almost believed him myself. He promised Lonergan the problem would be dealt with by Monday.

I replayed the conversation a couple of times, not for what was being said but to identify the background noise at Pergo's end, which I couldn't quite make out. Finally I gave up and switched off the phone. 'Who's for pizza?' I said, coming back into the living room.

'The lamb shanks should be ready in a wee while, Alby,' Mrs T said.

'Sorry, Mrs T, but right now we're in a situation that can only be resolved with a home-delivered pizza. Anyone not like anchovies?'

Chapter Twenty-One

You're totally spoiled for choice when it comes to pizza in Bondi. Gelbison do a fabulous house special with garlic, tomatoes, mozzarella and seasoned potato chunks, Pompei make a calzone to die for, and the Tratt has a fantastic goat's cheese and prosciutto with rocket, but they don't do home delivery. I ordered from Bazza's Pizza-rama because they guarantee twenty-minute delivery and they have the most powerful scooters.

The delivery boy looked down at the hundred-dollar note in my hand and shook his head. 'I only carry ten bucks in change, didn't they tell you?'

'How do you feel about a nice home-cooked meal with two lovely ladies and an extremely large tip? You like lamb shanks?'

My friends in the Astra would have logged a pizza boy in and a pizza boy out. A fifteen-minute scooter ride later, I was hammering on the steel door of Boxer's Surry Hills apartment.

'I didn't order a pizza,' Boxer said, and then when I took my helmet off, 'Jesus, and I thought times were tough in the film industry.'

Boxer's loft was a huge un-renovated warehouse space with worn wooden floorboards, high ceilings and large windows. The central living area was filled with various decrepit chairs and sofas rescued from council pick-ups surrounding a giant plasma-screen TV, and the kitchen featured a full-sized, four-group restaurant espresso machine. Benches and old wooden tables around the loft's walls were strewn with a jumble of electrical equipment, soldering irons, vintage reel-to-reel tape recorders, modern Nagra recorders and assorted microphones. As usual, there were numerous computers in various stages of disassembly and reassembly.

'Interrupt a nap, did I?' I said.

Boxer was wearing a long Japanese Yakuta robe. 'Not exactly.'

There was giggling from the curtained-off area that served as his bedroom.

'One of the waitresses?'

He grinned. 'The good-looking one.'

'Come on, Boxer, they were both pretty good— Oh.'

His grin widened. 'They've got a couple of days off. Me too.'

I tossed him my mobile. 'Sort this for me and I'll get out of your hair. Last recorded call between Lonergan and Pergo. See if you can figure out what the background noise is.'

Boxer connected the phone to a computer and put on headphones. While he worked I ate a couple of slices of pizza. Halfway through I had to check whether I was chewing the crust or the cardboard box.

'Easy as, Alby,' Boxer said after five minutes. 'Airport boarding call. "Final call for passengers on flight DJ872 to Hobart." '

I phoned Julie. 'Sounds like Pergo's on his way to Hobart. Priday said Cristobel was spending some time whale-watching in Tasmania, with Artemisia.'

'Hobart? Hang on a tick,' she said. I could hear the shuffling of papers. 'This might explain why everyone seems to be heading south. Artemisia has a place just off the coast of Tassie called Adamek Island. The Gaarg Foundation bought the lease off the government – it's an abandoned whaling station.'

'That's a bit poetic. Champion of the whales buying a joint where they used to slaughter the damn things. What does she need her own island for?'

'This press release says she's establishing a self-sustaining vegetarian community.'

'Why Tasmania?'

'Just a sec...it says here that global warming is going to make everywhere north of Albury uninhabitable within thirty years...blah, blah, blah...they also chose the island for the prevailing winds...the community's power is supplied by solar panels and wind turbines.'

'With everyone chowing down on lentil burgers and soy beans, you'd think a lack of wind would be the least of their problems,' I said. 'But an isolated private island would be the ideal place to ...' I moved away from Boxer and lowered my voice, '...stash a couple of stolen nukes. Check the charter companies. See what movements they've had heading south out of Mascot or Bankstown, over the past twenty-four hours. Call me back.'

Just as I pressed END my mobile beeped. A text message from Gudrun. Holy fuck!

Julie called back. 'A private jet on charter to the Gaarg Foundation left Bankstown Airport for Hobart twenty-five minutes after your little fracas at Soggy Togs.'

I walked to the far end of the loft to make sure I was totally out of earshot of Boxer and his playmates.

'I just got a text message from Gudrun,' I told Julie. 'They've identified the dead choirboy who was pulled out of the water off Eden. He was a weapons specialist, the only one in the group.'

'And that would explain why they needed Clare,' Jules said after a pause

'I'm not following you.'

'With nuclear warheads it's a bit more complicated than just lighting the wick and standing clear,' she explained. 'There are safety interlocks and codes to be keyed in. Our dead weapons specialist would have had the know-how to detonate a nuke.'

'And you think Clare is capable of doing that?'

'She's got a degree in electrical engineering from MIT, plus another in weapons engineering from Annapolis. It could mean she has the training.'

'Can you get me on the first available flight to Hobart tomorrow, Jules, and I'll need access to some serious firepower.

'Leave it with me. But I've just found something else you have to see.

'What?'

'I'll email you the link. Is Boxer's computer on?'

'Yep. What's it about?' I headed back to the workbench.

'It's a video on the World Whale Conference website. Apparently the Japanese government chose the week of the conference last year to announce it was increasing its scientific whaling quota to close to a thousand minke whales, and it was adding fifty humpbacks and fifty fin whales – an endangered species. The video's of Artemisia's speech to the conference after that announcement.'

The email arrived and I opened the link. The video showed a speaker reading out the new quotas at the conference and Artemisia immediately rising to her feet to seize the microphone. She made an impassioned plea to the delegates to find ways to persuade the Japanese to stop slaughtering the whales.

There was no doubting her conviction, and her anger and frustration were clear to see. Her voice wavered with emotion as she finished her speech with: 'Japanese whalers fire explosive-tipped harpoons into the hearts of these magnificent creatures.' She paused, looked at the crowd, then said, 'I wonder how the Japanese government would feel about an explosive-tipped harpoon being fired into the heart of their nation?'

You could see the fire in her eyes as the crowd leapt to their feet, whistling, cheering and applauding, but there was something about the look on her face that was chilling. I felt sick to my stomach.

'Jesus, Jules.'

'I know.'

'I'm on my way back. See you in fifteen.'

'Be careful, Alby.'

I ended the call. Boxer had wandered up to watch the video of Artemisia over my shoulder. 'She's certainly committed,' he said.

'Or needs to be.' I looked at Boxer. 'Mate,' I said, 'I really hate to do this, but about your plans for the weekend …'

I scootered back to Bondi, slipped the pizza guy an extra fifty bucks, and was packing for Hobart when my phone beeped. It was Lonergan making a call, so I listened in.

A male voice answered. 'Bondi Trattoria.'

'Hi,' Carter said. 'What time do you guys open for breakfast tomorrow?'

'We're open from seven, sir.'

'Great. Can I book a table for two around seven-thirty?'

'We're not too busy at that time, you don't really need to book,' the guy said.

'No,' Lonergan said, 'I'd like to. Table for two, a private corner if you have one. In the name of Murdoch.'

There was a pause, and then Lonergan said, 'Seven-thirty going to be okay for you, Alby?'

At 7.30 next morning I was sitting in the Bondi Trattoria, sipping a cappuccino and waiting for Carter Lonergan. He arrived ten minutes late and joined me at a corner table at the back. The waiter handed us a couple of menus.

'Everything's good here,' I said. 'The chilli beans on polenta with parmesan are very tasty, and the breakfast pizza should keep you going till dinner.'

Lonergan smiled. 'You have a taste for pizza lately, I hear.'

So Gwenda's bozos weren't the only people watching me.

'I find the home-delivery service very handy.'

'I'll bet.'

Lonergan ordered extra-crispy bacon with fried eggs, a potato pancake, and a flat white. For once I wasn't hungry.

'Any word on Clare?' I asked.

'Nothing.'

'So you still buying the ransom scenario?'

'No. But Pergo's still trying to sell it to me. That's why I'm talking to you.'

'Lieutenant Kingston has the ability to arm the warheads, right?'

He nodded. 'Yes, she does. And I don't like where this is leading.'

'Me neither.'

'Look, Alby, I'm going out on a limb here and handing you a chainsaw. Langley warned me about you when I was posted down here, and Pergo and his buddies in the Defence Department say you're a loose cannon.'

'Is that what you think?'

'I think there's a loose cannon somewhere, but I'm not sure it's you.'

'What were you arguing about with Pergo out on the tanker on Monday?'

He smiled. 'You don't miss a trick, do you?'

'I like to keep on top of things.'

'Okay, when I told Pergo I'd brought you in on the investigation, he lost it. Said you were the last person we needed sniffing around, and from the look of things he was right. I just didn't know why.'

'And now you do?'

He gave a brief nod. 'We've just turned up a connection between Pergo and Chief Warrant Officer Brames from the *Altoona*.'

'Iraq?'

He nodded again. 'Pergo had Brames onboard in a scheme to chopper antiquities looted from the Baghdad museum out of the country. NCIS got wind of it and Brames managed to get himself clear before charges were laid.'

Lonergan was going out on a very long limb by telling me this, so I decided to trust him. 'Your instincts are right, Carter. I'm not a hundred percent sure what's going on, but I know Pergo is up to his neck in it. He's on his way to Tasmania and I've got a fair idea the nukes and Clare are down there already. I'm on the ten o'clock to Hobart.'

'You need some back-up down south?'

'Not on the ground. I'll move faster on my own. But if you can keep Pergo thinking you're buying his ransom bullshit, he might leave his guard down.'

'Right.'

'The minute I've got proof that Pergo is involved I'll let you know.'

'Okay. Watch your back, Alby. If this goes down the tubes we'll both go down with it. It will bury us.'

'Yeah. Literally.' I looked at my watch. 'Got a plane to catch.'

I headed towards the door then turned back. 'How did you pick up the bug in the phone? Boxer said it was undetectable.'

'Educated guess. When my cell phone is out of my sight for more than sixty seconds I automatically consider it compromised. Standard operating procedure.'

He smiled. 'But I didn't know for sure until you turned up for breakfast.'

Chapter Twenty-Two

'Cruising men's toilets, Boxer? That's twice in one week. I'm shocked.'

Boxer glared at me. 'This is the last favour I ever do for you, Alby, you bastard. Now, where's your boarding pass?'

It was early Saturday morning and we were in the men's room by the departure gates at the domestic terminal. I'd bought a ticket to Perth online and I checked in for the flight with carry-on luggage only. Boxer had done the same thing, but for a flight to Hobart. Having passed through security, we were now exchanging boarding passes, coats and hats. Boxer would fly to Perth on my ticket and in my coat and hat, and I'd be heading south.

Boxer was pissed off because I was wearing a truly daggy, red terry-towelling sunhat and a white blazer. He was a pretty cool dresser and the very idea of having to wear that hat and blazer in public was killing him. The outfit would severely reduce his chances of making up for the missed weekend with the waitresses by renewing his membership in the mile-high club with one of the cabin attendants.

Julie had organised for a camera case to be waiting for collection at the airfreight counter in Hobart. It had been packed and dispatched by Graeme Rutherford, an ex-field agent who worked in D-E-D's Melbourne office. Graeme had spent four months in a coma after a nasty incident earlier this year, then in true Melburnian fashion, on the day of the AFL grand final he'd suddenly woken up in the ICU, watched his team get thrashed on TV, then checked himself out of hospital. He was as good as new now and still the best – he could pack five cameras into a case built for two and still leave room for an MP7 compact submachine gun and three 40-round mags. Our security-cleared freight-forwarding agents would helpfully ignore the disassembled weapon packed amongst the Nikons.

The approach in to Hobart was a bit bumpy When we came out of the clouds I was looking down at a very wild ocean with big, white-tipped waves being whipped up by the wind.

We touched down right on time and I was walking past the baggage carousel when I heard a whistle. A tall, solidly built man in a battered chauffeur's cap was holding up a sign reading ALIBI MUDROCK. It was written in crayon on a piece of cardboard torn from a Cascade beer carton. I walked towards the man, who smiled politely as I approached.

'Would sir like me to collect his luggage?' he asked.

'That would be nice,' I smiled back.

The man shook his head. 'Well, I'm afraid on that point, sir would be shit-out-of-luck. Who died and made sir King?' And then he grabbed me.

A hug from Ed Wardell is a bit like being wrapped in a giant bearskin rug and stuffed into a car crusher. He eased up the pressure just as I felt certain my ribs were going to snap .

'How ya doin', ya old bastard?' he asked, pumping my hand and grinning. 'I fumigated the sheets, locked up the virgins and stocked the larder, so Chez Ed is yours while you're in town.'

Ed was about forty, bearded and tanned. Built like the proverbial brick outhouse, he had slimmed down recently. There was still that larrikin twinkle in his eye that said if an opportunity for mischief was coming his way he wasn't about to step off the footpath and let it go by.

Ed's older brother Harry had been in D-E-D with me, right from the time I joined. Harry was a good mate and good at his job, which led to him being gunned down in a Double Bay café at the start of the Bitter Springs fiasco. It was only six months ago, and the pain was still raw for both of us, but being Aussie blokes, we'd avoid mentioning the whole business, apart from the odd clinking of glasses in the pub. And if I knew Ed, the pub would be our first stop. It was getting towards lunchtime and I suddenly fancied a big charred steak, all bloody in the middle.

We headed to the airfreight counter where my camera case was waiting. I moved away to unlock it and check the contents. Earlier this year, one of my cases had exploded minutes after coming off a Hong Kong-bound 767 and I wasn't taking any chances.

Ed insisted on carrying the case and my duffle bag to the car. His shiny new Jeep Cherokee was just outside the terminal, conveniently parked in a no-stopping zone with the bonnet up.

'Still having engine problems, I see.'

Ed grinned and tossed my luggage into the back of the vehicle before closing the hood on the engine compartment and climbing into the driver's seat. The Jeep's motor started smoothly at the turn of the key. Ed had a bit of a problem with rules and regulations of any kind, and claimed to have never paid for street parking in his life. All his vehicles, regardless of their age and condition, suffered catastrophic but temporary engine failure at the sight of a parking meter.

Not that the bloke was short of a quid. Fifteen or so years back he'd been working on an airline check-in desk in American Samoa when a famous Hollywood director on a location search had taken exception to his flight home being delayed by weather problems. Words were spoken, demands were made, and finally a punch was thrown. Ed went down like a sack of potatoes, even though he was twice the size of the wunderkind director and had been a promising light heavyweight in his younger days. The out-of-court settlement was massive. Ed came home to Tassie, bought himself a waterfront home, a boat, made some very wise investments, and settled down to enjoy himself. And for Ed, that meant getting into trouble.

He'd been arrested by the marine police a couple of years back for allegedly poaching abalone and had unexpectedly confessed. The cops couldn't believe their luck and the inexperienced police prosecutor didn't even bother to prepare a case. In court Ed politely explained to the magistrate that yes, he did indeed poach abalone, since he'd found that if you fried or grilled it the shellfish tended to toughen up.

Ed's description of simmering the abalone briefly in lemongrass, ginger, white wine and cream was countered by the magistrate's suggestion of a classic Court bouillon. Perhaps with a touch of Pernod, he added before dismissing the case. The cops were livid, and Ed spent a couple of months in Sydney with Harry until things cooled down.

'So what's on the agenda?' Ed said as I made sure my seatbelt was nice and snug. I'd driven with Ed before and I knew what to expect.

'Lunch might be nice, for starters.'

He gunned the engine. 'Now, how'd I know you were gonna say that?'

He pulled out into the traffic with a cursory look over his right shoulder, the acceleration slamming me back in my seat. He grinned at the screeching of tires and the angry horn blasts which accompanied most of his lane changes. One of Ed's early plans when he came into all that money was to open Australia's first offensive driving school.

The top was off the Cherokee and we screamed over the Tasman Bridge with Ed standing up and waving to the speed camera.

'I'm trying out this new paint that's supposed to make the number plates impossible to photograph,' he said.

'Selflessly working for the greater good of your fellow Taswegians, I see.'

'Yep, I'm the Apple Isle's own Mother Theresa!'

'Still got the place at Battery Point?'

Ed shook his head. 'Moved out of town. Down to Peppermint Bay. This joint is getting too bloody crowded for my liking.'

Crowded was one thing Hobart wasn't. On first impressions, you might get the idea the place is a big country town. It's low-rise, with lots of convict-era buildings, wide streets and public parks. For my money it's the perfect size for a city, big enough to support a vibrant arts community, a range of great places to eat, and all the public services you need, while still maintaining its heritage and being compact enough to wander on foot without the feeling of isolation you can get in Sydney or Melbourne.

Ed screeched to a halt at a pedestrian crossing, to the sound of more angry honking from behind. A tall, gamine, twenty-something in Ugg boots and a short denim skirt crossed in front of us and Ed wound down his window and whistled. The girl gave him the finger and he chuckled.

'Wild thing, eh? Jeez, mate, if that skirt was one millimetre shorter we'd be able to see the old map of Tasmania.'

It seemed odd hearing the expression used in Tasmania by a Tasmanian about a Tasmanian. Odder still was having Ed swerve into a parking space outside a downtown vegetarian café.

My lentil burger might have been about as good as a lentil burger ever can be, but since I'd had my heart set on a hunk of very rare, Cape Grimm grass-fed sirloin, maybe served on a sweet potato, apple and sage rosti, with a red wine sauce and caramelised onions, I was never going to eat more than a mouthful. Ed munched his way glumly but resolutely through a huge mixed salad. He used to boast that he hadn't eaten anything green since he was five, apart from lime jelly. In the old days, his idea of meat and three veg was a T-bone steak with French fries, roasted spuds and a creamy, cheesy potato gratin. Recently adult-onset diabetes had forced him to change his ways. Under protest and doctor's orders, he'd switched to a healthy diet to save his life and he reckoned it was slowly killing him.

Over lunch Ed brought me up to speed on what he knew of the Gaarg Foundation's foray into Tasmania.

'They bought Adamek Island from the government about a year or so back. Ninety clicks off the coast, out that-away.' He pointed towards the south-east. 'It's basically just a bloody big rock sticking out of the Southern Ocean – an abandoned whaling station with a lighthouse that was automated in the seventies, a bunch of cottages in various stages of falling down, a mutton-bird colony, and more friggin' nasty black tiger snakes than you can shake a stick at, if shaking a stick at a joe blake is your idea of a good time. Plus,' he continued, 'the island gets gales blowing up from the Antarctic that would freeze the balls off a brass monkey.'

'Sounds attractive,' I said. 'Can you get me out there?' I wasn't happy about involving Ed after what had happened to his brother, but I didn't have much choice.

'Sure. But it'll depend on the weather. Today's out of the question, I'm afraid, there's a big swell running. There's supposed to be a change on the way, though. I reckon we could have a go in the morning. It'll cost you, big time.'

'Name your price.'

'Dinner. You're cooking.'

A sign outside the gallery read LUCAS BAYVEL – NEW IMAGES and the framed photographs that covered the walls inside had three things in common: they were stunning, they'd all been taken from the air, and every single one of them featured a lighthouse.

'I wonder what Freud would have made of a man obsessed with photographing lighthouses?' I said, looking round.

A tall, thin man in his forties sitting behind the desk near the entrance looked up. 'Probably the same thing he would have made of photographers who run around in shooting vests with dozens of pockets all over them,' he said. 'It was all bloody sex with Freud.'

He stood up and walked around the desk. 'You know, Tasmania started as a dumping ground for the very worst of the worst, the vilest of the vile, the most incorrigible of miscreants for whom there was absolutely no chance of redemption. And now you're here! You're only about two hundreds year late, Alby.'

Lucas and I shook hands and I introduced Ed.

'Wardell?' Lucas said. 'Not related to Harry, by any chance?'

Ed nodded. 'My brother.'

'Good bloke, Harry,' Lucas said. 'You could rely on him. I was sorry to hear about it.'

'How's Joy?' I asked. 'Still flying?'

Lucas was a WorldPix and D-E-D veteran who specialised in aerial photography. He'd had a rule about not flying with female pilots until he turned up one day to do a shoot of Uluru and found all five-foot-nothing of Joy Janssen doing a pre-flight on the Cessna. What happened thirty minutes later was legend, with either little Joy or six-foot-two Lucas accidentally knocking the Cessna's radio to 'transmit', broadcasting Lucas's induction into the mile-high club to the bemused crews of almost a dozen domestic and international aircraft in the vicinity. Civil Aviation Safety Authority Investigators had been unable to trace the aircraft or the pilot, and Joy and Lucas were married within a month. Lucas retired from the spy game and together they now ran JoyFlights Aerial Expeditions out of Hobart airport. They also worked together on Lucas's obsession: photographing every lighthouse in Australia.

'So what brings you to Tassie?' Lucas asked. 'Business or business?'

'Adamek Island,' I said. 'But that's for your ears only. Anything you can tell me?'

'She's a nice-looking light. Twenty-two metres high, sixty metres above sea level, constructed from cast-iron segments. Originally used a Chance Brothers lens and a vaporised kerosene light source. She's now fully automated, running a quartz halogen lamp powered by a solar array, flashing one in nine seconds at 63 000 candelas, visible for thirty-three nautical miles.'

'I actually meant the island,' I said. 'Got any snaps?'

Lucas placed a large folder on the desk and rifled through dozens of prints before pulling one out. 'Here you go. Taken in 1996 on the twentieth anniversary of the de-manning of the station. Bastard of a place, really. Cold, bleak, and bloody windy. Posting of last resort for lighthouse keepers in the old days.'

The photograph showed a large barren rocky outcrop in the middle of the vast blue sea. There were steep cliffs on all sides, with white water everywhere as the waves of the Southern Ocean battered the shoreline. A white tower stood high above what looked like a ruined settlement on a small harbour. Lucas handed me a magnifying glass.

'That's the old whaling station, abandoned in the 1850s. Apparently the island was heavily forested before the whalers came. They chopped everything down for fuel to fire the try pots for rendering down the blubber. They reckon you could smell the island twenty miles off.'

I ran the magnifying glass over the coastline. 'Any place a bloke could go ashore if he didn't want to go up to the front door?'

Lucas looked at me for a minute before leafing through more prints. He pulled out another and pointed to a small inlet. 'It's on the eastern side, 'bout halfway round. Might be possible to climb up the cliff face from this little beach. A tinny or zodiac could make it in, but it'd be hairy. You'd want a calm day.'

Ed picked up the magnifying glass, had a look and grunted.

'You know that the Gaarg Foundation moved in a while back?' Lucas said.

'Joy and I flew out there about six months ago to update the photos for the new book I'm working on. There was a hell of a lot of activity happening – new buildings, wind turbines, helicopter landing pad.'

'Got any pictures of all that?'

Lucas shook his head. 'A chopper took off from the island and some bloke pointed what looked like an M16 at us, so we figured it wasn't worth it. That water is bloody icy and you wouldn't last five minutes in it, even if you survived the impact. I must getting old, Alby, but no photo's worth dying for.'

'I'm with you there, mate,' I said. 'Thanks for the info, say hello to Joy for me.'

'Will do. And if you decide to go out there uninvited Alby, take a box of chocolates.'

'Got one,' I said.

'Hard centres?'

'Armour piercing.'

'Good.'

'I don't miss the old days, Alby, not one bit,' Lucas called after me as we walked out the door. 'You look after yourself on that island.'

As we headed to the Salamanca Markets I was thinking about Harry and young Max and some of the other Dedheads who were no longer around. That was the thing about not missing the old days, you had to be alive to do it.

It was a sunny afternoon and the markets were packed with tourists and locals. By the time we got to the food vans at the bottom of the hill I was certain we weren't being followed. With apologies to Ed and his diet, I grabbed a roll stuffed with slices of freshly roasted lamb and a serve of delicious tiny Dutch pancakes called poffertjes, and ate as we walked. Once I had a proper lunch in my belly, we headed over to Constitution Dock and pick up the ingredients for dinner.

On one of the fish punts moored at the dock, a bloke in a blue plastic apron was filleting salmon, occasionally tossing a carcass out into the water where a sleek, happy-looking seal was waiting patiently. When it scored it floated on its back to tear the fish carcass into bite-size chunks. Looking at the seal's fat, wet, round belly, I realised I probably shouldn't have eaten all those poffertjes.

I bought snapper and Spanish mackerel fillets from Shane's Punt, along with prawns, scallops and mussels, and some fish heads and trimmings to make a stock. Walking back through the markets, I grabbed a baguette, tomatoes, leeks, fennel, garlic and saffron. As we headed to the jeep, Ed told me about meeting Artemisia at several rowdy anti-logging meetings.

'The old Artemisia can get pretty bolshie when she's wound up,' he said.

'You never struck me as the environmentalist type.'

Ed shrugged. 'I reckon those conservationists might have a point. If we keep chopping into the old-growth forests the way we are, the old map of Tasmania may wind up with a full Brazilian.'

Chapter Twenty-Three

THE ROAD TO PEPPERMINT BAY FOLLOWS THE COAST. OUT IN THE distance, across the channel, you can see Bruny Island, where they farm the best oysters I've ever tasted. The coastal views range from extraordinary to unbelievable, and they change every time you crest a rise or turn a corner on the winding road.

The sun was low in the sky, and to our right tall stands of trees cast long shadows across the rocky outcrops and sandy bays. For a minute I allowed myself to imagine being here under different circumstances, heading for dinner with an old friend before setting out on a trek down the Franklin, maybe to photograph the ancient Huon pines.

Ed's place was a few clicks past Peppermint Bay, a two-storey weatherboard set on pilings on the water side of the road. There was a long jetty sticking out into the channel with an elegant cabin cruiser moored at the end. Elegant or not, it was still smaller than an aircraft carrier, which put it into my category of modes of transport best avoided whenever possible. But if I was going to find out what was happening on Adamek Island I really didn't have a choice.

Dinner Chez Ed was my take on a bouillabaisse, which was really a fish stew since we were a long way from Marseille, and anyway, as my mate Armando would be happy to tell you, the French ripped off bouillabaisse from the Italian zuppa di pesche. Ed's state-of-the-art kitchen had every pot, pan and gadget a man could ask for, and even if I wasn't dragging on a Gauloises or sucking down some Pastis 51 while I cooked, the local seafood and the saffron-infused tomato, garlic and anise-flavoured fish soup all came together with a nice gutsy, Mediterranean feel. I found a Jansz rosé in Ed's wine cellar to help wash it down.

We had dinner out on the deck overlooking the water, and afterwards we reminisced about Harry over a half-bottle of an excellent vintage port. When the subject of Harry's affair with Julie came up, Ed said that Harry reckoned she was just filling in time, and she was carrying a torch for someone else. Not that he'd complained – Harry had been going through yet another relationship break-up and he appreciated having such a soft shoulder to cry on. None of us Dedheads could lay claim to a decent long-term relationship.

I turned in around eleven. I hadn't had much sleep over the previous two nights and I needed to have my wits about me the next day. Ed's guest bedroom was huge, with a king-sized bed and a balcony overlooking the channel. It must have been the fresh air and the wine and the gentle lapping of water, because I went out like a light, right in the middle of musing about Julie and her torch-carrying.

Sunday morning we were up at sparrow's fart, and while Ed rechecked the weather forecast I made coffee and raided his fridge for breakfast fixings. I figured Ed deserved a decent breakfast, as well as dinner, for his trouble.

It was a crisp, clear morning and we ate out on the deck again: whole-wheat toast triangles topped with slices of avocado, crispy rashers of bacon, poached eggs, Thai sweet chilli sauce, and a sprig of coriander.

After breakfast we walked down the jetty to the forty-foot Riviera Flybridge Cruiser tied up at the end. The name painted on the stern and the life preservers was Suzie-QC. Ed had named the boat after Susan Winter, the barrister who'd won him another impressive settlement a few years back, in one of those legal actions he enjoyed so much. The twin Cummins B370 diesels had a very reassuring rumble to them as we pushed off from the dock just after nine, heading south and towing a Zodiac inflatable with an outboard motor.

The sky was clear, the sea as smooth as glass, and all the signs pointed to me being able to keep my breakfast to myself. My last boat trip in ocean waters had been from Bali to Broome on a yacht that was attacked by a speedboat full of heavily armed pirates. We barely escaped with our lives, and now even a trip cross the harbour on the Manly ferry tended to make me a bit edgy.

Up in the wheelhouse, I pulled the MP7 from its holster and checked it out. With a folding front grip and a retractable rear stock, the MP7 is not a whole lot bigger than a hefty combat pistol.

'Is that thing bloody plastic?' Ed laughed. 'It looks like a toy.'

'They use a lot of polymer,' I said, 'so I guess it's sort of plastic but it's no toy.' I pushed a magazine into the base of the grip. 'Heckler and Koch PDW personal defence weapon, 950 high-velocity rounds a minute on full auto. Forty-round magazine, and the bullets will punch through serious body armour at up to a couple of hundred metres.'

'Oh,' Ed said. 'That's a lot of personal defence.'

'Works for me.'

Around eleven, as I was brewing coffee in the galley, Ed called me up on deck. He had a pair of binoculars focused on something off the starboard bow.

'Take a butcher's at that,' he said. 'Looks like old Artemisia's sent out a welcoming committee.' He handed me the binoculars. 'Thar she blows.'

It took a moment to find them and then I saw the plume of white spray, and then another and another, and then suddenly a huge flat grey tail broke the water.

'Humpbacks,' Ed said. '*Megaptera novaeangliae.* Heading back south to feed after having their babies up in warmer water. Let's see if we can get any closer.'

Fifteen minutes later, he had brought the boat near the edge of the pod. He shut down the engines and let us drift. There were a dozen whales in the group, including a couple of young calves, who stuck close to their mothers, but none of them seemed too fussed by our presence.

We stood out on the bow and I wondered if I should shoot some pictures, but decided against it. Having your eye up to a viewfinder means you get pictures of an event but sometimes no actual experience of it. And this was something that was worth experiencing.

I felt an almost imperceptible lifting motion on the boat, and down through the deep blue water I saw the shape of a huge whale slowly rising up towards us. He stopped just a few feet under the surface, rolled slightly, and then I was looking into a great big inky eye. We studied each other for what seemed like hours but was probably only seconds, and then the giant bulk of the whale faded back into the blue-grey depths.

It was an amazing feeling, looking into that eye. I had a sense that there was a soul inside that great body, and the whale was checking me out to see what I was doing in his backyard. Seconds later, the boat rocked violently as the whale leapt up out of the water not ten metres off our bow, twisting in the air like a twenty-ton ballerina before splashing back down into the waves. I had to get a good grip on the deck rail to stop going over the side

'Showing off,' Ed yelled. 'Maybe she fancies you.'

We were completely surrounded by whales now, showered with spray from their blowholes, the air filled with the sound of their exhaling breath and their massive tails slapping down on the water. It was breathtaking, and yet at the same time somehow intensely peaceful. Any one of these huge creatures could smash the little Suzie-QC to pieces with a flick of the tail, but they seemed perfectly content to have us floating along with them on the gentle swell.

Several whales were lifting their heads up out of the water, then arching their bodies before plunging back into the foaming sea. 'That bending motion when they dive is why they call 'em humpbacks,' Ed said.

We drifted along for about fifteen minutes, with the pod slowly drawing away from us as they headed south. When they disappeared over the horizon Ed restarted the engines, and about an hour later he pointed to a grey bump in the distance.

'Adamek Island. You can see why the whalers chose it. The whales came to them. All they had to do was row out and harpoon the poor buggers while they were cruising past.'

Ed explained that the Tasmanian whaling industry had boomed for forty years in the 1800s, until the development of kerosene wiped out the market for whale oil as a lamp fuel. Adamek Island, being isolated and difficult to access in bad weather, was one of the first stations to close down. A lighthouse had been built in 1869 and the keepers and their families had been the only human inhabitants of the windswept rocky outcrop for the next hundred years.

The lighthouse was the first structure we saw as we motored towards the island. It seemed to be flashing as we got closer, even though it was a bright sunny day. Ed focused his binoculars and grunted.

'They've got radar mounted on top of the lighthouse. They already know we're here, mate. Take a look.'

The rotating radar dish was clearly visible through the binoculars. One edge of the metal dish was catching the sun on each rotation, hence the flashing.

Ed took the boat round the southern end of the island, keeping about a kilometre offshore. The entrance to the main harbour faced south and was just a narrow gap in the rock face. Barely 250 metres wide, even on a calm day it looked menacing.

'Christ,' Ed said, throttling the engines back slightly, 'I wouldn't fancy going in or out of that with even a mild swell running. Imagine doing it under sail, or in a whaleboat using oars. Get a decent sea up, and some wind, and you'd have better odds playing Russian roulette.'

He put the engines back to full revs and we skirted the bottom of the island and headed north. The drop-off and pick-up point was the small inlet that Lucas had pointed out and Ed figured if we kept well in to the shore we'd be under the radar for the drop-off. Then the plan was he'd take the Suzie-QC back towards Hobart, as if he'd just done a leisurely cruise around the island, and heave-to over the horizon to wait for my signal. Once I had the information I needed and was ready to leave I'd activate a homing device and disable the radar dish so Ed could cruise back in and pick me up undetected. It seemed a simple enough plan – but I think that may have been what General Custer said before he rode into the Little Big Horn.

I changed into black jeans, a black hoodie and my hiking boots. On the rear deck of the Suzie-QC was a spray jacket, a two-way radio, a flare pistol and a lifejacket. I gave Ed the receiver linked to the homing device under my belt buckle and he gave me a quick refresher on handling the inflatable. He was reluctant to leave me but I promised to keep out of trouble and to have the Zodiac back in the garage by midnight with a full tank of petrol and no scratches on it.

I'm not sure he was convinced and frankly neither was I. Who know what the hell I was going to run into on that lump of rock, apart from Artemisia Gaarg, Pergo, the choirboys and a couple of nukes. The MP7 was wrapped up tight in plastic inside its holster and as I strapped it on I hoped I'd brought enough ammo.

Chapter Twenty-Four

I HALF JUMPED, HALF FELL INTO THE ZODIAC FROM THE STERN OF THE Suzie-QC and Ed started laughing. I hate rubber boats. He was still laughing when I pushed away from the cabin cruiser, twisted the throttle on the outboard and turned in towards the island. Bastard.

The waves were small and even though they'd had no effect on the Suzie-QC, they caused quite a bit of buffeting on the little inflatable as I headed towards the narrow opening in the rock face. The inlet was a miniature version of Adamek Island's main harbour, with the same towering stone walls and foaming white water where the ocean swirled in and out. It was ten percent seamanship and ninety percent blind luck that got me through the twenty-metre gap in the cliff face and onto the tiny pebble beach in one piece.

After making the Zodiac secure, I took off my lifejacket, wrapped the flare pistol in the spray jacket and stowed them in the bottom of the boat. I checked and loaded the MP7, then started on the climb up the cliff. I had thermals on under my black jeans and hoodie and I was sweating by the time I reached the top.

The lighthouse appeared to be a three of four k's off and I headed that way. The island was almost devoid of trees, apart from occasional clumps of withered shrubs with spindly roots wrapped around the weathered rocks. They looked like they were hanging on for grim death in anticipation of the next big blow from the freezing south.

I'd been walking for about five minutes when I heard the chopper. The island didn't offer a lot of hiding places so I sprinted towards a clump of shrubs, hoping my black clothes would camouflage me in the broken shadows of the bushes. The helicopter, heading north, passed over me without stopping. I breathed a sigh of relief and then stopped mid-exhalation when I noticed the unblinking eye of the fat black tiger snake at my elbow.

I was wondering whether I could jump faster than a snake could strike – which I wouldn't want to put money on – and whether my thermals would deflect fangs – also a long shot – when the snake opened its mouth and then disintegrated into a writhing mass of white flesh and entrails. The noise of the pistol shot bounced off the boulders and then there was silence.

'I hate those fuckers,' the man with the gun said, and spat. I moved my left hand very slowly up to my face and wiped snake guts off my cheek.

'And if you so much as twitch another muscle, you prick, you'll get the same.'

There were two of them, wearing camouflage combat gear, Raybans and bandanas. They looked like a couple of escapees from *Survivor*, but the pistols made me take them a little more seriously. And the fact that the bloke who'd shot the snake was Chief Petty Officer O'Reilly.

I got up with my hands in the air and O'Reilly kept me covered while the other bloke unhitched my MP7 and frisked me. He wasn't very good at it. I once had an English bobby doing security at Heathrow give me what appeared to be a casual pat-down but when he'd finished I reckon he knew exactly how much change I had in my pockets and how many fillings I had.

This bloke did find my two-way radio, which was no coup given it was the size of a packet of cigarettes. He smashed it on the rocks and handed the MP7 to O'Reilly.

'Nice gun,' O'Reilly said. 'You take him in,' he told the other bloke, gesturing towards the main harbour, 'and if he gives you any grief waste him.'

We'd been walking for a couple of minutes when I heard a long burst of submachine gun fire coming from the direction of the inlet. The all-steel spitzer-pointed ammo in the MP7 is designed to penetrate body armour so the rubber Zodiac didn't stand a chance. It was a good thing I was in training for the Bondi to Bronte ocean swim, because that was the only way I had now of getting out to the Suzie-QC for the pick-up.

I hadn't expected to see a township, but Adamek Island's harbour was surrounded by ten or twelve substantial stone buildings, which must have been built in the whaling days. They looked like they were in good condition, with new roofs, windows and doors, and fresh white mortar joining the stones and blocking out the weather. There were also another dozen modern, prefabricated buildings, which looked to be a mixture of housing and workshops.

Solar panels lined most of the roofs, and on a hilltop in the distance I could see the slowly-turning blades of a row of wind turbines. Two helicopters were parked on concrete pads near a large aircraft hangar. One was a nifty little Bell 430, which still had its rotor blades turning, and the other was a huge Russian Mi-26 Halo heavy-lifter. With its twin turbo-shaft engines powering an eight-blade rotor, the Halo could lift up to twenty tons of cargo, which would make resupplying Artemisia's little enterprise a walk in the park.

The village was set in a depression, which sheltered it from the worst of the wind, and there were orchards full of healthy-looking fruit trees and acres of thriving, neatly laid-out vegetable gardens. The whole scene would have been quite idyllic if it weren't for the man with the gun walking behind me.

The harbour widened substantially once you were through the narrow opening, and there was a jetty with a single-masted, wooden-hulled sailboat, about ten metres in length, tied up to it. The lacquered planking on the hull was a rich golden-brown and it looked like an old whaleboat that had been lovingly restored.

To the left of the jetty was a cobbled slipway leading down to the water, and the remains of rusty railway tracks. Shiny new tracks ran out from the doors of a large workshop set back from the slipway, but rather than running down to the water to receive whales, these tracks arched upwards on a support structure of steel girders, ending abruptly after about fifty metres. I'd seen a construction like it before, but I couldn't remember where.

As we walked past the workshop, a man in blue overalls stepped out of a side door. Behind him I could see flickering cold white light and hear the crackling of arc welding and the screech of an angle grinder cutting into metal. Sunday definitely wasn't a day of rest on Adamek Island.

I was led into what looked to be a staff dining room in the main stone building. There were about a dozen or so large communal tables and a self-service hot food bar. I took a squiz at what was on offer and instantly regretted the decision. A self-service vegetarian cafeteria. That was two vegetarian joints in two days. What a nightmare. It was lucky the goons had taken the MP7 off me or I might have been tempted to blow my brains out.

Artemisia Gaarg was waiting for me at a private table tucked away in an alcove and set with a crisp white linen tablecloth. A waiter pushed in my chair for me, deftly placed a napkin on my lap, handed me a menu and suggested I might like to start with an aperitif. I opted for a tomato juice – a Goodie, of course.

After delivering me to Artemisia, my escort had positioned himself next to the main door, and it was pretty obvious that was where he was going to stay. Artemisia hadn't spoken since I was ushered into her presence. Perhaps she had a copy of *The Boy's Own Book of Office Power Plays* too. A second waiter appeared, so I glanced over towards my hostess and said, 'After you, please.'

She smiled and ordered garlic and potato soup and frittata. I ordered the soup and the stew and let the waiter choose the wine, since I had no idea what the hell would go with eggplant and black-eyed peas.

'Interesting menu,' I said, by way of a conversation starter.

'If we were in a primary school dining room in Japan, Mr Murdoch, the menu would offer whale meat.'

'I had a close encounter with some whales on my way out here, Miss Gaarg,' I said, 'and I have to tell you that even a small one would make a hell of a sushi platter – I'm not sure the kids would be able to get through it in a single sitting.'

She smiled politely but there was no sign of humour in those hazel eyes.

'Whales, Mr Murdoch, are thinking, caring, kind and loving creatures. They sing, they play, they gently romance their mates and make love with amazing grace, and they nurture their young with a dedication that would put many a mother in our society to shame.'

'You'll get no argument from me there, Miss Gaarg. They're unique creatures.'

The whale that checked me out on the boat had looked at me with more than just the passing interest of a dumb animal. I'd had a similar incident in a refuge for orangutans orphaned and dispossessed by illegal logging in West Kalimantan. A six-month-old orangutan held my hand and I'd have sworn he was saying, 'Why are you letting this happen to us? You know it's not right,' as he looked up at me with his big sad eyes.

'In the name of spurious scientific research and cultural heritage, Mr Murdoch,' Artemisia continued, 'Japanese whalers hunt down these amazing animals and fire explosive-tipped harpoons into their huge hearts.'

I'd seen her give that speech before, on video, with the same fire in her eyes.

Just then the dining-room door burst open and about twenty men and women, some in white coats, some in blue overalls, walked in. It must have been lunchtime for the workers. One of the blokes in a white coat looked familiar. He studied the blackboard and shook his head.

'Jesus Christ, not more fucking tofu,' he groaned. 'I could bloody murder a meat pie.'

'Meat *is* murder, Mr Sheehan,' Artemisia called out.

Now I had a name for that familiar face: Francis Aloysius Sheehan. And I suddenly realised what that ramp and the railway tracks were all about.

The Nazis had used similar ramps to launch V1 flying bombs at London towards the end of World War II. The V1 was powered by a simple pulse-jet engine and was blasted up a launching ramp by a steam-powered catapult. A small, propeller-like device in the nose roughly measured distance, and once over the target the V1 would dive, starving the engine of fuel. Seconds later, the one-ton, high-explosive warhead would detonate. A lot of V1s were built in the Volkswagen factory, and though crude they were the forerunner of today's cruise missile.

Modern cruise missiles, like the American Tomahawk, fly at subsonic speeds and low altitude to avoid radar detection, self-navigating using inertial guidance to follow a preset course. The inertial system is supported by GPS, guiding the missile to the target with almost pinpoint accuracy. But those babies cost at least a million bucks a unit, so only the big boys can afford them, and they like to keep them to themselves.

Francis Sheehan, a former aeronautical engineer from the old Gaarg Aerospace operation, had earned a lot of publicity a few years back by claiming he could put together a homemade, accurate, long-range cruise missile from off-the-shelf parts. And he reckoned he could do it for under twenty-five grand a pop.

The entire government security apparatus had fallen on Sheehan from a great height. In the interests of national security they confiscated every drawing, plan and piece of paper he had to his name, and Sheehan had disappeared off the face of the planet. And now here he was – on a rock in the Southern Ocean with a fully equipped workshop, an employer with very deep pockets, and a rather nifty launching ramp pointing north.

But even if Sheehan was knocking together a Meccano-set cruise missile or two it wasn't the end of the world. One more cruise missile, more or less, wasn't going to make much difference to the planet. What would make a difference was a couple of nuclear warheads, just the right size to fit on a cruise missile. By the time my entree turned up, I'd lost my appetite.

Between sips of her soup Artemisia told me a lot more about the evils of whaling than I really wanted to know. When the waiter took away her empty bowl and my barely touched one I switched the conversation to Sheehan and the launching pad out on the slipway.

'I gave Mr Sheehan an open cheque, as well as a promised bonus for on-schedule delivery,' she said, 'but he seems to take pride in bringing the project in on budget.'

'The project being a cruise missile, made with loving hands at home?' I said.

Artemisia gave me a pleasant smile as she calmly buttered a piece of bread. 'For years now I have argued and protested and made appeals to governments and politicians and the UN. All to no avail. We blockade their ships and try to drive away their quarry, and still they persist. And now it has become clear that the Japanese government intends to buy its way into dominance of the World Whaling Commission as a way of again legalising whaling. They must be stopped. When reasoned arguments fail, Mr Murdoch, stronger measures are called for.'

'So you think nuclear blackmail's the answer?'

'Blackmail and threats are only delaying tactics, Mr Murdoch, and they give an adversary time to plan a response. Every day we prevaricate another dozen whales are slaughtered. It's my intention, therefore, to give the Japanese government other things besides scientific research and school lunches to occupy its mind.'

'It's a pretty long haul for a homemade cruise missile from here to Japan,' I pointed out.

'Mr Sheehan's missile is designed to make use of something called the surface effect to extend its range, and, coincidentally, to reduce its radar signature to nil.'

At the right speed, and with the right wing design, surface-effect craft travel over water or land on a slim cushion of air that reduces drag and extends their range dramatically. The Russians had built a number of seagoing vehicles, including large cargo freighters, to examine the concept, and the Japanese were looking at using it for a new version of frictionless bullet trains. It was feasible that it would work for a cruise missile. Shit!

'As to range,' she continued, 'the missile doesn't need to reach the Japanese mainland for me to achieve my purpose. Are you aware of the island of Iwo Jima, Mr Murdoch?'

'The place the Yanks captured from the Japanese army in 1945? Where they took the photo of the flag raising on Mount Suribachi?'

'Very good, Mr Murdoch. How fortunate we were to go to school at a time when so much emphasis was placed on history and geography. Iwo Jima is part of Japan's Volcano Islands, and has two sister islands, Kita Iwo Jima and Minami Iwo Jima. The area has considerable surface and subsurface volcanic activity,' Artemisia continued. 'Iwo Jima is a rather flat little island, apart from Mount Suribachi, but Minami Iwo Jima rises straight out of the sea, with almost sheer sides reaching to a height of close to one thousand metres. When I sold off my father's companies I retained Gaarg Satellite Imaging, with the intention of studying global warming and conducting a census of the world's whale population. In early 2005, one of our people noticed a major geological fault cutting across the north face of Minami Iwo Jima, the side facing the Japanese mainland.'

History and geography were actually two of my best subjects at school. Mathematics was totally beyond me, but right now I was starting to put two and two together and I was coming up with a terrifying four. 'Oh,' I said.

Artemisia smiled. 'Oh indeed, Mr Murdoch.'

'So, you're intending to use your homemade cruise missile to drop a nuclear warhead into a fault in the side of a volcano, causing the major part of the island to collapse into the sea … creating …

'A massive tsunami, a tidal wave. Precisely, Mr Murdoch.' Her voice was calm and steady but the look of demented righteousness in her eyes chilled me to the bone.

'When I approached Mr Sheehan with my plan he agreed that his cruise missile could reach the target so I put him to work. We were well advanced on the project before I learned that the cruise missile's load capacity was half a tonne of conventional explosives, which was nowhere near enough to achieve the result I wanted. I was stymied for a week or two, and then Mr Pergo approached me regarding financing a business plan he was working on with Reverend Priday. When he revealed the details of their scheme I realised he had the solution to my problem.

'So you made him a better offer?'

'Exactly, Mr Murdoch. Mr Pergo's past in Iraq was catching up with him and it was only a matter of time before he would be invited to appear before the War Crimes Tribunal in the Hague. It was all but game over for him and he needed to make a large amount of money in a short amount of time. With his connections to one of the crew on the American warship, and access to my resources, Mr Pergo was able to put all the elements together very quickly. We saw it as a mutually beneficial opportunity.'

'Not so beneficial to the millions of Japanese likely to be killed when your tidal wave hits the Japanese coast?'

'Detonation of the warhead and the subsequent landslip will register instantly on seismographs in Tokyo and other major Japanese cities, triggering the automatic tsunami alarms. It will happen at exactly noon on a weekday, so the alarms will set in motion the well-rehearsed emergency evacuation plans the Japanese are famous for, ensuring that all coastal cities in the path of the tidal wave suffer minimal loss of life. Infrastructure and economic damage will be severe, however, and as a consequence I'm sure the people of Japan will lose their taste for whale meat.'

The coldness in her voice as she said 'minimal loss of life' made my blood run cold. 'Minimal loss of life', like 'collateral damage', was one of those elastic concepts that meant different things to different people --words that turned human lives into statistical equations in a cost-benefit analysis. Exactly how many people was this woman willing to kill in order to save the whales? At what point did commitment and dedication to a cause, even the noblest of causes, flip over into obsession and then total insanity?

Telling crazy people that they're crazy isn't something the mental-health experts recommend, but it just kind of slipped out. Artemisia took it well, given that I phrased it in terms of her being out of her tiny fucking mind.

'And you're not expecting a lot of very angry people to come looking for you?' I said.

'That doesn't really matter to me, Mr Murdoch. My job will be done. Besides, I think the world will have more than enough on its plate coping with the collapse of the Japanese economy.'

She was right about that.

'We are totally self-sustaining on this island, Mr Murdoch, and we can ride out any storm until calmer and more rational views prevail. After all, isn't today's terrorist simply tomorrow's visionary? And remember, I'll still have one remaining warhead, which I'm sure will be useful as an insurance policy against unwelcome callers.'

No argument there. A nuke in the cupboard was as handy a deterrent as a pit bull to a postie.

'I'm guessing that old Aldo Ray movie gave you the idea for using the tanker as a distraction,' I said.

'I was always a fan, Mr Murdoch. I watched *The Siege of Pinchgut* many times as a child. Worked rather well, don't you think?'

I had to admit it had worked like a charm. But it wasn't a good feeling knowing that I, along with the Australian and US governments, had been duped by the plot of a 1950s B-grade movie.

One of the guards came over to our table and whispered in Artemisia's ear. She nodded and stood up.

'There's something I need to attend to, Mr Murdoch. You will, of course, be our guest on Adamek Island tonight.' It wasn't a question.

When she'd left, the guard motioned to me to get up and go with him. He did this with a wave of his pistol, which was pretty persuasive. I'd been hoping to check out the dessert menu, but a nine millimetre Browning trumps a carob-chip brownie every time.

Chapter Fifty-Five

THE ISLAND'S GUEST QUARTERS WERE NOWHERE NEAR AS SCHMICK AS A suite at the Hyatt, but mine did have an ensuite bathroom, fluffy white robes, a minibar, tea-making facilities, a very solid door and 24-hour security. The security, of course, was to stop me going out rather than anyone coming in. My guard was standing in the doorway explaining the house rules when I glanced down beside the bed.

'Jesus, how'd that snake get in here?' I said, and as he stepped forward, eyes to the floor and pistol raised warily, I swung the heavy door round as hard as I could. He saw it coming out of the corner of his eye and turned just in time for the edge to catch him on the temple. There was a nasty thud of wood on bone, another thud as his Browning hit the carpet, and then he was on his knees, a glassy look in his eyes.

I walked out of the guest quarters ten minutes later, wearing the guard's camouflage fatigues and carrying the Browning in his holster. I'd left him under the doona on the bed, gagged and trussed up with his belt and the cotton tie from a bathrobe. I kept my own belt, since the homing device fitted under the buckle was the only way I had of making contact with Ed and getting off the island.

And getting off the island was something I had to do fast because we'd have to call in the big boys to sort out this little viper's nest. I needed to get to the lighthouse – that's where the radar dish was and the high vantage point would give me the range for the homing device.

The few people I bumped into ignored me, so I decided to risk a peek in the big workshop before taking the path up to the lighthouse. A side door opened onto a large workspace crammed with machinery, including lathes, drill presses and computer-controlled cutting devices. The workers inside ignored me as well.

Artemisia's little cruise missile was sitting under a bank of lights in the middle of the workshop. It was about ninety metres in length and its cylindrical fuselage had stubby, delta-shaped wings attached, which made it look a bit like a scale model of the old Concorde. There was a raised air intake for the turbofan engine at the rear of the craft, and the delta wings were turned up at the tips. The black paint covering the fuselage and wings was probably radar-absorbing, and while the missile appeared rather crudely engineered and put together, the damned thing did look like it could fly. Worse than that, it looked like it was ready to fly.

Towards the front of the fuselage, a hinged panel lay open and a couple of white-coated bods were fiddling around in a space that looked big enough to hold a beer keg, or something the size of a beer keg. If the warheads were on the island, which now seemed likely, and my pal Lieutenant Kingston was also in the vicinity, then things were coming to a head.

On the far wall of the workshop there was a large mirror, and next to it a door marked PROJECT MANAGER. The mirror was no doubt one-way glass so the manager could keep an eye on his minions. Under PROJECT MANAGER it said NO ADMITTANCE, so I went right in. Sheehan had his feet up on a desk and was busily folding a sheet of A4 paper into the shape of a plane.

'Aerodynamic research?' I said.

He launched the paper plane, which did two quick spiral loops of the office before dropping neatly into a wastepaper basket under the window.

'Forget I asked,' I said. If Sheehan could get performance like that out of a paper plane, then his homemade missile would probably be able to go the distance.

Through the one-way mirror, I could see that a third person had joined the two boffins at the business end of the missile. It was Chapman Pergo.

'So how's it all going, Mr Sheehan?' I said, turning back in his direction. 'Launch on schedule?'

Sheehan took his feet off the desk and indicated the whiteboard behind him with a tilt of his head. A chart on the board showed target dates and stages of construction and testing, with COMPLETED marked next to most of them. Tomorrow's date had RTL 7.30 AM next to it with a question mark. I figured RTL stood for 'ready to launch'.

'You one of the new security team?' he asked.

I nodded and he smiled. He looked at me more carefully and I could see he was putting two and two together. 'No, I don't think you are. You don't sound like a Yank.'

He reached for the phone on his desk and I pointed the guard's Browning right between his eyes.

'You got me. I'm just an Aussie bloke with a big fucking gun, so don't even think about touching that phone. You and I need to talk.'

Sheehan settled back in his chair. 'Mate,' he said, 'I don't know what your problem is, but this place is sealed up tight as a fish's arsehole, so why don't you hand over the gun and let me call security?'

'Think your homemade missile can make Japan?'

He shrugged. 'Buggered if I know, but if Ms Gaarg reckons her looney-tunes fantasy of a tidal wave flattening Yokohama will help her cause, and she thinks my little bottle rocket out there can do it, then I'm willing to play along. She's a very generous woman, our Miss Gaarg.'

'So you think the tidal-wave idea's a fantasy?' I said.

'Look, mate, once we fuel her up with enough gas to get to Iwo Jima, she can only carry half a ton of explosives. Even if she detonates right on target we'll only get a bang big enough to scare the shit out of the seagulls.'

'See the bloke talking to your techies out there?' I said. 'You know who that is?'

'That's Chapman Pergo. Nasty bastard, that one. Not someone you'd want to cross, that's for sure.'

'Well, Mr Pergo there has recently pinched a couple of nuclear warheads from the US Navy, and when your missile takes off it's going to have one of them installed in the nose, primed and ready to blow. Think we'll just have a fantasy tidal wave if a nuke detonates in that fault?'

Sheehan sat bolt upright. 'Holy Mother of God, are you having me on?'

'I'm afraid not.'

There was a clock on the wall above Sheehan's head. If the launch was scheduled for breakfast time tomorrow morning that gave me less than eighteen hours to stop it. I'd spotted at least twenty camouflage-clad goons and they were all armed, so I was outnumbered and outgunned. What I needed was some serious back-up.

'That thing make calls off the island?' I said, pointing to the phone on Sheehan's desk.

'No. It's just for round the settlement. We use satellite phones to call the mainland.' He indicated his desk drawer and I nodded. The phone he pulled out was a small Samsung with a built-in camera.

I walked across to the mirrored window and used the phone to take a quick shot of Pergo leaning over the cruise missile.

There were two doors at the back of office, one marked EXIT and the other ABSOLUTELY NO ADMITTANCE – PROJECT HEAD ONLY. That door had some serious-looking locks on it.

'What's in there?' I said.

Sheehan looked a bit embarrassed. 'Electronic stuff, and plans and junk. Nothing interesting.'

I'm always intrigued by doors that are triple-locked to keep nothing secure.

'Open it.'

He stood up and pulled a bunch of keys from his pocket. I kept well back as he crossed the room but I was pretty sure Sheehan wasn't going to give me any trouble. I think he was still reeling from what I'd just told him.

He undid the locks and I ushered him into the cupboard. 'I hope you're not claustrophobic.'

The walls were solid enough to contain any yelling, and there was no sign of a phone. Shelving reached right up to the ceiling, stacked with electronic junk, just like he'd said, and rolls of plans and drawings. A piece of brown hessian was covering something on one of the top shelves and I reached up and pulled it off. Underneath was a neat pile of familiar-looking rectangular metal containers.

'You bastard!' I said.

He shrugged. 'A bloke can only eat so much bloody tofu.'

Francis Aloysius Sheehan's storage cupboard was stacked to the rafters with cans of Spam.

With Sheehan and the guard secured, I only had everybody else on the island to worry about as I headed up towards the lighthouse. The sun was hot, the path was steep, and I was breathing heavily by the time I reached the cliff top. I moved around until I got a signal on the satellite phone, then I sent the image of Pergo and the missile to Julie, along with the text, *Adamek Island.* I started to punch in her number again to fill her in but the handset beeped once, the battery light flashed, and it died.

Typical. Sheehan could build a homemade cruise missile but he couldn't remember to charge his damn phone. Now my only way of getting in touch with the outside world was the radio on Ed's boat.

Twenty-two-metres tall and painted white, the lighthouse was on the highest point of the island, and even from ground level you could see the ocean on all sides. Ed would be waiting somewhere over the horizon for my signal, and I should have just enough time to make my way to the tiny beach for the pick-up. All I needed to do was climb the tower, send the signal, disable the radar, then try not to irritate any sunning tiger snakes on my cross-island jaunt.

The lighthouse door was unlocked and I started up the cast-iron spiral stairway. I was wheezing like old Dougal when I finally reached the observation deck, but the view was spectacular, the horizon visible in every direction. The steel walkway around the top of the lighthouse had the original, ornate, wrought-iron balustrade, and the glass-walled lamp chamber housed the multifaceted prism reflectors that sent a powerful beam of light out into the blackness of night.

My breathing was just getting back to normal when I realised I wasn't the only person on top of the tower.

'Good afternoon, Miss Priday,' I said. 'Watching out for our friends the whales?'

Wearing shorts, hiking boots and a hooded sweatshirt, her hair tossed by the wind, Cristobel was as spectacular as the 360 degree view. Maybe more so. She lowered her binoculars and gave me that wonderful smile.

'A pod passed us earlier this morning, Mr Murdoch. They had a pair of calves with them, which was an amazing thing to behold.'

'I saw them on my way out here,' I said. 'And I agree with you – a sight to behold.'

'So you understand now why Miss Gaarg has to put such a strong argument to the people of Japan on the whales' behalf?'

'Smiting your enemy's coastline with a forty metre wall of water does present a powerful argument.'

Cristobel looked confused. 'What forty metre wall of water?

'The tidal wave that will result from the detonation of that cruise missile's nuclear warhead in a geological fault off the coast of Japan.'

Cristobel shook her head. 'Miss Gaarg is intending to release leaflets over the Emperor's palace to persuade the Japanese people that whales have a right to their place in the world like every other creature.'

'There *are* no leaflets, Cristobel.'

'Yes there are, Mr Murdoch. Miss Gaarg says that the breaching of the air-security cordon over Honshu and Tokyo by Mr Sheehan's rocket will cause confusion and anger amongst the populace, who, after reading our leaflets, will turn against their government.'

'Don't you think they might be a bit more confused and angry if a tidal wave obliterated their coast?'

'I'm afraid you're wrong. Miss Gaarg would never do anything as terrible as that. And besides, where would she get a nuclear warhead?'

'Have you ever heard of someone named Chapman Pergo?'

'Miss Gaarg met with Mr Pergo in Canberra this week. Mr Pergo has been helping us make our case to the government for the whale sanctuary. I think perhaps it was Mr Pergo who telephoned Miss Gaarg the night I … came to your room.'

And then, God love her, she blushed scarlet right down to her roots.

It wasn't the perfect moment to undo my belt but the homing device was located just under the buckle and it was time to activate it. 'I think we both know your heart was in it, Cristobel.'

'No.' She looked at the ground.

'Don't be embarrassed. That's a compliment. You're not cut out for a life of deception and lies. Unfortunately a lot of people around you are. The truth is, Chapman Pergo is Special Assistant to the Defence Minister. He has nothing to do with whale sanctuaries or the Antarctic. He's a traitor and a liar who arranged to steal two nuclear warheads from the American Navy for Miss Gaarg. They're somewhere on this island right now, along with a kidnapped weapons officer who knows how to arm them. Tomorrow morning around breakfast time, Miss Gaarg intends to launch one of the warheads in a cruise missile aimed at an island near Japan, in the hope of causing that tidal wave.'

Cristobel was staring intently out over the ocean but not really seeing anything. Her eyes were filled with tears and she looked like the bottom had dropped out of her world.

Somewhere down in the village a klaxon started sounding. Bugger. They'd discovered either Sheehan or the trussed-up guard and now the shit was hitting the fan.

I walked around the observation deck until I found a thick electrical cable running down from the radar unit on top of the light house. One decent tug and the cable ripped away from a junction box above me, and I could see the rotating dish beginning to slow down. At least Ed would be off their radar when he motored in to pick me up.

I had to shake Cristobel by the shoulders to get her to focus. 'Do you have a phone or any way of making calls off this island?'

'I have a satellite phone in my room so I can speak to Daddy,' she said.

I gave her a card with Julie's mobile number on it. 'Call this number and tell the person who answers that tomorrow morning 7.30 is game time. And tell them not to dick about.'

Cristobel looked at me defiantly. 'You have to be wrong about Miss Gaarg, Mr Murdoch. She could never do anything that awful.'

'Look, kiddie-wink,' I said, 'I really don't have time to argue. If I don't get where I'm going then your phone call might be the only thing that can prevent the deaths of hundreds of thousands of people.'

I could see the security guards spreading out from the village, forming up into search parties. It was at least a couple of k's to the inlet where Ed would be waiting, and most of it was across open ground so I had to hustle. I grabbed Cristobel's binoculars before leaving her on the lighthouse.

Getting down the stairs was a lot quicker than getting up, and once back on solid earth I started moving briskly north-east. Running over unfamiliar ground is a great way to break an ankle, plus there were all those friggin' snakes to contend with.

I was hot and totally knackered by the time I made the inlet. I used the binoculars to scan the water for Ed. There was no sign of him or his boat but I could see something bobbing in the waves close to shore. I adjusted the focus and just as I got a sharp image my view was obscured by a helicopter rising up from under the cliff and filling my whole field of vision. I didn't need binoculars to make out the bloke in the rear cabin pointing an M16 in my direction.

I was outgunned and I knew it. I put the Browning on the ground and my hands in the air. The chopper landed on the cliff top and I was frisked, disarmed, handcuffed, and given a clip over the ears for good measure, all in the space of thirty seconds. They tossed me into the helicopter, and five minutes later I was dumped out onto the helipad and back into the presence of Artemisia Gaarg.

'You are a very annoying person, Mr Murdoch,' she said, sounding a whole lot like Gwenda Felton.

It appeared that a couple of the guards were getting ready to demonstrate the level of her annoyance with me using their fists when I was saved by Cristobel. She must have run all the way from the lighthouse.

'Miss Gaarg,' she gasped, 'Mr Murdoch has been telling me a terrible tale about a nuclear bomb and a tidal wave.'

Artemisia gave me a disappointed look. 'I'm sorry, dear,' she said to Cristobel. 'I had hoped to spare you any of this unpleasantness until after the event.'

'But a tidal wave?' Cristobel said.

'I'm afraid you can't make an omelette without breaking eggs.'

I guess that made Artemisia an ovo-vegetarian. 'If you do this, Miss Gaarg,' I said, 'you'll be breaking a lot more than just eggs. This will be mass murder.'

'Please, please reconsider,' Cristobel begged her. 'This is not God's will, and I'm afraid you risk bringing down retribution from on high.'

'You're risking more than that,' I said. 'I don't know if you remember all *your* high-school geography, but Japan's nearest neighbours are China and North Korea, both of whom have nuclear weapons, nervous dispositions, and pretty shaky chains of command. If some low-level flunkey gets spooked by an unexpected atomic explosion in their sphere of operations, anything could happen.'

'And then the Japanese would have even less reason to bother with the slaughter of whales,' Artemisia said.

'You can't do this, Miss Gaarg,' Cristobel pleaded.

'I'm afraid it's too late to stop me, dear. I'm sorry, but I'm going to have to lock you in your room until this is all over. I hope you can forgive me.'

She motioned to one of the guards, who led Cristobel away while I was hustled in the direction of a stone building with barred windows. I just hoped my trousers wouldn't fall down before we got there. When they frisked me on the cliff top one of the guards had taken my belt and spotted the homing device. He crushed it under his heel and tossed my belt over the cliff.

It really didn't matter now, anyway. And pulling down the power cable to knock out the radar also seemed a futile gesture. I was pretty sure that the thing I'd seen floating in the waves at the inlet just before the helicopter turned up was a life preserver from the Suzie-QC. It was a wonder the bloody thing was still afloat, given the number of bullet holes in it.

I was hoping like hell that Ed hadn't suffered the same fate.

Chapter Twenty-Six

Adamek Island had all the comforts any self-respecting, self-sustaining vegetarian colony could ask for, including a nice little jail. The building had a narrow corridor with a couple of cells on either side. Mine had barred windows, bunk beds, a sink, a toilet and a small table. It also featured a very damp and seriously pissed off Ed Wardell. Ed was wrapped in a blanket and he scowled when I walked in.

'They sank the bloody Suzie-QC,' he said. 'Chopper flew up and shot her full of holes at the waterline. I went over the side in my lifejacket, thought they were gonna plug me too. Bastards pulled me out of the drink on a cable and dumped me in here.' He shook his head. 'Gunna sue these pricks for every penny they've got, Alby.'

Ed's saying my name got a reaction from the cell opposite. 'Alby? That you?'

There was a small barred opening in the cell doors and I looked across the corridor into the eyes of Lieutenant Clare Kingston.

'I was hoping you'd show up,' she said. 'What's going on?'

'Well, in a nutshell, we're the guests of a crazy woman with a couple of nukes, a homemade cruise missile, and a bone to pick with the Japanese about whaling.'

'Holy heck!'

'And, unless I miss my guess, you're here to arm one of the nukes.'

'And why would I do that?'

'I'm afraid that's where I come in.'

If there was anyone I didn't need to see right now it was Chapman F. Pergo.

When he stepped into view he wasn't alone. He had Cristobel by the arm and she looked like she'd been crying. Pergo held up a satellite phone, dropped it on the rough stone floor and crushed it underfoot.

Cristobel looked at me. 'I'm sorry, Mr Murdoch, but I did try.'

'And Murdoch is right in his assessment of the situation regarding the warheads, Lieutenant Kingston,' Pergo continued. 'We have the manuals, of course, and the recently deceased weapons officer wrote out the procedure and codes but we'd prefer someone with some expertise doing the job. We wouldn't want any slip-ups, would we?'

He did have a point, especially when a slip-up might result in Adamek Island being vaporised, along with everyone on it.

'And why would you think I'd cooperate?' Clare said.

'Well, for a start, because we've got your boyfriend captive in a warehouse in San Diego – here he is with a gun at his head.' He held up a phone and showed her a video picture. 'Excellent image quality, I think you'll agree?'

Clare gasped, and so did I.

'You've got a boyfriend?' This was a turn-up for the books.

'Sorry, Alby. I was going to tell you at breakfast but we were interrupted.'

'So what was that between us?'

'Well, like you said, I'd been at sea a long time.'

'So you just wanted me for my body?'

'Geez,' Ed muttered, 'she must have been at sea a bloody long time.'

Clare looked down at the phone again. 'How do I know that's real?'

'You don't,' Pergo said. 'But are you willing to gamble on your boyfriend's life?'

Clare looked at me and I could see the uncertainty in her eyes.

'Let me throw in a sweetener for you,' Pergo said. 'If I feel you're not displaying a high enough level of enthusiasm for the task, I'll bring in your toy boy here.' He nodded in my direction. 'Every time I catch you deviating from the manual, I'll take my bolt-cutters and snip off one of his toes right in front of you.'

From the sounds coming from Clare's cell, she was vomiting in the toilet. I have to admit I wasn't feeling too flash myself.

Ed pushed me to one side and glared out into the corridor. 'Listen, arsehole,' he yelled, 'if you lay a finger on one of Alby's toes I'll rip your bloody arms off.'

If things weren't so serious I might have found it funny.

Pergo ignored Ed's outburst. 'My bolt-cutters and your little piggies,' he went on calmly, 'will make for a very persuasive, if rather messy, inducement. And if she won't do it for you, Murdoch, then perhaps we could get young Cristobel here to play.'

Cristobel whimpered. Pergo opened Clare's cell door, pushing her roughly inside.

'So,' I said, 'you've got the CIA and the Australian government convinced that you're on the case and close to finding the missing nukes, and all the time you've got them in the back of your ute selling them to the highest bidder.'

'Precisely,' Pergo said. 'But when you put it that way, Murdoch, you make it sound like a bad thing. I prefer to think of it as an exercise in prudent retirement planning.'

'And the kid in the car park?'

'Collateral damage, I'm afraid. I meant to tell him I'd cancelled the assignment, but with all the excitement it slipped my mind. When I realised my mistake I had to rectify it.'

That pretty much summed Pergo up. Max's death was merely a procedural necessity.

'And it was you who put that charge under the seat of my rental car?' I said.

Pergo laughed. 'Not me personally. Let's just say the Minister has his way of warning you off the case and I have mine.'

Warnings don't come much sterner than half a kilo of plastique going off in your back pocket.

'But Mr Pergo …' Cristobel's voice was wavering. 'What about our Antarctic sanctuary? I thought you cared about the whales?'

'Cristobel,' I said, 'I'm afraid all Mr Pergo cares about is Mr Pergo's bank balance.'

'Now, that's not fair, Murdoch. I do share Miss Gaarg's passion for our finned friends. In fact, when I was a child I had an aquarium. One by one all my fish died. It was fascinating. If fish are hungry enough, eventually they wind up eating each other. It truly was survival of the fittest in that tank.' He smiled at me, and it wasn't a nice smile.' Of course,' he went on, 'of all the sea's creatures, my favourites are the sharks.'

Somehow that didn't come as a big surprise.

'There are some magnificent Great Whites in these waters, Murdoch, sometimes up to eight metres and more. We often spot them from the helicopters. Beautiful to watch, and extremely efficient killing machines.' He smiled that smile again.

'You know, Murdoch, a shark like that would take less than five minutes to finish off a person your size, and it wouldn't leave a trace.'

Great. Only Pergo could come up with a scenario that made an encounter between my toes and a set of bolt-cutters sound like the lesser of two evils.

Chapter Twenty-Seven

We spent a long, uncomfortable night, made even less comfortable by the fact that dinner was bread and water. We didn't get any cutlery, but when Ed found a discarded plastic knife under his bunk he suggested we tunnel our way out. Since Adamek Island was basically one big rock, that didn't seem too feasible, and even though I'm a big fan of *The Great Escape* we had limited time at our disposal.

From our cell window, I could see lights and activity in the main workshop where the boffins and engineers were pulling an all-nighter to get the cruise missile ready for the early-morning launch. It was a warm night, the cell was stuffy, and sleeping was impossible, so Ed and I rehearsed a little performance for when the goons walked in with the bolt-cutters. Pergo hadn't bothered to post an overnight guard on the cellblock, and given the solidness of the barred windows and the steel doors, I could see why.

They took Clare away just after six in the morning, and when no one came for me and my toes I figured she must have cooperated. Around seven, one of Pergo's men brought her back to her cell. She was bruised and bleeding from a split lip.

She looked at me and shook her head. 'What choice did I have?'

'Looks like you live to tango another day, Alby,' Ed muttered quietly. He was on his bunk under a blanket.

While it was nice to still have all ten toes, it wasn't what I'd expected from Clare. She was career Navy – Annapolis. Why had she caved in so easily?

When the guard had locked Clare in her cell I whistled to him. 'Hey, tough guy, my mate's in bad shape. Reckon you can get someone to take a look at him?'

The guard peered warily in through the small opening just as Ed let out a low moan.

'What's wrong with him?' the guard asked.

'Beats me. He just started feeling crook in the night. I think he's got a fever.'

Under instructions, I put my hands on my head and stood facing the wall while the guard unlocked the door and edged in.

'Crikey, maybe he got bitten by that snake!' I yelled, pointing to the corner of the cell. I don't like using the same ruse twice, but we had limited options. As the guard swung the muzzle of his Walther submachine gun away from me, I kicked him in the nuts and then biffed him with the cell door while he was on his knees. Not an elegant tactic, but it worked.

Ed sat up on his bunk. 'Jeez, mate, that was more Three Stooges than 007. I'm a bit disappointed.'

'Wait till you see my Abbott and Costello,' I said as I frisked the guard. 'That always lays 'em in the aisles.'

We tied the guard's hands with his belt and put him on my bunk, tucked up under the blanket. I couldn't find a phone on him, or any more ammo for the Walther, so I was stuck with what was in the magazine. The Walter is a good close-in weapon, but it only holds thirty rounds.

I left Ed locked in the cell with the unconscious guard for cover and started to work my way towards the launch site. I planned to get as close as I could, wait till they rolled the missile out, then try to put all my bullets into the engine. My plan hit a slight snag before I'd gone twenty paces when someone else with a Walther tried to put all their bullets into me.

I ducked behind the nearest rocky outcrop and squeezed off a three-round burst in the direction of the shooter, who had his own rock to hide behind. Only twenty-seven shots left and a lot of open ground to cover, which wasn't the way I'd planned it.

I popped my head up for a quick look and got a lot of encouragement to keep it down. Two or three shooters had me spotted now, and another three-round burst from me brought about a hundred in return. Bullets, ricochets and rock splinters were suddenly flying in all directions, and I hunkered down in a cleft in the rock.

Around twenty-four shots left. Between bursts of fire I risked another peek and really didn't like what I saw. The steel doors to the workshop building slid silently open and half a dozen of Artemisia's armed heavies spread out to form a protective circle. A bunch of nervous-looking, white-coated technicians pushed the missile down the railway tracks to the launching ramp. Sheehan was in the group, with one of the guards holding a gun on him. His face was puffy and bruised and I wondered if he'd had a discussion with Pergo about nukes.

The warhead compartment on the missile was shut and it looked like everything was in place for the Japanese to get their lunchtime surprise. The boffins made some last-minute adjustments and then withdrew into the workshop, followed by the guards. The steel doors were closed to protect the workers from the red-hot backwash of the solid-fuel booster rocket that would get the missile airborne.

At exactly 7.25, according to my watch, a loud klaxon blast echoed across the island. The five-minute warning for the launch. By now I calculated I had fifteen rounds left in the magazine. At this range I had no chance of hitting the engine on the missile, but if I left the shelter of the rock there was no way the goons could miss me. It was all about to hit the fan in a very big way and there was bugger all I could do about it.

Cristobel's prediction of retribution from on high came to pass with a vengeance, and not a moment too soon. It actually started at ground level, with short bursts of submachine gun fire from commandos in camouflage battledress. The main attack force came from three Blackhawks which raced in at high speed and low level, hovering just long enough and low enough for black-clad SAS teams to rappel quickly down ropes slung from each door of the choppers' main cabins.

The twenty-four SAS guys split into teams of four as soon as they hit the ground, spreading out and racing towards the different buildings, with the Blackhawks screaming away immediately the ropes were clear. The air- and ground-assault teams quickly linked up and suddenly doors were being kicked open, stun grenades tossed in, the soldiers charging straight into the smoke and confusion that followed the blasts.

Two teams of four broke away from the rest and sprinted towards the jail, disappearing round a corner. I heard the crunch of boots on the gravel path, followed by about ten seconds of silence, then an almighty bang. There was smoke and yelling from inside the jail, then two smaller bangs and more yelling. *'Get out, get out, get out.'*

Then troopers were half dragging, half throwing Ed, Cristobel and Clare from the smoke-filled building. They stumbled, dazed and shaken by the explosions, and fell on their knees, coughing and wheezing and gasping for air.

I popped my head up a little higher from behind the rock, and when nobody tried to shoot it off I figured things were safe. Leaving the Walther behind and coming out with my hands up seemed the smart thing to do. I was still wearing the camouflage uniform of Artemisia's security goons and I didn't want anyone getting the wrong impression. Especially not someone packing an MP5.

With my hands in the air I joined the group outside the jail. Suddenly my feet went out from under me and my face was in the gravel. I started to get up but a boot in the small of my back suggested I reconsider the move. I was quickly and efficiently frisked by someone who knew exactly what they were doing and then I was hauled back onto my feet.

Three SAS men kept us covered while a fourth gestured to the other team, sending them off in the direction of the main workshop. I could see a line of about twenty white-coated men on their knees with their hands clasped on top of their heads. While others kept watch, a pair of SAS troopers worked their way methodically down the line, searching each of the prisoners and then securing their hands with plastic ties. One of the men was pulled out of the line and marched over to our little group.

'White isn't really your colour, Pergo,' I said when he joined us. Trust him to grab a dustcoat and try to look like one of the boffins. He started to take his hands off the top of his head but when one of the SAS bods raised his submachine gun he changed his mind. He didn't change his attitude, though.

'My name is Chapman F. Pergo and I'm a special assistant to the Minister for Defence,' he announced. 'I have full authority to take charge of this operation and I order you to release me immediately.'

The SAS men looked at the soldier who was covering Pergo. The trooper gave a negative shake of the head. There was something familiar about the slight, black-clad figure.

Ed climbed to his feet and addressed Pergo's guard. 'I was wondering if I might have a brief word with Mr Pergo there?'

The SAS trooper nodded. Pergo lowered his hands as Ed walked up.

'It's about my bloody boat, and those bolt-cutters you mentioned,' Ed said, and then his right shoulder dropped a bit and Pergo began raising his right hand. But it was a feint and Ed's left shot out, there was a solid crack as his fist connected with Pergo's chin, and the bastard went down like Sonny Liston to Ali in '65.

Ed started walking in circles, shaking his hand and cursing quietly to himself. Hopefully the damage to his knuckles would be less than that to Pergo's head. Pergo sat up slowly after a minute and rubbed his jaw.

'I guess that would make it eight losses Chapman,' I said.

He started to get to his feet but two SAS troopers forced him back on his knees. Besides their submachine guns, they had pistols strapped to their thighs. The holster on the trooper in front of Pergo held a black, Teflon-coated nine millimetre ASP.

'I'll have your balls for this, you bastards!' Pergo hissed at the soldiers.

'Not mine, you won't,' the trooper with the ASP said, pulling off her helmet and balaclava.

'Hello, Jules,' I said. 'You know, you look really good in basic black. And those stun grenades are a nice touch. Very elegant.'

Chapter Twenty-Eight

Julie hooked the compact MP5K to the front of her combat harness and scratched her face. 'Those damn wool balaclavas are really itchy,' she said.

Her sub-machine gun was customised with a nifty ACE skeleton folding stock and an Aimpoint comp sight. It was a very nice-looking little package with a lot of punch close-up. Not unlike Julie herself.

This scenario would explain all those trips she took to Perth whenever she had a break. She always said she was going surfing at Margaret River, but she'd often come back with bruises and sprains. Once she'd even shown up with a broken collarbone, saying that she'd got on a right-hander at North Point.

The SAS trained out of Campbell Barracks in Perth, and since I hadn't been smart enough to join the dots on that one, I wondered what the hell I'd been doing running an intelligence service.

'Exactly how long has this being going on?' I asked.

She smiled. 'A year or three. A girl's got to have a hobby.'

'Well, your timing, as always, is impeccable, Ms Danko.'

'I got alarmed yesterday afternoon when Ed's floating gin palace disappeared off American satellite surveillance. Then when Artemisia's radar went down and your homing beacon cut in and out I figured it was time to call in the heavy mob. But it was your happy snap of Pergo and the missile that clinched the deal. I forwarded it to Lonergan, who took it straight to the Defence Minister.'

'That must have been an interesting meeting.'

'I'd say so. Suddenly everyone was white and shaking and in full "get it sorted and let's pretend it never happened" mode. Next thing, Gwenda received an order authorising me to do whatever was necessary. She wasn't all that happy about it, though. I won't be hanging out for a Christmas bonus this year. Getting the ground-assault teams ashore held us up a little, but we got here in the end.'

'Who's we?' I said.

'Well, there's the SAS, as you can see. We choppered in out of Hobart. And Lonergan organised for the *Altoona* to make a high-speed run down from Sydney so she could send in commandos from 4 RAR by rubber boat for the land assault. The *Altoona's* been standing off just over the horizon, watching on radar for anything in the way of a rocket launch, with anti-missile missiles armed and ready, just in case.'

'SAS *and* commandos? You weren't taking any chances.'

'With Pergo and the choirboys here, I figured we'd need all the firepower we could muster.'

'You got that right.'

A figure dressed in US Marine combat fatigues and carrying an M4 carbine jogged up.

'Very glad to see you and the cavalry, Carter.'

'You too, Alby. You okay? All in one piece?'

'Yeah, thanks, mate. Rounded up your choirboys?'

'Yep. Every one of them. And let me tell you, they're singing like canaries.'

The US Navy would get the surviving members of the choir on charges of mutiny, murder and desertion. Once convicted in a closed court, I figured they'd be stuck in the federal penitentiary in Leavenworth until the next millennium or beyond.

There was a loud bang from the direction of the staff quarters. I looked around.

'Just our boys tidying up the loose ends,' Julie said.

A trooper broke away from the group of prisoners near the workshop and raced over to us. He spoke quietly to the bloke who'd been giving the orders, who glanced over at Julie and said, 'We can't account for Target One.'

'Artemisia?' I asked.

Julie nodded.

'And you've got all the chopper pilots?

'In their quarters, secured,' the SAS commander said.

'Where the hell is she?' Julie said.

There was another loud bang, this time from the direction of the launch ramp, followed by the rumbling roar of a booster rocket firing up. We all turned in the direction of the ramp.

'Looks like someone left the keys in the ignition,' Ed said.

Suddenly, with a deafening roar and billowing white smoke, Artemisia Gaarg's lesson to the world's whaling nations was blasting its way up the launch ramp and off into the clear blue Tasmanian sky.

Chapter Twenty-Nine

THE SOLID-FUEL BOOSTER ROCKET BURNED OUT AROUND THREE hundred metres into the air and fell away. There was a brief spluttering sound from the missile's engine, then a loud metallic bang, then silence. The momentum provided by the booster rocket kept the missile going forward and upward for another fifteen seconds or so, then it slowed, the nose dipped, and it began a slow descent towards the water.

It looked like Sheehan had pulled a bang-and-burn sabotage mission on his own cruise missile without Pergo noticing, and if he had I'd be willing to swallow my pride and make the man the best Spamburger he'd had in his life. Of course, how long that life was going to be was currently up for discussion.

I considered putting my fingers in my ears to block out the noise of the nuke going off when it hit the water, but decided it was probably pointless. Even the tough SAS men were staring wide-eyed at the falling missile. The only person who wasn't holding her breath was Clare. She either had nerves of steel or she knew something I didn't. I was really hoping it was the latter.

The missile was heading straight down now and it hit the water with all the grace of a high diver. There was one small splash of white water and then it was gone.

No one moved for a full sixty seconds after the impact, and when we hadn't been vaporised by that point it seemed safe to relax.

I looked at Clare. 'No bang?' I said. 'Not that I'm complaining.'

'The warhead is fitted with a standard category G permissive action link. You have to key in a twelve-digit code to arm it. It's a bit like a bank auto teller – you only get a couple of goes and then it locks up. But this one also has an AUD lock. If you hesitate for three seconds between the third, sixth and tenth digits, it reads it as Arming Under Duress. It finishes the procedure normally on the display but totally shuts down the detonation sequence. I had to let Pergo smack me around a bit for appearance's sake, and then I tripped the AUD code.'

'Any chance of the nuke breaking open and producing a generation of glow-in-the-dark whales?' I asked.

She shook her head. 'Minimal. The casing is designed to withstand substantial impact. Plus there's a homing device fitted, so we should be able to retrieve it pretty quickly with an unmanned submersible salvage vehicle.'

Now that the warhead was safe on the bottom of the ocean, that left Artemisia.

'With the chopper pilots locked up, there's only one way off this place,' I said, looking down towards the jetty, where a white sail was already being hoisted on the old whaleboat.

Julie was on the move, heading towards the jetty and unhooking her MP5K as she ran. Two SAS troopers were sprinting out towards the point, leaving the fourth to guard Pergo.

By the time I caught up with Julie at the beach, Artemisia had the whaleboat under sail and well away from the jetty. We had no way of stopping her. Julie took off again, sprinting towards the harbour entrance. It was obvious Artemisia was going to make the open ocean without any trouble, but what did it matter? She really had nowhere to run.

The craft cleared the harbour entrance and just as I was about to yell to Julie to radio the marine police its mast began rocking violently from side to side. There was a billowing of foam and white spray and suddenly the whaleboat was up in the air, then falling sideways as a huge humpback leapt almost clear of the waves. The tiny boat slid off the whale's back like it was just another droplet of water and landed on its side, sails flat to the waves. I could see a yellow flash of Artemisia's lifejacket as she was tossed into the maelstrom.

More whales were breaching now, some just blowing spray into the air while others leapt and twisted, the white flashes of their bellies showing through the blue-green water. Caught in the middle of these leviathan aquarobics was the tiny yellow dot that was their strongest champion. There must have been thirty of the huge mammals and I couldn't imagine what Artemisia must have been thinking, out there all alone with her beloved whales. There was one final flurry, a massive tail smacked down with a sound that carried clearly to the shore and then they were gone.

The ocean returned to a steady swell, and the hull of the capsized whaleboat bobbed on the waves, but there was nothing else. No sign of the yellow lifejacket or Artemisia's white hair. Did whales swim along with their mouths open? Could a whale actually swallow a person whole? There it was again – that question which had led to my traumatic expulsion from Sunday School and dashed my hopes of playing the Third Wise Man in the Christmas pageant.

On the horizon I could just make out the shape of the USS *Altoona*. Pretty soon there would be a heavily armed shore party trampling through the orchards and all over the vegetable garden, looking for the second missing warhead. Then everyone could return to the happy state of being able neither to confirm nor deny their existence.

Would the Americans take the nukes back now, I wondered, scared off by the close call? Or would Operation Chester still go ahead? We'd probably never know. All those involved in the scheme would close ranks and deny everything.

I heard the crunch of pebbles and Julie was beside me, her sub-machine gun hooked back across her chest in the combat harness.

'Well, it looks like you're going to be the golden-haired boy in Canberra for a minute or two,' she said.

'Only if I keep my mouth shut. And that's going to come at a price. I think Peter Sturdee is odds on to get reinstated and promoted, don't you?'

'Definitely. But only after he and all the Sturdees have had a nice little holiday in Tahiti, with hot and cold running babysitters, all at the government's expense.'

'I like the way you think, Ms Danko.'

I picked up a flat pebble from the stony beach and spun it out onto the bay. It skipped four times across the water. Julie picked up a pebble, crouched low and let it go with a lightning flick of her wrist. Five, dammit.

'Not bad for a girl in full battledress and armed to the teeth,' I said.

She grinned. 'It's all in the wrist, Alby,' and I wasn't sure if we were still talking about skipping pebbles.

I was searching for just the right response when she was suddenly in my arms and I was falling backwards. As I hit the beach with Julie on top of me, I might have thought all my Christmases had come at once, if it hadn't been for the staccato, breathy, cough-like exhalations caused by the impact of the bullets from Chapman Pergo's submachine gun slamming into Julie's back.

Chapter Thirty

Pergo was firing on full auto and on the run, so how he managed to hit Julie right between the shoulder blades was beyond me. I could hear Ed yelling and then everything went into slow motion. Pergo was closing in on us, spurts of dust kicking up from under his pounding feet and a crazed look in his eyes. He might not have been much chop as a boxer, but a nine mil submachine gun at close range packs more than enough punch to put someone on the canvas and keep them there.

Julie's eyes were closed and her face was ashen. As I struggled to ease her off me, my hand closed round the grip of the sub-machine gun strapped to her chest. My thumb must have pushed the fire selector up from SAFE to FULL AUTO by reflex, and as Pergo lifted his weapon and screamed, *'Fuck You, Murdoch!'* I twisted Julie's inert body clear and squeezed the trigger.

The noise was deafening and I felt a sudden burning sensation in my chest. I thought for a moment that Pergo had shot me, but it was only the red-hot brass shell casings ejected from Julie's sub-machine gun pressing into my skin. The impact of my slugs knocked Pergo backwards, and from somewhere in the distance an SAS trooper emptied the magazine of his Browning into the bastard's back. It was damn good shooting at that range, and bloody amazing for someone firing from a sitting position. Pergo was down for the count, and this time it was permanent.

Ed was suddenly beside us and he pulled Julie's body off me. 'That Cristobel bird passed out,' he said, 'and when the SAS bloke turned to check on her Pergo biffed him with a rock and took his gun. Oh Jesus, Alby, is she hurt bad?'

Then an SAS medic was pushing me aside and tearing off Julie's gun harness and ripping at the Velcro side tabs on her bulletproof vest. I tilted her head back and made sure the airway was clear before I started giving her mouth-to-mouth. Her eyes flickered open for a moment and closed again. The Kevlar vest was off now and the medic expertly ran a pair of scissors up the front of her black rollneck. Underneath she was wearing a lacy black bra and for one bizarre moment I wondered if it was SAS issue.

'Roll her,' the medic grunted. 'But carefully.'

Even at a distance I could see the chopped flesh of Pergo's torso, but when we turned Julie over, although her back was a mass of rapidly blackening bruises, the skin was unbroken. The medic reached for the discarded bulletproof vest and inspected it. Through the torn fabric and ripped fibres, I could make out the nicked and dented ceramic insert plate that had saved her life. The medic counted the dents.

'Five hits,' he said. 'She's a bloody lucky lady.'

'No major damage, then?'

'Not that I can see. Hopefully it's nothing worse than bruising, and I think she was winded by the impact. Might have cracked a rib or two, though, so we need to get her to a hospital.'

More SAS troopers were around us now, and as they wrapped Julie in a silver space blanket, I heard someone radio for a medivac chopper. It was over us in seconds, lowering a metal stretcher basket by winch. As they strapped her in, her eyes flickered open again and she turned her head in my direction. A strap was holding her arms by her side and her right index finger beckoned me. I leaned over her, putting my ear close so I could hear above the noise of the chopper.

'Just a tip, Alby,' she whispered. 'Next time you give someone mouth-to-mouth, no tongues, eh?'

'You started it Jules.' I gave her a smile and then she was gone, the

Blackhawk heading for Hobart before they'd even finished winching in the stretcher.

Adamek Island was suddenly very quiet. The SAS medics were gathered round the injured trooper who'd somehow managed to down Pergo at maximum pistol range, even though he was slightly concussed. These blokes were bloody tough but then they'd have to be to keep up with Julie.

Thankfully, someone had thrown a tarp over Pergo's body, weighing it down with half a dozen rocks and improving the view considerably. I knew nothing could bring Max back but I was glad to see this evil prick dead.

With Artemisia and Pergo both gone, the Reverend Priday would now be sitting pretty. What could he actually be charged with? Nobody from the American side would be allowed to testify about events that had officially never happened, and we had no evidence of the conspiracy. All we had was a benign LNG tanker cluttering up Sydney Harbour on a holiday Monday morning.

I looked at my watch. Ten past eight and suddenly I was starving. There was a lush little herb garden near the cafeteria, I remembered, with some nice flat-leaf parsley. Scrambled eggs were looking good, or maybe a cheese omelette. Too bad there wouldn't be any bacon, but I knew where to put my hands on some Spam if anyone was that desperate. I wondered if Ed and the commandos and SAS blokes would want breakfast, and then I realised it was a silly question.

END

About the Author

Melbourne-born author **Geoffrey McGeachin** always secretly wanted to be a writer but deftly avoided the issue by becoming a photographer.

After decades living and working in Asia and the US he settled in Sydney to teach photography and one day decided to sit down and see if he actually had a book in him. The comic caper novel ***Fat Fifty & Fucked!*** was the result, getting him an agent and a publishing deal.

This first book was followed by three tongue-in-check spy novels featuring photographer/secret agent Alby Murdoch: ***D-E-D Dead!***, ***Sensitive New Age Spy*** and ***Dead & Kicking***.

The Charlie Berlin historical crime trilogy came next, with ***The Diggers Rest Hotel***, ***Blackwattle Creek*** and ***St Kilda Blues***. The series, set in 1949, 1959 and 1969, earned him two prestigious Ned Kelly Awards for best Australian crime fiction.

Geoff now lives on the beautiful Central Coast of New South Wales.

Foreward – as an Afterword

The three Alby Murdoch spy novels – ***D-E-D Dead!, Sensitive New Age Spy*** and ***Dead & Kicking*** – are a satirical take on the espionage business, puffed-up politicians, government duplicity, inept public servants, insecure security agencies, and all the poor bastards forced to interact with them.

I originally wrote these books thinking I was being a very tongue-in-cheek and somewhat outrageous storyteller, but recent political developments worldwide have really blurred the line between the funny, the off-kilter and the totally bat-shit crazy. But the good news is politicians are still inept, the security services are still dodgy, football is still a religion and now tere are even more areas of Australian life needing to have the piss taken out of them.

Reviewers summed up Alby as, 'a genuine action hero with a truly Australian irreverence' and 'a highly competent larrikin,' descriptions I'm quite happy with.

I considered updating the books for these new editions but decided the originals hold up as written. However, technology has advanced in leaps and bounds over those two decades so *you*, dear reader, will have to deal with a time where fax machines are part of any home office, cassette tapes are still common, homes have landline telephones, there are no smart phones with GPS in people's pockets, and our national coffee obsession is still brewing. I'm sure you can deal with it. Enjoy.

Geoff

Acknowledgements

Many thanks to the amazing Selwa Anthony who set me off on this journey and to Lindy Cameron and Clan Destine Press for giving the Alby Murdoch books a second life in print.

From Geoff McGeachin and Clan Destine Press

www.ingramcontent.com/pod-product-compliance
Lightning Source LLC
LaVergne TN
LVHW090939080826
845145LV00003B/810

* 9 7 8 1 9 2 2 9 0 4 9 4 2 *